War on the Rio Grande

Laredo Under Fire

James Herrick

ISBN-10: 0996395210
ISBN-13: 978-0996395212

DEDICATION

To all Border Patrol Agents –
current, past, and future
– working in the field trying to do an impossible job.

Without you dedicated men and women there would be no border at all.
Thank you for keeping the violence, chaos, and bloodshed
to our South out of our streets and back yards.
Sometimes, doing the right thing hurts.

CONTENTS

ACKNOWLEDGMENTS

I would like to give a special nod to my editor, Jim DeBellis, who helped to make my book a reality. He gave depth and dimension to the storyline and characters; and he added the heart, humor, intrigue, and touch of romance that really brought my story to life. Thanks, Jim!

Preface

Mexico has been falling apart at the seams for decades. Maybe longer. 120 million good people are all trying to get by in a corrupt and dangerous ticking time-bomb of a society overrun by soulless, gun-happy cartels and gangs that will stop at nothing to keep their pockets lined with American dollars. A rich culture is crumbling under the weak and frightened governance of a splintered power that can no longer keep a centralized grip on the 1% – the drug lords, henchmen, and desperados who lawlessly and mercilessly rule the roost. It doesn't help that many workers on every level of government, from the lowest cop on the street and city inspector to the highest federal bureaucrat, have bought into the bribery and corruption as a way of life, or sometimes just to survive and protect their families.

It's no wonder that 10 percent of the Mexican population has already escaped to "a better life" of menial subsistence and looking over their shoulders in the U.S. – and millions more are clamoring to cross the border.

All the Band-Aids fell short. NAFTA and GATT were well-intentioned free trade and tariff agreements that should have bolstered a flailing Mexican economy. But the real economy was drugs. The drug lords don't pay taxes or tariffs, and their profits don't filter down to the general population. There was big Mexican oil, but that market had been commandeered by big government and the richest of the rich shortly after the first big deposits were discovered offshore a few decades ago. Societal factors and illegal drugs, along with greed and corruption, kept the masses all on the wrong side of the tracks with no way to participate in the economic perks and privileges.

But they did share in the pain. When the peso was greatly devalued in 1994 and 1995, it hit the entire economy like a wrecking ball. The engine stalled, and they couldn't get it going again. The response ended up being more corruption. The rich got richer and the poor got screwed. The economy for the poor depended more and more on money coming in from family members in America, and more desperate people flooded the border and crashed the gates.

The cartels loved the border chaos, of course. It made things easier for them. Cartels from Mexico to South America thrived from the disorder and the desperation of the poor, who would now do anything to feed their families or to just get out – including smuggling drugs and carrying cheap Russian arms, or weapons provided by the U.S. Government to protect their cargo. The cartels rose in power and wealth, evolving from the status of major corporations to that of far-reaching governmental powerhouses, with armies and treasuries that small nations could only dream of.

This slow decay and demise all traces back to the early 1980s. That's when the real shit hit the fan. The Institutional Revolutionary Party (PRI) had controlled the Mexican government for 70 years, holding it together with an iron fist. Although there were many cheap thugs in the government who enriched themselves with bribes and extortion, they did protect the rule of law…somewhat. They kept the cartels on the run, or at least in the shadows. When the PRI lost power, it was like the dismantling of the Berlin Wall in 1989. The dikes were blown, and power was up for grabs. The nation splintered into factions, one of which was ruled by the nefarious cartels. The black markets, not only in the drug trade but also in human trade, flourished. That opened the door for the coyotes to smuggle more families and individuals across the border.

Our southern border is 1,900 miles long with a 25-mile wide No-Man's Land separating the land of the free and the home of the brave from the scurrilous and perilous turmoil of our neighbor to the South. Once Pandora's Box has been opened, it's no easy task to put the chaos neatly back into the box in an orderly way. Even all the king's men can't put the pieces back together after a great fall.

So the pot just continues to boil. Drug money reigns supreme, second only to the guns and ammo – which are also in the hands of the drug lords and gangs of thugs who leave a trail of blood and tears in their wake. Competing cartels violently vie for territorial control of every dunghill from the Rio Grande to the Panama Canal – the post-apocalyptic war zone that lies between production centers in Colombia and the lucrative marketplace in the U.S.

Thousands of men, women, and children are en route to the border every day – often under the guidance and "care" of thugs and rapists who care only about the payday they will get for delivering their cargo to the doorstep of the Promised Land. Every night, hundreds of people amass at the border and rush across into the U.S., overwhelming the Border Patrol and leaving them with just a few illegal immigrants in custody out of the hundreds who cross. The Mexican government turns a blind eye, and America has no clue how deep the problem runs, choosing to believe that they can fix it with benevolent smiles and humanitarian ignorance.

Each person in those faceless masses has his or her own compelling and disturbing story. So do the Border Patrol agents who try to stem the flow and manage the incoming hordes without any real government support or road map. This is the fictional story of one of those real agents, whose life became inextricably tied to the evil forces behind the innocent human tsunami, and what he did to make a difference

THURSDAY, MAY 1

Chapter 1

It was always way too early when the alarm jolted him out of his comfortable dream world. But Kelly Smith was a Border Patrol Agent pulling the important night shift, and sleeping a minute longer was not an option. He opened one eye as he slammed his hand down on the alarm clock and looked at the big red digits: 12:15 a.m.

Kelly threw his legs off the side of the bed and sat with his elbows on his knees and face in his hands as he contemplated another day.

"Time to make the donuts."

He rose to his six-foot two-inch stature and stared blankly at his athletic body in the mirror for a long moment without moving. He turned slightly to look at the red heart tattooed on his arm that read: *Sarah...forever my love*. He kissed his fingers and patted his tattoo, and then he washed his face with cold water. His blond hair and stone-blue eyes gave the appearance of a youthful, carefree young man...but with his face close to the mirror for his morning shave he could see the deep wrinkles around his eyes and the hollow expression that made him look all of his 42 years, and then some.

His partner, Ruben Garcia, would be there to pick him up in a few minutes, so he put on his deodorant and quickly slipped into his slightly stale uniform. He saw Ruben pulling up just as he finished getting ready and headed out the door.

"I guess I'll be driving today, bro; you look like you're still in zombie land. Come on, come on! Ándale!"

They had local duty that morning, which meant that they were not going to go outside the Laredo city limits. The Rio Grande River, separating the U.S. from Mexico, would not be on their itinerary today. It was stacking up to be an uneventful day in town.

Ruben was driving on the access road along IH-35, about three miles up the road from International Bridge II in Laredo, Texas, while Kelly tried to stay awake. It was now past four in the morning, after three hours of uneventful rounds.

Ruben was 36 years old and had a brown complexion and sparse moustache. He stood only 5'8" tall, but he was built like a brick fortress. He looked like he could take a cannonball to the midsection without flinching, and local legend had it that a blow from his powerful fists had the power of a cement cinderblock at 50 miles per hour.

Ruben and Kelly were good friends. Ruben was a family man with a wife and two kids, and Kelly spent a lot of time at their house. Kelly enjoyed feeling like part of a family, since he didn't have many friends or a family of his own anymore. When he wasn't with Ruben, he was just alone with his haunting memories.

As they rode along, the dispatcher's voice came over the radio. "All Agents, we have a BOLO just in: a port runner from International Bridge II. A 1998 Chevrolet Suburban, dark blue, Texas plates, KILO-ALPHA-ROMEO-3-2-5. One Hispanic male."

A port runner is a vehicle coming from Mexico that runs through the International Port of Entry, over the bridge into the United States, without stopping for inspection.

Ruben hit Kelly's shoulder to wake him.

"Okay, Kelly; wake up! We got something here."

"Yeah, yeah, I heard."

Port runners were hardly ever caught. They were usually trying to bring in illegal aliens or contraband. The usual tactic to avoid being caught was to get off the highway as soon as possible and hide in the neighborhoods adjacent to the highways. But that wouldn't be the case this time.

"There he goes! Let's get him!" Ruben said excitedly as he punched the gas pedal.

Kelly flipped on the overhead red lights and siren. The lack of traffic in the quiet early morning hours allowed them to fly through red lights as they hit the on-ramp to the highway with the runner a thousand feet ahead and widening his lead.

"That guy is flying. Tell the radio room that we have the Suburban in sight."

"Way ahead of you," Kelly responded as he relayed the information.

"...and, Sandy, if you got somebody near the Bullock Loop you might be able to cut him off there. He's gonna be flying over the Lafayette Street overpass in about one minute, and nobody's gonna catch up to him from this end. Will try to keep target in sight. Out."

He put the radio microphone back in its cradle and turned to his partner, whose eyes were transfixed on the road. "That guy has to be doing over 100 miles per hour, Rube. It's going to be tough to catch up to him."

"Just keep those binoculars on him, Robin. This guy ain't getting away from the Batmobile."

"Funny. You think you're Batman, just cuz you're driving? Ain't no Batman got a wide ass like yours. Besides: Ruben/Robin; it's pretty clear who's who. And I've got the superhero jawline, dude."

"You, the Dark Knight? With that blond hair and those angel eyes? Ha! Sorry, bro, but I'm the Caped Crusader of this dynamic duo. Just wait. Someday I'll have a black Crown Victoria convertible with all the bells and whistles – then there'll be no denying who the real Batman is."

The young Hispanic driving the Suburban was scared. Even though he had a history of other crimes, he had never run the port before. Experienced or not, driving a Suburban at 116 miles per hour with hot pursuit on his tail had to be new to him. Agency policy strictly limited the Border Agents to 90 mph, so they would not be able to keep up with the terrified maniac ahead of them.

"Looks like he's going airborne over Lafayette, Ruben."

"Don't go giving away my secret identity, man!"

The Suburban landed in a hail of sparks, making it difficult for the driver to maintain control. A white Toyota Corolla was entering the highway from the right lane at exactly the wrong moment, and the unsteady momentum of the Suburban took him right into the path of the unsuspecting Toyota Corolla sedan. They collided, fender to fender, in a horrendous clash, which was too far below the crest of the hill for Kelly to see. The impact threw the compact car rolling over to the right-hand shoulder of the highway and down the embankment onto the access road. The driver and passenger in the Toyota never had a chance. They were dead before they knew what hit them.

The Suburban fishtailed sideways into the left lane and flipped forward several times. On the final roll it seemed to leap skyward and came down on all four wheels with an incredible thud, landing in the grassy median of the highway.

The runner put his bloody arm through the window of the vehicle and had just pulled his battered face off the steering wheel when the Suburban burst into flames and was consumed by a fireball that lit up the whole town an hour ahead of the scheduled sunrise. The 625 pounds of marijuana in the Suburban caught fire, adding billows of white smoke and a thick, sweet scent to the air.

Kelly and Ruben were still nearly a mile back and looked at each other with eyes wide when they saw the flames touch the sky. They left the pavement briefly as they topped the hill of the overpass at 90 mph, landing in the midst of debris from the high-speed collision and rollover. Ruben had to react quickly to avoid a bumper, hubcaps, most of a windshield, and other large pieces of the fresh wreckage while Kelly looked in amazement at the crashed vehicle to his right and the flaming wreckage to his left.

"Holy shit! What happened?"

"Fuck! I don't know. Call the fire department." Ruben said excitedly. They slowed down and approached the scene. "Yeah, and Highway Patrol too. This is no longer a Border Patrol matter."

Ruben parked the patrol unit along the shoulder of the highway and radioed for backup units and emergency services. Kelly got out of the sedan and was immediately hit with the smell of burning marijuana.

Well, at least we know it wasn't kids and families he was hauling, he thought to himself.

Kelly Smith had been in the Border Patrol for eighteen years. He had seen a lot of changes in the Patrol and in his own life since he had joined. Tensions had escalated along the Border, but it was still basically the same. Masses of poor people were trying to enter the United States illegally, and the "Trafficantes" were still smuggling their drugs into the United States. The difference was that, before, the poor only came to flee the poverty and find jobs; now they were also fleeing the drug war violence. The drug lords had become more brazen, empowered by the fact that 500 Mexican police officers were dead in one year from assassination.

Kelly's mind wandered back through the devastation and broken pieces of his own life to the time three years ago, in 2016, when his optimistic outlook on life had been changed forever. He was a part of the Border Patrol Tactical Unit (BORTAC), a special ops group that went behind enemy lines in drug-producing countries.

Kelly had served for two years in Venezuela and Colombia. The group he led in Colombia was responsible for destroying the country's largest cocaine processing plant. The Colombian organization lost 300 million dollars because of Kelly and his group. The loss to the cartel was so large that the operation became very high profile. Kelly gained media recognition. His identity became public.

Upon returning to Laredo, he found that his home had been invaded and his wife, Sarah – a beautiful blonde-haired schoolteacher who was five months pregnant at the time – lay brutally tortured and killed on the kitchen floor. It was unheard of for the cartels to retaliate against U.S. Law Enforcement on U.S. soil.

The act caused an international uproar that the cartels did not want. It made doing their business that much harder. Their business was primarily smuggling drugs, not violence, and they would rather remain low profile and undetected. But a loss of 300 million dollars was significant enough for some cartel big-wigs to exact revenge.

There were no suspects in the murder of Kelly's wife, and the attack was not against the agent himself, so the allegation of retaliation against Kelly could not be made. He quit BORTAC the next day. The Patrol sent Kelly to headquarters in Washington D.C. after the attack to get him out of the way. This was not an unusual practice. Whenever significant events occurred and they needed to quiet things down, they sent the agent to "The Land of Broken Toys," as it was referred to in these cases.

Kelly had met his wife in D.C. when she worked as Chief of Staff in Senator Cuellar's office, so he couldn't really escape his demons there. He didn't do anything for a year; he just hung out in D.C. He made a few contacts and drank. A lot. The staff up there welcomed him and allowed him to cool off as much as was possible under the circumstances.

A short time later the Mexican cartels began their internal conflicts to gain control of the border region. The violence in Nuevo Laredo affected everyone. People started to run scared. But bigger, more international criminal elements saw an opportunity. Their idea was to bring in enough cocaine to flood the market with very low prices and eliminate the competition. The biggest such master plan ever was secretly unfolding right now on the Laredo border.

The lights and sirens of the arriving emergency units snapped Kelly back to reality.

"You okay, Buddy?' asked Ruben. "Let's get outta here."

Chapter 2

It was nearly 10:00 a.m. when Kelly got home that Thursday morning, with memories of the blazing Suburban filled with marijuana still burned into his mind. He knew that the young driver was just an innocent and frightened pawn either trying to provide for or protect his family. *Dying for half a ton of some kind of weed,* Kelly thought as he shook his head. *It's such a horrible, fucked up game.*

He went about his usual routine: read the newspaper, drank a few beers, and went to bed. Sleep takes on a bigger significance to people who work nights. They tend to plan their lives around getting enough sleep. It had been a long night. One consolation was that he had the next two nights off, and he was going to Ruben's house for dinner tonight.

Kelly woke up five hours later, showered, and made his way over to Ruben's house only two blocks away. Even though it was very near, he still drove his old Jeep there. In the back of his mind he had plans for later that night.

Ruben's two boys – Ruben Jr., 11, and Chuy, 9 – both charged at Kelly as he opened the front door to his friend's house. Kelly stooped and scooped both of them up and kept walking through the house. Kelly was a regular and welcome fixture at the Garcia home. Ruben's wife, Sylvia, was in the kitchen cutting and seasoning the fajita meat they would have for dinner that night. Ruben was still in the shower.

"Hi there," announced Kelly as he entered the kitchen.

"Hi yourself," retorted Sylvia. "Boys...you're all too big for that. Get down off Kelly now before you break his back. I hear you all had some excitement last night, Kelly" she said with raised eyebrows and a smile, hoping that Kelly would give her more details than her husband had offered.

"Oh, just a little bit. It was all over before it even got started," Kelly replied, not wanting to burden Ruben's wife with the grisly details of the Suburban chase.

Seeing through his ho-hum attitude about the incident, Sylvia replied, "You guys make what us ordinary people think is so exciting seem so boring. Would you do me a favor and start the fire outside?"

"Sure." Kelly went off to the backyard to start the barbeque with his two young assistants. He loaded the briquettes into the grill pan, stacked them neatly for a proper burn, and squirted on some lighter fluid.

"Let me light it!" said the elder son excitedly.

"Your mom might skin me alive if I let you do that," said Kelly.

"Nah-ah, my dad always lets me do it, honest!"

"Well, let's do it together, Ruben." Kelly took the long-nozzled fireplace lighter, clicked on the flame, and held it between his and the boy's hand, while Chuy took two steps back. "Okay...let's stand as far back as we can. One...two...THREE!" They touched the charcoal with their magic wand and the flames leaped with a whoosh. Kelly was again reminded of the burning Suburban. "Great job! Let's get back inside."

Ruben was finally out of the shower and had made his way to the kitchen with Sylvia.

"Hey, partner," Ruben greeted Kelly.

Without giving him a chance to say a word, Sylvia started asking Kelly about a nightclub called *The Roundup* and a waitress named

Cristina. Sylvia was interested in seeing Kelly start dating again, and Ruben had told her that Kelly had been going to the Roundup now and again to look in on this mystery waitress. After she was done interrogating him, Kelly gave Ruben a hard look.

"Why is your wife asking all these questions?"

"Why, uh…well, uh…I guess I told her that you had been going there," Ruben responded with a guilty and perplexed look.

Kelly knew he was not going to get out of this without a decent response to Sylvia. "The Roundup is just a club, and Cristina works there. She's a waitress there."

"Mmm hmm. Just a waitress…and the first woman that's caught your eye in three years. I expect to see Miss Cristina right here at my dinner table with you before the end of the month. Sooner is even better." Sylvia had a way of laying down the law and making people face reality in a loving yet firm way.

The meat was cooked and the *pico de gallo* and tortillas served; it was a comfortable meal. Kelly did not usually stay very long after dinner. As often as he came, he did not want to wear out his welcome. He also made a point of bringing groceries and beer to the Garcia household from time to time. Ruben would have refused money from his guest, but the food was different. Kelly frequently enjoyed Sylvia's good cooking, so it just seemed right.

Chapter 3

It was about nine-thirty when Kelly left Ruben's house. He said nothing about it all night, but he could tell from Sylvia's big smile when he left that she knew he was on his way to the Roundup to see Cristina. The parking lot was full when Kelly pulled in. In Laredo, the weekend started early, so the clubs were always packed on a Thursday night. It was more crowded than usual, perhaps in anticipation of the Cinco de Mayo celebration coming up on Monday. Kelly spotted the young parking lot attendant and all-around helper who waved him into a spot right next to the building. The tall, lanky teen turned the dumpster sideways to make room for Kelly's Jeep.

"Thanks, Carlos," Kelly said with a nod as he handed him a five-spot. The boy's eyes and huge grin was all the thanks that Kelly needed, and he headed for the front door. "You keep an eye on it for me now."

As Kelly opened the glass door he was greeted by blaring music, the slurred chatter of drunk patrons, a smoke-filled room with a low ceiling – and a 300-pound behemoth called "Tiny" who patted him for weapons and drugs.

People in these parts worked hard, and they liked to party long and hard in Laredo. The place had an earthy, down-home ambience, and it was filled to the rafters with people ready to let their hair down for a night of fun. The Roundup was a Country and Western bar with a mix of Tejano music.

A cute young Mexicana in a short sparkly dress on stage finished singing Selena's *Bid Bidi Bom Bom* and announced that they would be taking a break, which made Kelly very happy. It was nearly impossible to hold a conversation when the music was playing.

The bar was across the room, and Kelly worked his way slowly through the crowd to give himself a chance to check out the patrons. Over the years he had met a few unfriendly people who were unhappy about how well he did his job, especially when it affected their illegal activity. Kelly finally made it to the bar and ordered a long neck Budweiser, his favorite beer and weapon of choice in a bar fight. Guns were not allowed in the bar, and the heavy security and frisk search at the door assured this. With his back to the bar, Kelly continued to check out the crowd, not only for "unfriendlies," but also for general interest. Kelly was a people watcher.

Strategically standing next to the waitress station at the bar, Kelly knew that if Cristina was working she would stop there. Sure enough, she did.

"Are these mine, Flaco?" asked the Mexican beauty in her alluring Salma Hayek accent, pointing to the tray of four Buds and two strawberry Margaritas. Then she looked at Kelly in a flirty and solicitous manner as she brushed her silky smooth hand across his unshaven cheek. "How are you doing, Mr. Smith?"

Kelly was drawn like a magnet to this untamed 30-year-old feral female. She stood only 5-feet 2-inches tall – a full foot shorter than him – but she seemed so much larger than life. She had a very narrow waist with extremely ample round curves above and below. Her skin was a satiny caramel brown, and her dark brown eyes peered up playfully from behind her mid-back-length black hair, which had a natural and sensuous wave. She wore a black halter, just a bit too small to contain her full breasts; and had a bottle of Cuervo in a holster and a belt lined with shot glasses below her bare midriff with an emerald in her pierced navel. Daisy Dukes and cowboy boots completed the look.

"I'm pretty good, Mizz Chavez. How about yourself?" Kelly couldn't help but let his eyes wander all up and down her perfect body.

"A little horny. Can I have my clothes back now?"

Kelly smiled and looked in her eyes, which made his heart race even more.

Cristina put two fingers behind his big bronze belt buckle and rubbed her thumb on the Budweiser logo. "You know what they say about men with a big belt buckle – they're trying to make up for their shortcomings."

"I can hold my own in that department..." Kelly replied with a confident chuckle.

"Or I could hold it for you; just let me know if you need a little help sometime..."

Kelly appreciated her Mae West candor and wit. "There were nine ugly women born on the same day as you, Cristina, because God gave you the beauty of ten women."

Cristina was flattered. "Well, at least you notice me, but a girl needs more than nice words and a smile, Kelly Smith." She patted his belt buckle and looked at him with raised eyebrows so that he couldn't miss her not-so-subtle meaning. Then she took her tray and went off to serve more drinks.

Cristina liked this Texas cowboy a lot, and she knew that he liked her too. He was different from all the half-drunk lechers who were fast with their hands and even faster with their lewd comments. But the one guy she would welcome advances from always seemed so shy and reserved. He kept coming to the rodeo, but he never got on the horse. Something always seemed to be holding him back.

Kelly took a swig of his beer and started checking out the crowd once more. His eyes set upon a group of men sitting at a table in the furthest and quietest corner. His instincts immediately told him that this was not a friendly group. Two large goons with dark glasses and their arms folded across their chests were facing the action. Across the table with their backs toward the crowd sat a squatty Hispanic male, receiving a neck massage and the fawning attention of two saloon girls, and a lanky white businessman. They seemed to be embroiled in a heavy conversation.

Kelly fought off a compulsion to approach the men, but his instincts told him they were up to no good. He wanted to avoid an off-duty confrontation in a public place, so he decided to leave. This was no big deal to Kelly; he had walked away from many potentially bad situations, never feeling that he was acting cowardly. There were times and places to confront these situations.

Kelly walked toward the door with his eyes squarely fixed on the table of men. Just before he exited, the squatty man turned his head briefly in Kelly's direction. He started to turn back towards the table but then abruptly turned his face to look at the cowboy. Kelly stopped as a big smile grew on the man's devious face and the glint of a gold incisor next to his smoke stained front teeth. He gave Kelly a nod of acknowledgment and went back to his conversation.

Kelly went outside into the hot, muggy night air and broke into a cold sweat. He knew that face, though he didn't know why – but the rush of adrenaline and the warning bells going off in his head told him that this was a bad man. A very bad man. And a man who clearly knew him.

Then it came to him like a hot kiss on the end of a cold fist. This was not some local punk he had busted for smuggling a few aliens or for a load of dope. The civilian clothes had thrown him, but that familiar face belonged to an infamous and treacherous criminal named Hector Escobar, a Colonel in the Colombian Army who used his position of power to work closely with the biggest and meanest of the drug cartels.

Kelly had run across Escobar when he was still working for BORTAC in Colombia and actually had a chance to put a bullet in his head the night the 300-million-dollar warehouse was seized. Escobar gave him that same cocky smile that night when Kelly decided to lower his gun rather than kill a foreign military leader.

Escobar had a reputation for being cold, calculating and brutal. He was in charge of security operations back in Colombia. On the side, he provided security for the Cartels. He had been educated in the US, attended a number of army tactical schools in the US, and the Israeli Insurgent Tactics School. Kelly knew that Escobar lost a lot of money and credibility with the cartels in the 300-million-dollar operation that he had closed down, and he always suspected that he had ordered the hit on his wife in personal retaliation.

Kelly turned around to go back inside, but he stopped himself as his hand met the pull-bar on the door. He realized that he was excited; too excited. He needed to collect himself and make a plan before he just went in and grabbed a man by the throat when he had two huge bodyguards with him.

He was a Border Agent and needed to remain cool. He walked back in without a glance toward Escobar and went back to his perch near Cristina to have another beer and sort out his thoughts. Cristina was placing another order.

"Flaco, get your sorry culo over here with my beers!" Then under her breath she added, "Maricón flojo."

"I see you're still your normal sweet self," Kelly said with a grin. "I guess I'll just order my own beer."

"I don't need your mierda, Gringo," Cristina said with glazed eyes as she whipped out and opened her little switchblade near Kelly's face. "I swear I'll cut you if you're not nice to me." She was upset because her love interest had left without a word. Again.

Kelly just stared back, thinking about how pretty she looked.

Then, just as quickly as she pulled it out, Cristina returned the blade to her pocket and gave Kelly a coy and sexy smile.

"You can be sure of one thing: If you see me pull it out again, I will use it." She swayed her hips and put both hands on his waist. Her bad mood was improving now that Kelly had returned.

"I thought you left," she said. Then she opened the bottom button on his shirt and rubbed his hairy belly with her silky hand.

Kelly loved it, but tried not to show it. "So, do you want to kill me or undress me?"

Cristina looked up at Kelly with her sexy eyes as Flaco walked towards the waitress station with four Buds. "It's a fine line, Mr. Smith…" she said.

"Cerveza, your majesty," Flaco said as he put the bottles on her tray.

"You're lucky, Flaco. If you had a dick I would cut it off. Here's twenty bucks for your share of the tips. Now go bother someone else."

"You share your tips?" asked Kelly.

"We don't have to, but Flaco is really a good bartender and a sweet guy, and he has a little girl at home."

"I would hate to see how you treat your enemies," Kelly said.

"I stab them," Cristina said, very matter-of-factly.

"So, how do you get that blade past Jabba the Hut anyway?"

"How do you think, Mr. Smith? I smile and I tell him a girl has to protect herself. And then I rub his thigh…like this," she said, sliding her hand all the way up Kelly's leg, "and I brush against him…like this." Cristina leaned in slowly and sensuously rubbed her double Ds against Kelly's abdomen as she looked directly into his eyes.

She delivered her beers and quickly returned with another order, which she shouted in to Flaco.

It was time for Kelly to turn his attention to the more serious business at hand.

"Cristina, do you recognize any of the men at that table over there?" He nodded toward Escobar's table very briefly. Kelly had never shown any particular interest in an individual in the bar before, and this sudden interest of Kelly's made Cristina wonder, especially since it was not another woman.

"The only one I really recognize is that guy, Docksneider; he has the white shirt and tie on. Why do you want to know?"

Kelly was not ready to explain the reasons behind his interest quite yet. "I'm pretty sure I've met him before, but can't remember where. What do you know about him?"

"He's a rich Knob Hill pendejo; my mother works for him. He has an import-export warehouse down past Bridge One by where they're building the new bridge. He likes little boys, if you know what I mean."

"I know what you mean. He must know our Deputy," Kelly said jokingly.

"He does. I take my mother to work sometimes, and I have seen the Deputy going in and out of his warehouse before."

Kelly couldn't help but flinch at Cristina's last statement. The Deputy's reputation was known, but to have it stated so publicly was shocking and embarrassing to Kelly.

Deputy Chief Patrol Agent of Laredo Sector, Rangel Marín, was suspected of being a pedophile. He had made it up high in the ranks of Border Patrol, but when suspicions of his activities with young males became widely known throughout the agency his career ladder stopped. He was a sexual predator. His political clout had kept him safe throughout his career. His family had high-level State Department contacts in Washington and Latin America.

Laredo was the largest land port in the nation. It was a business town. More import/export commerce flowed through Laredo than any other border town. Bridge One referred to the Customs and Immigration Port of Entry between Mexico and the United States in downtown Laredo. There were four international bridges in Laredo – two of them were downtown. Bridge One was the oldest, built in 1956. Having an import/export house next to the Port of Entry was strategically beneficial to the business. There was much more traffic and confusion around the bridges, which worked well for the black market.

Kelly decided to leave as the glares from the goons at the table became more fixed on him.

"Thank you, Cristina. I owe you one."

"Yes, you do, Kelly Smith," demanded Cristina, "and I expect to collect soon." Kelly gave her a closed mouth smile as he left.

Cristina was approaching 31 years and was the mother of a 12-year-old son, but she could still turn heads as well as any 22-year-old. Her jet-black hair, golden complexion, and wide dark eyes made her as big an attraction at the Roundup as the music. She weighed in at a perfect 103 pounds, but would probably be no more than 88 pounds without her buttocks and breasts. She appeared to carry much of her weight in her those areas.

She was not rich – not even solidly middle-class – and had always worked out of necessity. She grew up hard and knew how to take care of herself. She lived with her mother who helped take care of her son while she worked. It would have been easy for a girl like her to fall into the "get rich quick" underworld of the drug trade, but she had already lost her son's father and one brother to the drug business and had a lot of hate for everyone involved.

She was interested in Kelly. She knew that he had lost his wife. Other agents that came to the bar had told her…but she didn't know the details, only that he was a widower. She liked Kelly a lot. He wasn't one of the drunk flirts that was always coming on to her. And he wasn't playing hard to get; he just was hard to get.

Chapter 4

Kelly climbed into his Jeep but did not leave the parking lot. He decided to wait for the table of criminals to leave and find out what they were up to. A cartel bigwig and a guy with a warehouse by the bridge added up to no good, and Kelly knew it.

He positioned his vehicle in the shadows of the pole sign near the parking lot entrance so that he had a good view of the front door and could inconspicuously fall in line behind his targets when they drove away. It was 10:45, and he figured he had a few hours to wait until the bar closed. He hoped that Escobar would want to leave before that time. Kelly pulled his binoculars out of his tricky bag, the gym bag he used to carry his work equipment, and started glassing the front entrance of the bar. He had a good view of the entrance, but he wasn't close enough to be conspicuous.

Kelly didn't have to wait long. At 11:33 Escobar walked out with Docksneider and his goons. Kelly could see by their movements that Docksneider and Escobar were fairly inebriated. Escobar was unusually stiff as if trying to maintain an air of authority in an uncontrollable situation, and Docksneider showed a certain cavalier style that would make one think that he was overly confident or trying to impress someone. Kelly chuckled at their drunkenness. It wasn't unfamiliar to him.

All four walked over to a late model midnight blue BMW sedan and got in.

Damn. Now that's a car, Kelly thought.

Kelly took down the license plate number and watched as Docksneider got into the driver's seat and Escobar got into the backseat with the bigger bodyguard. The other unidentified man had a military demeanor. He stood at the side of the car and closed the back door, then did a 360 look-around before he took the passenger's seat in front.

The driver started the car and let it warm momentarily, and then he pulled out of the parking spot. Kelly hesitated. He did not want to be spotted. As the BMW turned onto the roadway, he gave them a little lead and then pulled in behind them. He knew the neighborhood that Docksneider lived in, so he figured that they would head over in that direction.

The BMW generally headed in the expected direction of the Knob Hill subdivision, but when the vehicle took a turn into one of the more middle-class neighborhoods Kelly had to rethink his suspicions. He knew the neighborhood he was going into. He had been there before. He had followed the Mayor's secretary home one night after the bars closed and spent the night with her. They were taking the same general direction through the neighborhood that he had driven through that night.

When they pulled up a few houses down from her house, he started to freak out a little bit. The house they had stopped at was the home of Deputy Chief Rangel Marín. *What the hell are they doing here? The deputy isn't that dirty, is he?* When the Deputy answered the door and greeted them heartily, Kelly's heart sank. He knew.

Kelly sat back in his Jeep's bucket seat and watched as the BMW parked on the street in front of the house. The driveway was full, with a late model emerald green Jeep Cherokee parked behind the Deputy's car. Kelly wondered what his next step was. This was all going way too fast. He knew if he reported any of this the Deputy would shut the whole deal down and wait it out – or worse: he might make something happen to Kelly. He needed more information. He needed to know what was going on inside the Deputy's house right now.

Escobar's right-hand man in Laredo, Miguel Valdéz, and Deputy Marín were inside waiting. Escobar and Docksneider were the other principals involved in pulling off the biggest drug smuggling operation of the century.

All eyes were on Escobar as he sat in the most comfortable chair while a military bodyguard on each side. Docksneider and Valdéz stood several feet away, and Deputy Marín poured a few ounces of wine into each of their stemmed glasses as he joined the triumvirate. There was silence as Escobar crossed one ankle over his stubby knee and puffed several times on his expensive cigar. Then he spoke.

"We will soon have 1.6 billion dollars worth of cocaine waiting just across the border. We would never put so much at risk in one shipment unless we could be absolutely sure that everything will go off smoothly without any problems. When we accomplish this, we will drive our competitors out of business by undercutting their prices, and we will own most of the huge U.S. market"

Escobar looked for an ashtray to flick his cigar ash as billows of smoke rolled out of his mouth and nostrils. One of his bodyguards extended his open palm for the Colonel to use. His beady eyes scrutinized the white faces of Marín and Docksneider, and he turned toward Valdéz. "You think this skinny white man and this American-born Mexican deputy really have the cojones and the brains to do the simple job we ask of them? Should we really risk so much in one crossing?"

Valdéz smiled broadly with confidence and put his arms around both of his accomplices. "Colonel, it is your brilliant plan for our own private bridge which makes it both necessary and safe to send all six semi loads across at one time. Rangel has the power to keep law enforcement away from our operation, and my friend Jerrod just has to allow us to use his secure warehouse location. Their jobs, though important, are very easy. It is you and I and our Colombian soldiers who will take care of the logistics and execution. We will only have this one brief opportunity, Colonel, so we must take the whole load now while we have the bridge for our private use."

"Men have died for much less, Miguel." Escobar looked menacingly at Docksneider and Marín. "And I have what you call a *zero tolerance* policy for failure. You will either get very rich or very dead, my friends." The Colonel leaned back in his comfortable chair. He uncrossed his legs and pulled the cigar from his mouth as he let out a bellowing laugh. Then he jumped to his feet and held out his wine glass.

"Gentlemen…to your health!"

Kelly knew he had to work fast on this. His only chance was to get Cristina's mother to use her connection to Docksneider to secure the intel he needed. He went back to the bar and found Cristina. He knew he couldn't just blurt out his suspicions and try to convince her to recruit her mother to help him. He actually had to try to be charming and win her over.

As he walked back into the bar he kept telling himself, *Yeah, you can do this. You told her you owed her one for the information, so just tell her you want to pay down your debt and take her out to dinner.*

He slipped up to the waitress station at the bar, and Cristina came up to get another order.

"Back again? What's going on with you?" she asked.

"Well, you said I owed you. I couldn't stop thinking about you. You really want to get together?"

Cristina's eyes narrowed with suspicion as she looked at him.

She didn't want to appear too eager and continued thoughtfully. "Hmm, why all of a sudden, Kelly?"

"Well, why don't you let me take you out, and I'll explain," he responded.

"Okay. I'm off Saturday. Give me your phone," Cristina said with her hand extended. Kelly gave it to her, and she called her phone with his. When she felt the vibration in her pocket, she hung up and handed the phone back. "Your last outgoing call is to me. Save the number. Now I've got your number, and you've got mine. Call me in the morning – late." Then she turned and left with another round of drinks.

She felt a rush of excitement as she walked away. The man she was interested in was finally coming around. Kelly cradled his head in his hand at the bar and thought to himself: *What the fuck am I getting myself into?* Kelly felt a mix of excitement, guilt, and fear. He had slept with a few women in the past year, but he hadn't dated a woman that he cared about since his wife's death.

Kelly finished his beer and headed home.

FRIDAY, MAY 2

Chapter 5

The next morning Kelly awoke at 6:00 a.m. thinking about Escobar and the Deputy. He had worked seven days straight, and now he had a three-day weekend. But he wouldn't use it for relaxation; he had to hatch a plan to find out what Escobar was up to and then crush him in the act. He wasn't really scared for himself – although he should have been. But he was anxious about being in the middle of a very big situation without a real plan of action on how to approach it. He had to do some serious thinking. He didn't like it, but he knew he had to take advantage of Cristina's mother's work connection with the skinny warehouse owner and ask the two women to be a part of this potentially big and dangerous bust.

Walking away from what appeared to be a conspiracy was not an option. He had a score to settle with the cartel, and he knew that they had a $300-million axe to grind with him too. They might just want to get him out of the way and avoid another run-in. They were surely still feeling the sting of the crippling loss he had dealt them.

Once he started thinking along those lines, he realized that he had no choice but to pursue this as a matter of survival. He had to know where these guys were at all times. He was going to need more available time to follow the "bad guys." His job as a Border Patrol Agent was going to get in the way unless he could actually use work time to do his personal investigating. Maybe he could turn his work time and connections into a plus.

Kelly remembered that there were a couple of detail positions coming up that would give him more freedom to do what he wanted and needed to do. These details were referred to as "tits" because you were sucking off the tit and not really working. There was a six-month detail to the Intelligence Unit, a one-year detail to Recruitment, and then there was the Training Unit detail. He could get any one of those spots, and he had the connections to make it happen today. He had the seniority, hadn't asked for a detail in years, and was liked well enough by management that they would give him what he wanted. They owed him that much.

The Intelligence Unit detail, referred to as "Intel" by the Patrol, would give him resources to do his investigation...but he was afraid that the supervisors there might monitor him more closely. The Recruitment detail would allow him the most freedom of movement. It would sometimes require him to travel out of town, but at a time like this he wanted to be right there in Laredo to watch what was happening. Kelly didn't even consider the training unit – too many trainees to deal with all the time. The Intel detail would also allow him to be in plain clothes in a take-home unmarked vehicle, whereas the recruitment detail required him to be in a dress uniform. His mind made up, he made a few phone calls to his supervisors to clear the way for him to start the Intel detail after the weekend.

Intelligence Unit work was not usually the spying and intrigue it sounded like. It was more of a numbers crunching and logistics job: They had to take the number and locations of alien apprehensions and drug loads seized and develop trends as to where the action was happening and not happening anymore. This information was used for deployment of manpower and also to justify budget requests. More apprehensions meant more funding and resources. Intel also did some liaison work with Mexican law enforcement and with the Immigration and Customs Enforcement (ICE) Unit associated with Border Patrol. These connections would be assets to Kelly if used right. And the Intel Unit also had some surveillance equipment that he would make use of that they used to gather intelligence when they had to.

Kelly took a shower and drank a pot of coffee; then he drove over to the area where Docksneider's warehouse and office were located. From outside the front gate to the truck yard Kelly could see the blue BMW from last night parked under a canopy out front. He made a mental note that he had to get the BMW bugged with a tracking device and, if possible, a listening device inside. This is where the Intel resources would come in handy. It wouldn't be easy getting that close to the BMW without raising suspicion.

The cell phone in Kelly's shirt pocket went off.

"Hello."

"Kelly, this is Tom Bird. How's it going?"

"All right. What's up, Tom?"

Kelly had known Tom for his entire career. He had been in the Patrol longer than Kelly and had been able to make it up the management ladder far enough. But then Tom fell from grace. Now they just move him around from unit to unit at the Chief's whim to keep Tom from establishing himself in any one place.

"Hey, I hear you're coming over to the Intel Unit."

"News travels fast."

"Yeah, it does. I'm glad to hear it. They got me babysitting over here at Intel now, so I saw your name come up, and I just wanted to let you know that you can start whenever you want. I can put the transfer through right now if you want."

"Well, I'm on my days off right now, so in three days I can show up. I'll see you on Monday."

"Make it Tuesday, then. I just got a memo from the Deputy Chief that he's giving us Monday off for Cinco de Mayo for some reason. I guess they expect our neighbors to be busy celebrating."

"Sounds good to me. It's great news to find out you're there; I thought I might be working for iPod."

"iPod?"

Kelly chuckled. "Yeah. Some of the guys call Casillas the International Prince of Darkness – iPod for short."

"Huh. They got him on training detail, so I'm plugging the hole. Anyway, why don't you come on over sooner and have a cup of coffee if you can; check the place out. I'm in all day today."

"I'll do that, Tom; see you later."

Chapter 6

The Border Patrol was a small army of 20,000 Agents. The significant increase from 9,000 to the current level during the Bush years was helping a lot. Deterrence of illegal entry into the US from the Mexican side had pushed the alien smuggling operation into more contained areas. The border, far from being under control, was nowhere near as wide open as it was a decade before.

The big-time smugglers wanted their operations to be nearer to urban areas where there was better support and transportation. Prior to the increase in Border Patrol manpower, Border Patrol operations were going back and forth from patrols in and around the urban areas then back out to the rural areas. When agents patrolled further out, alien smugglers would switch back to the urban areas. Local officials would start to complain about the increased vagrancy, trespassing, petty theft, and general increase in crime. Border Patrol operations responded by moving manpower and other operational resources back to the urban areas. It became an endless game of Whack-a-Mole. We would beat back the problem in one area, and it would rear its ugly head somewhere else. Rinse and repeat.

The increased manpower allowed the Border Patrol to maintain a show of force in both the urban areas and out in the more rural areas as well. The alien smugglers were being squeezed, but manpower numbers still were not enough.

Certain areas of the Rio Grande were lower and narrower, and Laredo had some prime shallow routes for crossing over to the US. The banks of the river were not as steep in these areas. On average, the river was about 300 feet across from shore to shore. The barrios and bridges tended to develop around these low-lying areas because it was easier to cross the river and easier to build over it. These were popular spots for human trafficking and drug smuggling.

There were still good spots near the urban areas to cross large numbers of aliens, but the crossing areas were getting crowded, and groups of aliens waiting to cross would start to fight for position. This also often instigated riots. Groups waiting to cross in some areas would be staged in barrios right on the border. Their presence right in the middle of already congested slum areas would agitate residents living there.

The smugglers would agitate the groups to further their position or just to watch the fight. What was supposed to be a discreet illegal crossing into the U.S. would then evolve into a neighborhood riot. Border Patrol would respond to the area of the riot on the other side of the border that separated the U.S. and Mexico to try and deter the rioters from bleeding over into Texas. Sometimes the riots would start in the surrounding neighborhoods and end up on the bridges.

It was nearing 11 o'clock in the morning, so Kelly figured he had time and might as well go over and see Tom – maybe see what they have in surveillance equipment. As he pulled into the parking lot of the Intel Unit, Kelly saw a few familiar faces walking out. He waved and they waved back and continued to walk. The Intel office was located in a warehouse on the East side of town next to his station. Warehouses were everywhere in Laredo. Sitting amid the clutter of all the other warehouses in this industrial subdivision, the Intelligence Office blended in rather well.

But to the more trained or suspicious eye, this warehouse was unusual. There was only one tractor-trailer on site, and it hadn't moved in weeks. Most vehicles that went in and out were passenger vehicles, and occasionally there were marked Border Patrol units. Several sedans and SUVs were parked outside. The agents there were provided with fulltime vehicles, many of which had been confiscated from drug busts, so there were some pretty fancy vehicles for government workers.

Inside there was a small, sparsely adorned lobby with a receptionist window and security door eight feet ahead. The window was one-inch thick bullet-resistant glass, and the wall surrounding the window for four feet on each side, above, and below was covered with bullet-resistant Kevlar paneling. A rotund woman in her late twenties or so sat at the desk behind the glass. She was wearing a pumpkin-orange man's polo shirt and had an entire family-size Three Musketeers bar stuffed between her cheeks – with a stack of a half-dozen more on deck near her elbow.

Kelly walked into the small lobby. "Hi, Grace."

"Come on in, Kelly," she said. She buzzed him in through the electronically controlled security door.

"You here to see Chief Bird?" Grace asked, a bit flirtatiously.

"Yeah." Kelly responded.

"He's in his office down the hall, last on the right. Pretty empty here right now. Most everyone is on their two-hour lunch break."

"Thanks. See you later," he said as he began to exit the reception area toward the offices.

"I saw you at the Roundup last night," Grace said as he walked by.

Kelly shook his head and turned towards her with a smile. He thought to himself: *You can't go anywhere in this town.*

Kelly had been to the Intelligence Unit office only a few times before. Their office had been on the main facility before expansion caused them to move to this site.

He walked down the hall and turned into Tom Bird's office. Tom was sitting behind someone else's desk. Moving around all the time as he did, it still wasn't a comfortable situation sitting behind someone else's desk. He thought of it as sleeping in someone else's bed all the time.

"So, where is Casillas?" Kelly asked as he walked in. Casillas was the permanent Patrol Agent in charge of the Intelligence Unit that should be sitting behind the desk.

"They detailed him to D.C. for a few months. I think it was a punishment for something he did; or it could have been to just get him out of the way. Don't really know," Bird responded. Bird stood up and walked around the desk to shake hands with Kelly. He was a towering figure, 6'4" with a shaved head and the distinguished look of a life-long military man.

Kelly respected the hell out of Bird, who had a reputation for standing behind his men and risking his life to protect them. That's what happened a few years ago when Bird responded to a mayday from some agents whose drug bust was going south on the wrong side of the border. He rushed in with a small commando team to bail out the undercover Border Tactical Agents a couple miles deep into Mexican turf and slaughtered a few murderous criminals in the firestorm that followed. One of the casualties turned out to be a dirty Mexican Border Agent and nephew of the mayor of Nuevo Laredo. To avoid an international incident, Bird had to be sacrificed. If the Mexican government hadn't wanted to cover up their agent's role in the smuggling operation, it would have been a lot worse.

"How are you, Kelly?"

"All right. I'm looking to get off of a rotating shift for a while and do some low-key duty. You're nearing retirement, aren't you?"

"Eighteen months, so I'm retired on duty at this time."

Kelly started thinking he wouldn't have to worry much about being monitored too closely by this supervisor.

"It's pretty low key around here, Kelly. You'll do all right. I know how you work. I'm going to have you going around to the stations, acting as a kind of liaison officer. Do some face-to-face with the stations rather than just receive their reports and do the data input. We have a bunch of young guys around that do that. All they do is play on the computer all day anyways. You won't start doing that right away. Ease into it; see how the office works around here. Read the reports we have so you have a general idea of what's going on, then go talk to people."

Tom took on a look of concern and continued: "These river riots are one of our priorities right now. In the last year we've seen five riots. Some of this has to be staged for something else. What's the real reason for these river riots? I'm not buying this turf war thing among the alien smugglers and drug smugglers trying to use the best routes for crossing aliens; that's a lot of happy horseshit. It's a cover for something else. It seems they're trying to time the next one with Cinco de Mayo. This is a diversion of some sort, but we haven't seen any other activity along the border when these riots occur. That doesn't mean it isn't happening. I think the ones last month were just a decoy or dry run, but one of these days something's gonna pop. My money is on Monday – Cinco de Mayo. Some of it is just regular people trying to protect their neighborhood. They rile them up just to play into their game...you know."

"I love that kind of stuff, Tom. I can handle it."

"Thought you could. So, if no one is working on Monday, how are we going to cover that if something happens?"

Bird smiled. "Don't worry, Kelly. An old military man like me is always on duty. I emailed the Deputy to put a full crew on call."

"Well, okay," Kelly said, wondering how the dirty Deputy would handle the request. "You mind if I wander around, see where my office will be and all?"

"Nope; go right ahead. You have the office two doors down on the right."

Kelly shook hands with Tom and left. As he walked out of

Tom's office he passed an office with a young agent tapping away at his computer. The young man looked up and smiled, and then his eyes widened and his grin grew broader as he recognized the legendary Kelly Smith. Kelly was used to this from the young agents, and he gave the kid a smile and a nod.

Then Kelly found his office and immediately started looking for the equipment room. He found it right around the corner, marked with a big brass plate that said, "Equipment." He tried the doorknob and found it locked. He looked both ways and wondered how he was going to get into this room. He didn't want to pass Tom's office again, so he kept walking down the hall. Kelly knew that the offices were set up in a circle that would take him back to the reception area.

"Grace, I'm going to be in room 138. What's the extension there?"

Grace ran her finger down her list and stopped at the listing for 138. "8121, Kelly. When are you going to start?"

"I'll be here Tuesday. I'm on days off right now."

"You know, Cristina is my cousin."

"Who?"

"The one you were talking to at the Roundup last night. Don't play innocent with me. I saw how you guys were practically doing it right there at the bar."

"GEEZ! You can't go anywhere in this town!"

"Nope. What else do you need?"

"Let's see, umm, the equipment room – how can I get access to that?"

"I have the key; we have a checkout book. Whatever you check out, bring it up here and sign out for it."

"Sounds simple enough. Can I take a look-see?"

"Sure," Grace said as she handed him a ring of keys with one large room key and several smaller ones for cabinets.

"Okay. Let me go take a look, get my self situated."

"Okay. I can go with you if you want. You can pretend I'm Cristina, alone with you in the equipment room." Grace said with her eyes locked onto Kelly's as she slid her hand down over her crotch.

Kelly jerked his head toward the round ball of a woman. He was more than a little flustered as he responded, "Uh...uh...no time for that right now, Grace...but thanks."

"How about a blow job? I can blow any man in two minutes or less, guaranteed – and I never spit."

Kelly headed for the hallway to the offices at lightning speed. "Maybe some other time, Grace."

"I can stick my tongue up your ass, suck your balls, and jerk you off with my forehead," she offered, but Kelly didn't respond. Grace shrugged and opened another Three Musketeers.

Kelly headed back to the equipment room and let himself in. The room was nothing more than a large walk-in closet with locked cabinets. Each cabinet was labeled with a list of its contents. There were two large gun safes in the room also. Then he spotted a cabinet marked *Vehicle Tracking* and another marked *Listening*. Kelly opened both and found hard plastic Pelican cases marked with their contents. He grabbed them, closed the cabinets, left the Equipment Room, and walked over to his new office with the cases and put them behind the desk. He walked back to the reception desk and gave the keys back to Grace.

"Okay, well, let me see what I need for my office. Thanks."

"Okay," Grace said, rolling her tongue all the way around her lips, and then, making her tongue as cylindrical as possible and rubbing her breasts, she provocatively moved her tongue in and out of her mouth.

Kelly walked back to his office, grabbed the two cases, and headed for the back exit. He put the two cases outside the back door and walked back past his office into the reception area.

41

"Okay, well, I'll see you in a few days, Grace."

"We'll see you, Kelly." Grace got up and tried to strike a sexy pose as she stood with one arm on her desk between Kelly and his escape route through the security door. Kelly thought that she looked like a basketball with a kickstand and began to get very nervous and uncomfortable.

"And say hi to Cristina for me. Like I said, we're cousins, born 12 days apart. We've got the same genes, so...anything she can do for you, I can do just the same – right here in the office. That equipment room is pretty soundproof. We'll be alone a lot, you know. I'm pretty good with my mouth too, Kelly. The National Guard invites me to their camp one weekend a month for...'maneuvers.'" She licked her lips, flung her hair back, and gave Kelly her best "bad girl" look.

Kelly was flabbergasted and disgusted and just wanted to run out of there as fast as he could – but Grace was blocking his way. "Uhm...Ohhh...you Chavez girls are sure a fiery bunch. That sounds great, Grace, but I really can't afford to get into trouble with the agency. You know." He squeezed by her, brushing against her enormous breasts, but the experience was nothing like the one he shared with Cristina at the bar the other night.

Grabbing the front of her shirt, she picked up one breast off her belly with both hands and offered it to Kelly. "You can hold it if you want to."

He patted her on the cheek and gave his final farewell. "See you, Grace," he said, and walked through the security door into the lobby

"I'm wet for you right now, Kelly."

Kelly just kept walking and opened the front door as Grace let out a booming fart.

"Just give me five minutes and you'll never think about Cristina again." She held open the security door and shouted out the front entrance before the door closed behind Kelly. "That was just from my protein shake...*It smells good! Cinnamon spice!*"

The door clicked shut, and Grace returned to her paperwork.

"Your loss," she muttered to herself and opened another candy bar.

Kelly walked through the parking area in front of the Intelligence office as fast as he could and got into his Jeep. He pulled the Jeep over to the rear exit at the far end of the building, picked up the tracking and listening equipment he had left there, and drove off.

As soon as he got home he anxiously began looking at the equipment he had inappropriately "borrowed," and started to figure out how to use it.

By then, it was 1:30 in the afternoon. He needed to call Cristina. He was nervous about calling her, not only because of the help he needed from her, but also because he was definitely developing real feelings for the bright and beautiful waitress.

Chapter 7

"Hello." Cristina saw Kelly's name on her phone and wondered if he was going to finally man-up and ask her out on a real date.

"Cristina?" Kelly asked quietly, in his usual shy way.

"Yes. You called Cristina's number, so it's Cristina."

"It's Kelly. How are you?"

"I know who it is, Kelly. I'm fine,"

"Just fine?"

"Yeah, fine enough," Cristina said. She could see that this conversation was going nowhere, and she was getting impatient with the way Kelly would always beat around the bush before getting to the point. "I'm fine, my mama's fine, my hijo is fine – the whole damn world is fine. Is that what you called about?"

"Uh…no…no…of course not, Cristina." Kelly was caught a little off-guard by the feisty Latina.

"So, what then? The weather is hot and sticky, I'm overworked and underpaid at my job, and I don't give a crap about any of your sports teams. Does that about cover it?"

Kelly was just about to ask her what crawled up her ass when her mood seemed to change.

"I've been thinking about you," Cristina said, somewhat sweetly.

"You have?"

"Mmm hmm." Cristina knew that if this conversation was ever going to go anywhere, she would have to be the one to take the bull by the horns. This was going to be the conversation she wanted to have. "So…you have some explaining to do."

"I do?"

"Yeah, that's what you said last night."

"Oh! Yeah, uh, heh heh." Kelly cleared his throat, hoping his awkwardness around Cristina would be cleared away too. "I guess I do. So are you going to let me explain over dinner?"

"Well, I work tonight but I'm off tomorrow. But I have my son, so I would have to make arrangements. It might not work out."

"Well, what if I come over tomorrow and cook?"

"You cook? What are you going to cook, ketchup sandwiches and beer?"

"No. We can either have steak or spaghetti," Kelly said, now feeling quite proud and confident.

"You can really cook?" Cristina asked, doubtfully, wondering whether the meal would be fit for her growing son.

"Yes, I can cook."

"Well, It's been a long time since anyone has cooked for me, so if you want to cook spaghetti, that sounds good."

Kelly could hear her mother in the background, "Oh! So I never cook for you, muchacha?" followed by a lot of Spanish.

"Of course, my wonderful Mami cooks for me too," Cristina said loudly towards her mother, and then she turned back towards the phone and rolled her eyes. "You'll have to cook for me and mama and my son, you know."

"What time?"

"You're not going to Pizza Hut and buy this, are you?"

"Nooo. What time?"

"Whenever. You're cooking."

"Hehe. Okay, I'll have a few things to pick up, so I'll be over around 4:30. It's going to take some time to make my famous *Spaghetti Smitharelli*." Excitement and anticipation was already beginning to build inside Kelly.

"That's all right. You'll need the time to do your explaining anyways. I'll see you then, Kelly," Cristina said and hung up the phone.

I hope I wasn't too sassy with him, Cristina thought to herself. She liked Kelly and she wanted to light a fire under him, not chase him away. She wondered if too much of her frustration with his slow pace came through and put him off.

"Geez, sassy girl!" Kelly said to himself with a little chuckle and a big smile. He figured if she didn't feel close to him she would be all formal and polite, but this girl was giving him good-natured guff. *Must be a good sign*, he thought.

Kelly set aside his excitement and turned his attention back to the surveillance equipment. He opened the case of tracking equipment on the sofa next to him and pulled out a tracker. He read the directions and flipped on the switches only to discover that the batteries were dead.

"I bet they never use this stuff," he said to himself. Kelly opened up the battery compartment on the GPS vehicle tracker and saw that it ran on four AA-cell batteries. The tracker was about the size of a large bar of hand soap and had magnets on one side to hold it to the vehicle. It had a rugged appearance and was labeled *Unit #1*. "Good. Nothing too complicated here."

He set the unit on the coffee table and unpacked the rest of the equipment in the case. Two other similar units were labeled *Unit #2* and *Unit #3*. There were also three smaller units about the size of Bic lighters labeled *Unit #4, Unit #5,* and *Unit #6*.

Turning his attention to the base unit, Kelly saw that it gave him the option to plug it into a 12-volt car cigarette lighter outlet, run it on batteries, or plug it into a regular wall outlet with an AC adaptor. The unit was a little smaller than a laptop computer and could be mistaken for one. The top flipped up like a laptop to expose the monitor. On the keyboard there were several toggle switches and a rollerball similar to those found on old laptops. When he plugged the unit in and turned it on, the screen brought up some kind of grid.

Kelly grabbed a box of AA batteries from the kitchen junk drawer and installed them in the tracker. He flipped the switch on the side, and a moment later a green dot appeared on the monitor screen. Kelly saw a button on the base unit labeled *Locate*. He pressed the button and a triangle appeared on the screen with the message: "Wait a moment while triangulation occurs." Soon a map started to populate the screen, and as it became more complete Kelly recognized the map as the Laredo area. As Kelly tapped the *Zoom In* key, an area of the map expanded to show a smaller area with a flashing dot. That area appeared to be his neighborhood. The GPS system had correctly found his location.

"Cool. Now I just need to figure out what to use it for."

Then his cell phone rang. He recognized the phone number as Senator Cuellar's.

"Hello."

"Kelly, it's Cuellar. How are you doing?"

"Fine, sir; how about yourself? When are you inviting me to one of those fine parties of yours again?"

"Next time we have one in Laredo, I will; but honestly, how are you doing? I always worry about you."

Kelly paused for a second, wondering if he should say anything.

"Well, honestly, sir, I think we have a situation. You remember that guy, Escobar? I saw him last night here in Laredo. Something's not right about that."

"You saw him here? In the United States? There's no way that guy should be here!"

"Yes, I know, but he's here. I don't know much more than this, but I am working on it."

"Kelly, you stay out of that. You hear me? He's very possibly behind what happened to Sarah, and I don't want the same thing to happen to you. Please, Kelly…stay out of it."

"Sir, I can't. What if he's here for me? And you know I can't trust all of my own people."

Cuellar was silent for a long moment before he continued. "Kelly, be careful."

"Sir, I will. I may need to ask for favors."

"Of course, Kelly, of course. Your wife was my right hand. I wouldn't be here if it wasn't for her. She managed me like a mom with her kids. Is there anything I can do now?"

"No, not yet. I don't know enough, and it may just work out without having to call you."

"Well, you call me. Keep me in the loop. This isn't a small thing."

"I will, sir."

"Okay. We just can't seem to keep you out of trouble even when you're not looking for it."

"No, sir."

"Okay, well, I better get going here, Kelly; keep me posted."

"Yes, sir. Thanks for calling."

The time had flown by while Kelly got familiar with the equipment, and it was already mid-afternoon. Ruben would be done at the gym and should be arriving home with his kids after school about now. Kelly put the equipment slightly out of sight under the coffee table and figured he'd better go and tell his partner that he had transferred out.

Chapter 8

"Come on, dude. You gotta be kidding me. How can I do my job without my partner?" Ruben was clearly upset as he returned from the kitchen with two bottles of beer and handed one to Kelly. "Stay with me, man. I'll let you be Batman. I was just kidding about that 'Robin' thing, you know. And what's a sidekick going to do without his superhero?"

Kelly smiled at Ruben's flair for the dramatic. He had a tight relationship with his partner and felt horrible about leaving him in the lurch. "Man, I just need a little time to take care of this thing I'm dealing with. I'll be back before long."

"Bro, it's a six-month detail. I saw the posting on the bulletin board."

"Oh...so you were thinking about taking it yourself, and now you're giving me crap."

"No, it ain't like that. You know. In fact, I thought it would be great for you, but I didn't tell you about it because I need you here with me." Ruben shook his head in frustration as he set his beer on the side table. "Now I'll probably get stuck with Ronnie Knox or that rookie chick who failed target practice three times. If I get dead, it's your fault, bro. I'd never abandon my partner like this."

Sylvia came into the living room and put coasters under the beer bottles. "Oh, is my big Teddy Bear crying like a little girl? Hmm? You're the one who's been telling me that Kelly should take a break from the heavy action. It will be great for him to be working in an office for a while, if you ask me."

"Well, nobody asked you," Ruben retorted. He instantly recognized his mistake just before Sylvia shot a thousand poison arrows at him with a single look. "But, of course, your opinion is always welcome here, my darling." Ruben got up and patted his buddy on the back. "And, as usual, my better half is right and I'm wrong. I'll miss you, but I'm happy for you, pal. Are you going to stay for dinner?"

"Thanks, but not tonight," Kelly said.

"Eat with us, Kelly," Sylvia pleaded. "It's make-your-own-taco night at the Garcia house. There's plenty, and the kids would love it."

"It sounds tempting, Sylvia, but I've got a boatload of stuff to go through to get up to speed on this new detail. I'll take a rain check though." Then Kelly turned to Ruben. "Let me take you out for a beer after dinner. It'll be our own little going-away celebration...and I've got some things to talk over with you too."

"Sounds good to me. Pick me up at 7:00."

"6:30," Sylvia interjected. ""It's Friday night, so I don't want you getting caught up in the night crowd stuff. Have him home by 8:00, Kelly."

"Will do, Boss," Kelly said with a tip of his cowboy hat and a grin.

"Gee...I wonder where we'll be going," Ruben said to Sylvia with a wink.

Kelly got all of the surveillance equipment unpacked and puttered with it until he had it all figured out. He looked at his watch and saw that he had an hour left before he had to pick up Ruben. "Let's plant one of these suckers, see how it works."

He grabbed a GPS tracker, a listening device, and a slim-jim for unlocking a car and headed to Docksneider's warehouse. Kelly parked out of sight and approached the building from the side that had no windows. The BMW he had followed last night and the green Cherokee he had seen at Deputy Marín's house were both there, backed-up to the side of the building. But the BMW was visible from the front door of the warehouse office while the Jeep was screened by the Beemer. He sneaked slowly up to the Jeep Cherokee in the daylight. He looked and listened very carefully and then placed the tracker inside the chrome rear bumper. The heavy-duty magnets attached with a clunk that was a little too audible for Kelly's liking, but he could tell it was secured quite well.

His heart began to race as he went between the vehicles to break into the passenger's side of the Jeep to plant the microphone. His first two attempts with the slim-jim failed, maybe because he was nervous and his hands were sweating. Then he heard the front door of the building just around the corner, and several voices emerged. He couldn't run, or he would be seen. The BMW was too low to the ground, so he quickly rolled under the Jeep and held his breath.

"It's a good day to be bad, Señor Deputy," Valdéz snorted as he opened the driver's door of the Jeep."

"Just get me out of here before someone sees, Miguel," said Deputy Marín.

Valdéz started the Jeep and drove ahead, leaving Kelly exposed, and more than a little shaken.

I think I'll get Ruben and have a beer now, Kelly thought. *Thank God for the towing package – over-sized tires and a heavy-duty suspension.*

Kelly and Ruben made their way to a small table near the vacant dance floor at the Roundup, which just happened to be in Cristina's station. Ruben had on a short-sleeved button-down shirt with a bold pattern and way too much Axe cologne – which was pretty dressed-up for the casual homebody – and Kelly wore his usual pale blue jeans, light-colored plaid cowboy shirt with the sleeves rolled up to the elbow, along with the mandatory Stetson and boots. He was still a little dusty after his close call at the warehouse.

"I think I'm going to grab a little bite too. I've been kinda busy since I left your place," Kelly said.

"Oof...just beer for me," said Ruben patting his belly. "I filled up on tacos – steak, chicken, shrimp...you should have stayed, man. Sylvia is a good cook."

"Hello, gentlemen," said Cristina as she approached the table to take their order. "You're a little early tonight, Mr. Smith. Budweiser?"

"Yes, ma'am. And, Cristina, this is my partner, Ruben Garcia."

Ruben had been distracted looking at a table of young ladies across the way, and when he heard his name he turned to greet Cristina. As his eyes went from her shorts slowly up past her bare midriff to her breasts his eyes kept growing wider. He was finally able to pry his eyes off her breasts and look at her face, which made him even more awestruck.

"Glad to meet you, Ruben. Kelly seems to think you're a pretty great guy. What can I get for you?"

Ruben couldn't speak, as his eyes just darted between her face and her breasts.

"Budweiser, Ruben?" Cristina prodded.

Ruben just nodded as sweat began to bead up on his forehead.

"Sorry...he doesn't get out much, Cristina. Bring me some of those chili-cheese fries too, will you? And...no tequila belt today? It's been a rough afternoon; I could use a shot."

"I don't put it on until the music starts in a few hours. I'll bring you a shot of Jack. Texas cowboys over 25 seem to like that better anyway," said Cristina, and she was off to put in the order and give Flaco some good-natured grief.

Kelly swatted his buddy on the arm. "Geez, Ruben, you act like you've never seen a girl before."

Ruben took a deep breath to recover from the experience. "That is not a girl, man. That is a perfect pile of sex wrapped up in the silkiest skin and the finest lady parts I have ever seen. Bro, I could never date a woman like that. If I took her out to dinner, I would jizz in my shorts before I finished my salad. Holy crap, bro. That's your girl?"

"Just settle down, Ruben. I've got some things to tell you." Kelly looked over to the table where Escobar had been the night before and then glanced around the bar, but he saw no familiar faces. "Something big is coming down. Very soon."

Kelly explained the whole situation – Escobar, Docksneider, the BMW, his plans for Cristina's mother, the surveillance equipment – and the Deputy.

Cristina could see the men were in a deep conversation and set their order on the table without a word.

"No, man! No. Not Rangel. He might have made some sleazy mistakes with some young boys, but there's no way he's going to betray the Border Patrol and his country. He's just not that kind of dirty."

"Look, I hope you're right. I don't know everything yet, but as soon as I can get a microphone in a car and maybe in Docksneider's warehouse I'll know a lot more."

"Look, man, I thought you were getting away from the action, but this...this is some deep shit. It...it's suicide, man. You can't do this. Not this way. You ain't Robocop, man. Leave this for the Feds, the DEA, the FBI. You're going to get yourself killed."

"I'll be careful. And I'm going to need your help. Be close for the next few days."

The two men had another beer and walked out of the front door of the Roundup with plenty of time left to get Ruben home before his curfew. Kelly's Jeep was on the side of the building, and he heard some humming and singing behind the dumpster as he approached his vehicle.

"Carlos…what's up?" Kelly asked as he poked his head behind the dumpster.

The boy was quiet and clearly scared as he looked at the imposing figure of Kelly in the dusk. He was changing out of soaking wet clothes and putting on some dry clothes from a sealed plastic bag. Kelly quickly figured it out.

"No need to be afraid of me, amigo. I'm not going to tell on you. So, you live across the river and come over every night to work?"

Carlos, looked at Kelly and then at Ruben and slipped into his dry shirt. "But you are the Border Patrol, Mr. Kelly. Maybe you will shoot me or arrest me."

Kelly smiled and patted Carlos's shoulder reassuringly. "Of course not. We're friends. We help each other. We always have. Actually, I'm proud of you. If everybody who crossed the river went home every night, we wouldn't need a Border Patrol. You take care. Your secret is safe with me." Kelly nodded and took a step towards his Jeep, but Carlos had something to say.

"Mr. Kelly."

"Yes, Carlos?"

"I think something bad is going to happen very soon."

Kelly and Ruben leaned on the dumpster as Carlos laid his wet clothes over the electric meter to dry a little before he had to put them back on for the return trip later on.

"I go across by the new bridge they are building because it is low and narrow there. There are many men on the other side and more big trucks everyday. Trucks that carry a big load like that one over there," he said, pointing to a semi. "They are turning them into American trucks with license plates and writing on the doors and sides in inglés."

Carlos looked nervous, and Kelly and Ruben were very

interested as he continued.

"And in my village ten kilometers down the river, many people keep coming in. Whole families. Hundreds of people. Maybe more. And the bars are very busy because they all have money...twenty dollars...fifty dollars...and even many one-hundred dollar bills in American money. I talk to some of the kids. They don't know everything, but it seems they are waiting for more people, and then they will make a lot of trouble in our town and then many of them will go across the river all together at the same time. Mr. Kelly, please don't let them burn down our town, and don't send soldiers to shoot everyone because my family is there. The people in my village are not a part of this."

"Where is your village, Carlos?"

"It was just a squatters village on the end of Al Hipódromo," said Carlos, "right on the river."

Ruben looked at his partner. "Hipódromo?"

"It's across the river from the tail section of town, a few miles past the Community College. Go ahead, Carlos."

"But it is not so small anymore. It has grown big because the river is narrow there and the water is Mexican almost all the way across."

"When will they cross the river?"

"I don't know. I am afraid to ask too many questions."

"Are there any men in suits who are the leaders?"

"There is one man. They call him 'Jefe.' He looks Mexican, but his Spanish is not like ours. He is from somewhere else. He has girls and guns and a car."

Kelly and Ruben just looked at each other, and Ruben understood that what Kelly had told him was all for real – and maybe bigger than either of them had thought.

"Thanks, Carlos. Don't work too hard – and be careful over there." Kelly took a step and then turned back towards the boy. "If you ever need anything – in your village or here in Laredo – or if you find out some information I should know, give me a call," he said, handing Carlos his card. "Use the cell phone number."

The duo got into Kelly's Jeep and were in silent thought for a while.

"They're gonna run the port with some big rigs, bro, and we'll be ten kilometers away chasing grandmas and babies out of the river," Ruben finally said.

"The bridge isn't open yet where they're staging it, but they can't set it up right next to an operational port bridge. They'd get caught. My guess is they will use the bridge furthest from the village where the decoy disturbance will be. Maybe the World Trade Bridge eight miles in the other direction, and 15 miles from the mob."

Ruben turned pale and stared straight ahead. "Dude," he said, and slowly turned to face Kelly. "I went into the station this morning to finish up our report on that port runner that went up in flames yesterday. There was a memo on my desk. Bridge Number 3 will be closed for six hours on Monday night – Cinco de Mayo – for a big parade across the river in Nuevo Laredo, and they'll do some bridge maintenance too." Ruben exhaled and shook his head. "The memo was signed by Deputy Chief Patrol Agent, Rangel Marín."

Chapter 9

Kelly dropped Ruben off and went home to plan his next move. Something wasn't making sense to him. If there was going to be a parade in Nuevo Laredo, it would be by the two central bridges near their downtown area. There was nothing but an industrial park way up by the other bridge. And there would be plenty of room there for them to set up their trucks inconspicuously.

The Rio Grande, or Rio Bravo del Norte as the Mexicans called it, ran North to South along the west side of upper Laredo and then made a 90 degree elbow to the East. The big bend slowed the river down there, and it wasn't far past the bend where Docksneider's warehouse was located – where the San Francisco Javier Avenue loop connected Eagle Pass Avenue to Pedregal Street. It was only a couple miles from there to Slaughter Park where the river bent to the South again, along the lower part of Laredo and down past Carlos's village.

Kelly looked at the tracking base unit monitor and saw that the Jeep Cherokee was not moving. It was parked about halfway between Docksneider's warehouse and Slaughter Park.

Nothing to do here, he thought. He scratched his head and remembered that he had made a mental note of the license plate numbers of the two vehicles at the warehouse. Kelly called the radio room at his headquarters.

"Border Patrol. Can I help you?"

Kelly recognized the voice. "Elena, this is Kelly Smith. How are you tonight?"

"Mr. Smith, I'm good; how are you?"

"Elena, I have huge favor to ask. I just got put on detail to the Intelligence Unit. I have a case I'm already working on. Can you run a couple of plates for me?"

Elena was used to having agents call in to have plates checked. Sometimes the younger agents were trying to find out the identity of a girl they were interested in, but usually it was legitimate inquiries. And Kelly was never one for abusing the system like that.

"Sure, give me the plate."

"HK2 556."

"Stand by...A Jeep Cherokee...It comes back to Enterprise Rental Car."

"Oh, is it the local agency?"

"Let me see...Yes it is; airport location."

"Okay, the second plate is JKT 234."

"Stand by...I'm not getting anything. Let me check the pending file for new cars. Okay...it looks like a brand new BMW for Jerrod Docksneider. Do you want me to print this?"

"No, that's alright, Elena. Thanks, you've been a great help."

"We'll talk to you later. Bye."

Kelly knew what he had to do. Tomorrow he would go by the rental car agency and find out who had rented the Jeep. He wanted to get to bed early, but he still had an hour to kill, so he popped open a cold beer and called Cristina. She always took a break at 9 o'clock.

"Hi, Kelly. Yes, this is Cristina and I'm fine. What's are you doing now? Your friend seems a little strange."

"Hello, pretty girl. I guess I just wanted to hear your voice before I go to sleep. Give Ruben another chance; you'll like him. What are you doing?"

"Just sitting in my car, petting my kitty and thinking about you," she said provocatively.

Kelly was confused. "You never told me you had a cat. That might be a problem when I come over to cook tomorrow, 'cause I'm allergic to cat dander."

"Oh, you stupid man," she muttered. "I don't have a cat. I hate cats, except for throwing them through windows in vacant houses. But I have something warm and soft that needs to be touched sometimes...and you haven't been doing your job there."

"Uhhhhmm...you don't mean...uh...I, um...well."

"Yes, Kelly. I'm a woman. I need a man. Is that plain enough for you? Or should I draw you a picture?"

"Well, you could *send* me a picture if you want..." he mumbled softly.

"Again, please? I'm not sure I heard you."

"Oh, uh, nothing, Cristina..."

"I did hear you, you know. Most men I would hang up on now, but you...it just gives me hope that maybe you are human after all. If I wasn't working tonight, I would come over and give you what the other men in this bar only dream of. Look, Kelly, thank you for calling, but I have to go to work now. The music is going to start soon."

"Okay. Great talking to you. See you tomorrow."

Kelly realized that he had better pick up his game a bit if he wanted to get something going with Cristina. After all, she could have any guy she wanted anytime she wanted him. Just then his phone beeped with an incoming text message. It was a picture of Cristina's lower region with just a little bit of her white panties visible behind the narrow strip that was the crotch of her Daisy Dukes. The note said, "Make my sad kitty smile."

Kelly smiled and shook his head. "That I will gladly do, my

beautiful girl." She had activated the launch sequence, and Kelly had to adjust his trousers to make room for his growing manhood. "Now there's one more thing I have to do before can I sleep."

SATURDAY, MAY 3

Chapter 10

Kelly woke up the next morning wondering what his next move would be. He had determined that the Jeep Cherokee in front of the Deputy's house and at Docksneider's warehouse had been rented, but he had no real plan as to how he would pursue this investigation. It was only about thirty-six hours ago that he had jumped down this rabbit hole. For now, his plan would be no plan at all. He would just follow the leads he had and take things as they came, being sure to keep his eyes and ears open.

He took a shower, drank his coffee, and headed out the door late in the morning, about 9:15. He drove to the airport and went to the Enterprise Car Rental booth. There was a vibrant young girl behind the counter with a nametag that said *Sabrina*. She appeared to be about 23 years old with nicely kept shoulder-length blonde hair and a smile that could melt glaciers.

"Good morning, sir, and welcome to Enterprise! How can I help you today?" she said cheerfully.

Kelly envied her energy, but he wasn't in the mood for cheerful. He was going to be asking for information that she wasn't required to give without a warrant or subpoena, so he sized her up and decided to rely on his skill in the art of the bluff to get the information he needed out of her. Failing that, he could always fall back on his charm, but he didn't feel much like smiling right now. He tossed and turned most of the night, and his mind was overloaded.

He flashed his badge and credentials briefly and put on a gruff and dispassionate "all business" persona as he spoke to the girl. "I'm Agent Smith with the United States Border Patrol. I'm working on a classified investigation. A vehicle identified as one of yours is involved in the case. I need you to tell me who rented the vehicle. This is the license plate number." He handed her the piece of paper with the plate number on it.

The wide-eyed girl became nervous but cooperative. "Y-y-yes sir! Uh, okay. Uh, let me look." She tapped on her keyboard to access the rental database.

"It's a Jeep Cherokee, and it was rented Thursday afternoon by Docksneider Import /Export, Freight Forwarders, Inc."

She was a helpful and sweet kid, so Kelly smiled to calm her down. "Thank you, Sabrina. How long do they have it rented for?"

"They're supposed to return it Tuesday morning," she said, a bit more relaxed.

"Does it say who signed for it?"

Sabrina paused. "Am I supposed to be telling you all this stuff?"

"You're doing your country a great service ma'am, and probably saving some lives." Kelly knew she didn't have a chance against him, so he leaned over the counter and put his hand on her arm. Then, with a warm, professional smile he added, "I really need to know this right now, Sabrina, or it might be too late." She blinked; he won.

"Umm, it says Hector Escobar is the primary driver."

"You wouldn't happen to remember any of these guys, would you?"

"No, sir, I sure don't. We see a lot of people here, and that was a couple of days ago."

"Is there a contact number for them?"

"Yes, there is."

"I'll need that too."

"This is pretty unusual, sir, I'm not sure I should be doing this."

"I think I'm getting a text," Kelly lied. He fumbled through his pockets and set his badge and a set of handcuffs conspicuously in front of the young girl. "I guess not," he said, looking at his phone.

Sabrina was beginning to figure out Kelly. "I'm pretty sure you're not going to handcuff me, Officer Smith. I do trust you, and if this case involves the Border Patrol, I know it must be important. It's just that I don't want to lose my job...you know."

Kelly nodded understandingly and leaned on the counter. "Ma'am, this is a very big case. There are a lot of very bad people involved that have hurt a lot of people. If we can't get to them right away, a lot more people are going get hurt, a lot of innocent people. I would really appreciate your help."

"What's the case about?" she asked.

Time to lay on the charm, he thought. "Ma'am, we're the Border Patrol," he said with a smile. "Around these parts we primarily deal with criminals trafficking drugs or people. I can't tell you what the case is about, but it's not about people sneaking into the country."

The girl gave Kelly a serious look and then checked her left and right flank for supervisors. "Those drug bastards killed my cousin last year," she said as she wrote the number on a rental pamphlet and slid it to Kelly. "I hope you get them, Mr. Smith, and if I see them I'll call you."

"Thank you, Sabrina. I really appreciate that. You've been a lot of help. Here...this is my card. Please don't try to do anything heroic about any of this. I don't want you getting involved – because you will get hurt – but if you think of anything, call me."

"Sure; yes, sir."

"Will you be working the day they return the car?"

Sabrina thought for a moment. "Yes, I will."

"Can you call me the minute they return the car, you know, not right in front of them but after they leave?

"Well, I'll try."

"Okay, thanks. I better get going."

Kelly left the counter thinking he should try being charming more often. It seemed to get him further. He also started worrying that this young counter girl could screw things up so bad she could get herself killed.

Kelly got back into the car and looked at the phone number Sabrina had given him. It appeared to be a local number. He dialed it on an impulse, and somebody answered.

"DoubleTree Inn."

"Yes, Hector Escobar. Has he arrived yet?"

The voice on the other end of the line paused. "Let me look. Oh, yes. He has been here for a few days already. Would you like me to connect you with his room?"

"Yes, please."

"Hold On." After a silent pause, Kelly hung up.

A minute later his phone rang with a return call from the Inn, but he didn't answer.

Kelly needed to do some quick thinking on his next move. He headed over to the DoubleTree and started looking for the Jeep Cherokee in the parking lot. His tracking monitor showed that the Jeep was there.

Rolling through the lot, Kelly spotted the vehicle and kept driving by until he could pull into a parking space. Then he opened up the case with the surveillance equipment and pulled out the listening device marked #4. He still had the slim-jim with him to open the door of a locked vehicle.

He stepped out of his Jeep and turned his whole body all the way around counterclockwise, instead of just turning his head in a suspicious manner, slowly scanning the entire parking lot to see if anybody was watching. He walked up to the rented Cherokee from behind and reached under the rear bumper. The GPS tracking device was still solidly in place.

Now he needed to plant the microphone. The listening device was supposed to be able to pick up conversations inside the car if the device was secured to the roof and the vehicle was moving at a relatively slow speed, but Kelly didn't want to take any chances. He slipped the slim-jim down between the car door window and the weather strip molding. With a few tugs on the device, this time Kelly was able to unlock and open the door. He activated the listening device and wedged it under the front seat against the seat rails. He locked the door and closed it.

Returning to his Jeep, he turned on the laptop and waited for it to boot up. Once it had booted, he opened the file and selected *Unit #4* and pressed the *Activate* icon. On the left side of the screen there was a selection bar for the audio. The only option was volume. The middle of the screen started populating with a map that looked similar to any generic Google map or Yahoo map service, except this one had already gone to the Laredo area and had a red star with a "4" in the middle of the screen. Using the mouse pad and the *Zoom* option Kelly was able to take the map down to the exact intersection of the DoubleTree location, and a popup identified *La Posada DoubleTree* – the DoubleTree Inn.

Kelly plugged in an earpiece just as Escobar and four other men came out of the hotel and got into the Jeep. He turned up the volume and could hear chatter in Spanish. Trying to listen to and interpret several different conversations at the same time, Kelly was able make out one conversation about how hot-looking the receptionist was. The other conversation was about a *"puente pontón."* Kelly understood the word *"puente"* to be "bridge" in English, but wasn't sure about the word *"pontón."*

They're planning to run the port, Kelly thought. But he didn't know which bridge they would be using.

The other two men in the Jeep were quiet, possibly listening to the two leaders. They hadn't even left the parking lot, and they were talking about having to come back for the rest of the men. One of the men asked when they were going to get more vehicles. Transportation needed to be quicker, the one talking complained, saying that going back and forth to pick up people was a waste of time. He thought dedicated vehicles would be needed for surveillance. This same voice went on to say that surveillance needed to start right away, during daylight hours, in order to get to know the area better.

Another voice could be heard saying that those details should be taken care of today and that this was part of the reason why they were going to the warehouse, so Escobar could discuss what they need with Docksneider. As they pulled out onto the main street they picked up speed, and the road noise started drowning out the conversation. Kelly figured they were going to Docksneider's warehouse, and started heading to the store to buy what he needed for dinner at Cristina's house.

Kelly could see on the monitor that they were headed in the direction of Docksneider's warehouse, and he figured the conversation would soon be out of range. The Tracker used the GPS satellites, so that signal should remain steady, but he didn't know how far the microphone could transmit back to the base unit. As he turned North off Zaragosa Street, the sound took on a lot of static and then cleared up. Kelly looked at the monitor, and right above the red star with the "#4" the word "Roaming" appeared.

"Well, I'll be damned," said Kelly. "It's using the law enforcement subcarrier on the cell phone towers. Maybe these things aren't as ancient as I thought."

Chapter 11

Kelly picked up what he needed to make dinner and several packages of fresh AA batteries at Serena's Market on Sanchez, just across the tracks from Cristina's neighborhood. His excitement to see his favorite girl had him running about a half-hour ahead of schedule.

He pulled onto Garza Street, just across from Dovalina Elementary where Cristina's son went to school. The old neighborhood was snuggled between the river and the railroad tracks. It was about 4:00 in the afternoon when he pulled into her driveway. The house was old but neat. The neighborhood was as old as the house and typical of the older neighborhoods in Laredo: There were some very large newly-built homes next to run-down houses, as the people here liked to stay in the area where their families had lived for generations, even when they became successful. Further down the street there was a fancy modern Spanish-style villa with an old dilapidated garage.

Cristina's yard was fronted with an old picket fence in serious need of paint and repair, but most of the flaws were covered by vines that had overgrown the entire fence. A nicely groomed lawn overloaded with potted plants was behind the fence. The siding on the house was 3-inch board and batten with a worn whitewash finish, and

69

there was a small partially-enclosed porch at the front entry. The metal roof had a high pitch with four gables. A couple cats hung out on the porch and a couple more lounged around the front yard. It was a simple place that exuded the welcoming feel of several generations of family at the same location – not rich, but perhaps near middle class.

The surveillance monitor needed a recharge, so Kelly put it in a bag with the groceries, along with the charger cable. With two bags of groceries in one hand Kelly walked up to the front door and knocked. He shook his head and thought, *This is a hell of a way to have a first date: "Oh, and by the way, do you think you could help me take down a major drug cartel while we're at it?"*

Cristina's mother answered the door. She was a woman of about 50, maybe older, but a well-preserved image of Cristina with glasses. Still a fine-looking woman, she clearly cared more about family than appearance.

"Mr. Smith?"

"Yes, ma'am."

"Ah, my name is Magdalena Chavez. I am Cristina's mother. Please come in."

"Thank you, ma'am. I can see where Cristina gets her good looks."

"Cristina, I already don't like this man. He throws out compliments like *chicle* from a piñata!"

He walked past the rather grand wooden staircase, through the foyer, and into the living area. The living room had a vintage old couch and chair, probably from the 1940s, that showed some wear but still looked remarkably elegant. There was also a 1970s recliner, some blonde end tables, and a large glass coffee table with a tube steel frame that had not stood up as well as the older furniture. Family pictures and bric-a-brac adorned the shelves and walls.

Cristina walked out from the kitchen, unpinning the bun in her hair as she shook it loose and let it fall. She looked like a petite runway model in a tight fitting black dress with a scoop neckline and a hem about 4 inches above her knees. She was barefoot and bra-less, leaving Kelly to wonder if the dress might not be the only piece of clothing she had on.

"Sí, Mama, he's trying to be nice; don't start with him."

Oh, this is going to be interesting, Kelly thought to himself.

"Hi, Cristina," Kelly said trying to get past the first hurdle.

"Hi, Kelly. You're early, and you came prepared. You want to bring that stuff in here?"

"Sure, and I might as well get started. This is going to take a while."

"I will give you this, Mr. Smith: A man that cooks is not a bad thing," Cristina's mother said with a forced smile.

"Well, I'm getting somewhere with you, aren't I, Ms. Chavez?"

"My name is Magdalena. My friends call me Magda, but you can call me Magdalena."

Cristina gave her mother an annoyed and disapproving look, but Kelly was willing to take the time to win her acceptance.

"Okay, Ms. Chavez...uh...Magdalena."

She gave Kelly a long look over her glasses.

"Oh, hey, Cristina, would you mind if I charge up my little laptop here?"

"Give," she said with her hand extended. "I'll put it on the phone table by the stairs because it is easy to get to the plug. My phone is charging there too." she said as she quickly plugged it in and returned.

"Okay, spaghetti tonight," said Kelly, very theatrically as he rubbed his hands together, "but this is not just any spaghetti. It is my special 'Kelly Smith' spaghetti made from an old family recipe passed down to me from Rachel Rae on the Food Network!" Kelly seemed to be the only one amused as he looked at the stone faces on the two women. "*And* there's salad, bread, and, of course..." he said, pulling a bottle of Zinfandel out of a bag with a flourish, "…red wine!" Kelly put the bottle on the counter and thought about what he would need to prepare the meal. "First, I will need a cutting board, a good knife, and a can opener."

"No, first you will need a beer," Cristina said, handing him a cold Bud she had just pulled out of the refrigerator.

I think I could really like this girl, Kelly thought to himself.

"Thank you," Kelly said with an impressed and appreciative nod. "Magdalena, how long have you lived here?"

"I was born here, in this house. My grandfather bought this house in 1943 and gave it to his only son, my father. When he died my three other siblings had already moved on, so I moved in with my mother and so here we are."

"I like it. It has a nice feel about it," Kelly said, nodding and looking around.

"Thank you." She was checking this man out. Magda did not trust men. Most of the men she dealt with were trying to be *"macho, muy hombre,"* and she had no time for that. She was a proud woman trying to maintain what she had.

"Mijo! Max! Come here! We have a guest; come meet him!" Cristina yelled.

A moment later Maximino, or Max as his mother called him, walked into the kitchen. He was a good-looking boy with all the family resemblance showing through.

"Max, this is Mr. Smith."

"Hi," Max said.

"Hi, Max. That's a good, strong name for a handsome fellow like you," Kelly said.

"Ah, there he goes, throwing out compliments again."

"Mama!" scolded Cristina as she glared at her mother.

"Okay, what about a knife." Kelly said as he started pulling fresh green peppers, mushrooms, and garlic out of the bag.

Max was quick to direct him to the knives. "The drawer in front of you. You are making spaghetti for us tonight?"

"Yes, I am"

"Good. I like Spaghetti. Can I go now?"

"Are you watching TV or playing video games?" asked Kelly.

"I have homework."

"Wow, impressive. Nice meeting you, Max. I'll get busy on the spaghetti and call you when it's ready."

"Thanks." Max turned and left.

"Nice kid." Kelly said.

Max noticed the laptop-type device on the table and opened the monitor. The map of Laredo appeared, and a moment later he saw the red star flash with the message "audio detected." He was curious and wondered what kind of music his visitor listened to. His mother's phone was almost fully charged, so he pulled the large USB end from the plug and inserted it into the device. He looked over his shoulder and then found the record app on the phone and started recording the incoming audio and headed upstairs.

The women retired to the living room with one bottle of beer and two glasses as Kelly began the preparations. He browned a pork chop and a piece of beef in a little oil in a sauce pan and then sliced and sautéed the mushrooms and peppers in a small frying pan with the garlic and other herbs and spices. Then he put it all together with the meat in the saucepan and added a couple cans of crushed tomatoes and some tomato sauce.

Once the preparation of the sauce was out of the way and the sauce was simmering, he put on a large pot of water to boil and walked into the living room where the women were talking and holding empty beer glasses. "We'll let it simmer as long as possible and then eat at about 5:30," he said.

"Come here and talk to us," Cristina said with a pouty look, patting the couch cushion next her. "Mama was just telling me about her work."

"I still have to prepare the bread and the salad," Kelly said, "but I'd love to hear about her work. Let me grab you another beer, and then I'll join you for just a minute."

"Bring us two bottles, please. I want a whole one for myself this time," Magda said.

Kelly nodded and headed for the fridge while Cristina looked irritated. She didn't want Kelly to think they were big drinkers.

"Mama..." Cristina whined.

"It's my house. It's my beer. It's my way," said Magdalena firmly. "Your cowboy isn't going to care. I don't need a *pene* to drink some beer."

Kelly returned with three fresh beers, handed two to the ladies, and then raised his bottle toward them and took a swig.

"It's starting to smell good. Maybe you can cook, Kelly," Cristina said.

"Thank you, ma'am," Kelly said with a nod.

"Look on the TV, Mr. Border Patrol man. I think you are going to be busy soon. You have a lot of customers gathering just across the river," said Magdalena.

Kelly looked at the news report coming from the station in Nuevo Laredo on the Mexican side of the river. Large numbers of people seemed to be streaming into a village just a few miles down stream. Kelly knew that all of the street activity probably meant riots were likely to begin soon, and a rush on the border was all but a certainty.

Carlos was right, he thought. *Tom Bird too.*

If a thousand people cross at once, they know that most of them will get through. The news report said they were gathering for a Cinco de Mayo music festival, but three-generation families didn't look like a typical group of music fans to Kelly's trained eye. He figured he had two or three days at the most before some kind of hell broke loose.

The report ended and he turned to Magdalena. "So, you work at an import/export warehouse, Magdalena?"

"Yes, I work for that little weasel you saw in the bar last night. The one you asked Cristina about."

"Ah, yes. Docksneider, isn't it?"

"Yes...but most of the workers there call him 'Cock-biter.'"

Kelly did his best not to spew his mouthful of beer across the room. "I'd like to hear a little more about the operation there, but first I need Cristina to show me how to pre-heat the oven for the garlic bread." Kelly got up and offered his hand to Cristina, which she grabbed and pulled herself to her feet.

"With most guys this would be an excuse to get me alone," Cristina said to her mother, "but with this man...no such luck. He just wants a hot oven." She grabbed Kelly's sleeve to go, but then her mother began to speak.

"What's the matter, Mr. Smith? Don't you like my daughter?"

Cristina looked at Kelly with wide eyes and an inquisitive smile, putting him on the spot even more.

"Well...she's a very...pleasant girl," Kelly responded, his head still in a stunned daze from the question. Professing his feelings was not his strong suit.

Magdalena cackled loudly and slapped her knee. "I know my daughter, Señor. She is beautiful and smart and hard-working and headstrong – but she is very rarely pleasant. Put an ugly face on her, and she would have men running away screaming from her 'pleasantness.' But I still don't know if you like her. I have heard you compliment everyone in this house since you arrived – except for Cristina. Perhaps you have nothing nice to say about her, Mr. Smith...?"

Cristina clasped her hands behind her tailbone and swayed from side to side, like a shy schoolgirl. Kelly knew he had to say something that would satisfy both of them. He had been struggling to come to terms with his emotions for other women since his wife's death.

He put his hand on Cristina's shoulder, inhaled deeply, and looked her straight in the eye but directed his words towards her mother. "I think your daughter is the most beautiful, strongest, sweetest..." then he turned his gaze to Magdalena for a moment, "...and most pleasant woman alive on this earth." He looked back to Cristina and continued, "And, yes...I like her."

Magdalena hid a tear and shooed the couple off to the kitchen. "Well, if she is pleasant to you, then she must like you very much, Mr. Smith. Go light the oven now. Cristina, I will be in there in five minutes, and we will get the good dishes out and set the table." That was her hint to Cristina to get any kissing out of the way right now.

Cristina was floating on a cloud and did not speak as they went into the kitchen and out of her mother's line of sight. She faced Kelly and put her hands around his neck.

"So...you like me, Mr. Smith?"

Kelly was speechless in this bonding moment as Cupid attacked both of them with an all-out assault. They kissed tenderly for a long while, which felt like a timeless eternity in a far-off paradise, and then they held each other in a tender embrace.

"Here I come," announced Magdalena. "You forgot how the oven works, Cristina? What temperature, Mr. Smith?"

" Call me Kelly. 375 should be good."

"Okay, Kelly. And starting tomorrow you may call me Magda."

Cristina's jaw dropped, as her mother had never allowed one of her boyfriends to call her Magda before. The ladies got the plates and silverware and disappeared into the dining room to set the table.

Kelly put the pasta into the boiling water and cut the bread. Then the butter, garlic, and Italian seasoning were cooked together to drizzle over the crusty slices, which he would toast in the oven when it was hot.

The salad was a simple tossed salad with pitted black olives thrown in, then mixed with cottage cheese and Italian dressing.

He wished the sauce could simmer a while longer, but a quick taste test told him that it was good enough. He tested a strand of the spaghetti as it cooked to see if it was done, but it needed a couple more minutes. He put the sliced bread on a baking sheet and slathered on the buttery mixture, and then he sprinkled it with a little grated Parmesan and slid it into the hot oven. He took one more noodle from the boiling pot and tasted it.

"*Al dente*," he said. Then he kissed his closed fingers and thumb and quickly pulled them from his lips and spread them open, in a classic gesture indicating culinary perfection. He pulled the pasta off the stove and drained it.

"Almost ready, ladies. Call Max."

"I'm already here," said Max from the other room. "I smelled it and got hungry."

"Don't burn the bread," hollered Magda.

He poured the pasta into a large bowl, ladled sauce over it, mixed it together, and then put another ladle of sauce over the top. A little sprinkle of Parmesan was the finishing touch. He pulled the bread from the oven, and it was perfect – warm and slightly golden. Everyone came into the kitchen.

"Maximino, get three tongs for the salad, spaghetti, and bread," commanded Magda as she grabbed the salad.

Cristina placed the bread on a platter as Kelly triumphantly took his masterpiece, and everyone went to the dinner table.

The table was beautifully set and the wine was poured. Magdalena had already had a couple of beers and was relaxed and in a good mood.

Max and Kelly each had two helpings, and no one left anything on their plate.

"Thank you, Mr. Kelly," said Max. "You can come and cook again tomorrow! It was very delicious." Then he left the table. On the way to his room, he grabbed his mother's cell phone and went upstairs.

"Yes, that was very good, Kelly," said Magda. "Next time I will cook for you."

Cristina was very pleased and admired her cowboy in a whole new way. "I will get iced tea for everyone. I think that will be all the dessert any of us needs," she said as she headed off to the kitchen.

This was Kelly's chance to delve further into what Magda might know about Docksneider and Escobar. "Magdalena, your boss, Docksneider, he's a good man?"

"No, not at all. He pays me, but not enough for what it is I do. He is cheap. He doesn't pay any of us enough. Except of course his operations manager, Valdéz. Miguel Valdéz is actually my boss, and Docksneider is his boss. He is very *mammon.* He is always sucking up to Docksneider and hiding things from us about how things are going. It makes it very difficult to work there."

Cristina returned and set the beverages on the table. She moved her chair right up to Kelly's. Then she sat and listened quietly with her feet up and her knees on Kelly's lap.

"So, why do you stay?" asked Kelly.

"You know, wages are very low in this town. Even though he doesn't pay me enough, if I left he would badmouth me, and nobody would hire me. I'm stuck. He brings in these young boys and girls as my assistants. They are no good to me, but he uses them for what he wants, then gets rid of them."

Kelly saw an opening.

"Cristina, you know the other night, when I was in the bar and I asked you about Docksneider and the guys he was with?"

"Yeah."

"Well...those guys were heavily involved in the murder of my wife three years ago. I don't have the proof yet, but all the facts point that way. I followed them that night after they left the bar, and they went to our Deputy's house."

A silence fell on the table. Both women started to understand why Kelly was there but did not quite get the full magnitude of it all.

Kelly went on: "Those guys are some of the biggest cartel bosses around. They're up to something. This gathering down the river might have something to do with it."

"And you want to include us in your *venganza?*" Magdalena probed.

Kelly wanted to say "yes," but he thought it better to let the reality sink in. He was asking an awful lot of these people who had everything to lose and nothing to gain.

Cristina's rational side was taking the lead. She had her son to consider, the risk she would be putting her son into, the risk to herself, and her mother's safety. It would be her mother that would be taking most of the risk. She was the one that worked right in the middle of Docksneider's snake pit.

Her emotional side was also tugging at her. She really liked Kelly. He was a good man, and she wanted to be with him.

"Look. I've said too much. I should leave. Can I help clear the table?"

"No. We can clear it, Mr. Smith," Magdalena said.

Kelly took the hint. He was "Mr. Smith" again. "Well, then, I'd better leave. Thank you." Kelly got up and started for the door.

Cristina had said nothing up to this point. She got up and followed Kelly to the door. "Here's your laptop and charger, Kelly...I'll call you. Thank you for coming over. I mean it." She hugged him and then slid her hand against his face. They smiled reticently at each other for a moment, then Kelly left and Cristina closed the door.

"Él es un Loco!" Magdalena exclaimed as Cristina walked back towards the table. "He wants to include us in his war against the cartels."

Kelly skulked into his Jeep for a long silent ride home. He was feeling as though he had made a huge mistake by trying to recruit the help of Cristina and Magda. But his mission had to continue, one way or another. He turned on his monitoring equipment and headed for home.

Chapter 12

Cristina and her mother silently cleaned up the dinner table. Cristina said nothing about what Kelly had said to them.

"You say nothing. You can't be considering what he said," Magdalena said, more as a statement than a question.

"The dinner was good, don't you think?"

Magdalena just looked at her daughter who knew she couldn't avoid the issue. There was a long pause before Cristina spoke.

"We would all be taking a risk, but it's you that would be taking the biggest risk. You work for those people. He would be asking you to do the most. And what about Max? They could hurt him. That would be the first thing they might do besides kill us. And we have lost so much already. I have lost a husband and you a son. Everything tells me not to do this. But something else tells me I should. But the decision has to be yours. You are risking everything. Still…"

"Mija, don't let your heart pull you into this."

"I know. But it's not just my heart. They're bastards; they took so much from us."

"Yes they are, but they could take even more. Think about Max."

"If it got that bad we could send him away."

Deep inside her heart of hearts, Magdalena wanted to get back at them also but could not convince herself to act. She knew how dangerous and heartless these people were.

"Cristina, this is too much...I cannot...I don't know." Magdalena fell silent and went about washing dishes.

Cristina did not press the issue further, but Magda's most painful memories were invading her mind and twisting her heart. The boyish but mature cowboy had impressed her with his demeanor, his respect, his cooking, and his genuine affection for her daughter. She needed to think. They finished up, and their night ended with a worried silence.

Just then Max galloped down the stairs and entered the room. He was wearing earbuds, which were connected to Cristina's cellphone in his hand. His face was ashen and his expression dire and wide-eyed.

"Mama! They are going to bring big trucks full of drugs across the river. Are good people like my papa going to die again? Mama? Are they? There will be many men with machine guns and rocket-propelled grenades. And...and...they were talking about Mr. Kelly too...they don't like him because he is good. They are afraid he might get in their way."

The women looked at each other, and Magda and Max rushed to Cristina for a three-generation embrace.

*   *   *   *

Miguel Valdéz and other top henchmen were in the fanciest suite in La Posada DoubleTree with their leader, Hector Escobar. Valdéz was a 38-year-old bisexual. His deep-set shifty eyes, acne-scarred face, large bent nose, and furry unibrow made the man quite unattractive and gave him a menacing look. And he had a broad girth of a waistline, which magnified his short stature.

He was also a master of logistics. Before coming to Laredo he worked in the trucking industry in Venezuela. He knew how to handle materials. He had been in Laredo for five years working for different freight forwarders and trucking outfits, learning the areas and identifying people that they could trust. He was the one that identified

Docksneider. He had seen an unscrupulous side to him that could be approached and exploited. To all appearances, he works for Docksneider managing the dock, but in reality Docksneider now works for him – and Hector Escobar.

Docksneider also had the connections in the trucking industry and a warehouse on the Rio Grande that would be indispensible in carrying out an operation as large as the one they had planned and were preparing to execute. Docksneider was the final piece of their plan, and when the deal was done, Valdéz went to work for Docksneider to set the plan in motion. Escobar spoke first:

"It's a simple plan that has not been exploited yet. If we don't do it soon someone else will, or the 'Migra' will start posting patrols in the area making it impossible. We need to do it now, or the opportunity will be lost. If we can get the Mexicans to do their part and create a large enough riot down river, the border will be open up river. I don't trust those Mexicans. They're likely to try and take over this operation and steal everything."

Valdéz, Escobar's Operations Manager and asset on the ground in Laredo, spoke up. "Don't worry, Colonel Escobar. The deal we have with the Mexicans that are working for us is like the Americans and Russians – what do they call it? – Mutually Assured Destruction. They have all their Nukes pointed at each other knowing if one pulls the trigger the other will too and they will both be very, very dead.

"But with our deal, each side comes out very, very rich if they do what they are supposed to do. If they don't, they get nothing, and somebody will also be dead. And I assure you, Colonel, it will not be you or me that is dead. That being said, I know you want to be here to see thing go as planned, but you are a target and you would be better off away from here. We have been planning this for months. Every detail has been thought of and addressed. Your distance from here will assure compliance because you will not be so accessible to any threat."

Escobar had heard this all before and knew it all made sense, but with so much at stake the thrill of the operation intrigued him and kept him close to the action.

"Miguel, you are a salesman and a genius of an operator, but there is no way that I can stay away with so much at stake. We're talking 1.6 billion dollars worth of cocaine across the border at one time and getting into the interior of the United States in one fell swoop! This is immense! If we do this just this one time we don't have to do it again…but just think if we can do it several times!"

Only a few places along the Rio Grande River were low enough, shallow enough, and narrow enough to allow the plan to work. It just so happened that this location was the construction site of the next international bridge that would connect the U.S. and Mexico – right next to Docksneider's warehouse. It was exactly what engineers look for in bridge crossings. Heavy equipment was everywhere, which hid the fact that many trucks were being gathered to stage the operation. Much of the site had been cleared, graded, and prepped to allow this operation to happen.

"Your plan is brilliant, Colonel," Valdéz said as he poured several glasses of wine and handed one to Escobar. "One by one, our caravan of semi trucks loaded with pure Colombian cocaine will cross the river from Mexico on a bridge that was made in America."

Escobar smiled devilishly as he bit down on his stub of a cigar. "Sometimes the famous American ingenuity can be very helpful to us," he said.

"Especially when it is combined with our own great criminal genius," Valdéz added. He and Escobar clinked their wine glasses and downed the ruby red beverage.

One by one, loaded semi trucks from Mexico would cross the bridge. Once across, the trucks would immediately head out of town on IH-35 where checkpoints will have been shut down in order to respond to the riot, by order of Deputy Marín. From there they offload into several dozen smaller trucks that are not weighed, logged, or regulated. Then they will scatter onto US 83 and 59, Hwy 44, IH-10 and other disparate routes to cities all across America.

Escobar redirected his attention to his Lieutenant, Juan Chavarria. The Colonel had brought his own military thugs in to handle the more technical parts of the operation. His team was a platoon of Colombian Special Operations soldiers lead by Captain Chavarria that Escobar had paid off to do this mission.

Colombia flew the team to The United States to buy American military supplies needed for military rescue, reconnaissance, scouting, and even drug interdiction operations. The Colombian government did not know that they would be using the equipment for their own pernicious operation.

"Chavarria, have you and your men checked the merchandise? How does it look? Are you ready?"

Chavarria was a rather tall Hispanic with a fit military look about him.

"Colonel, as I have told you before, we are familiar with this equipment. We have used these before in Colombia when the Americans came down to ford rivers there. The ones we have bought will work fine. If this operation is a success and we can take them back to Colombia, they will pay for themselves again for the good of Colombia. We have been checking the equipment out as it comes into the warehouse yard to see if all is functional. But it looks fine; we checked it out before we bought it too. The Americans take good care of their equipment. If everything goes according to plan, once we start the deployment we will have it up in 45 minutes and back down in about the same time. My part is to assemble and disassemble it quickly and accurately. Everyone else needs to do his part. The truckers need to drive, the rioters need to riot, and so on. If you can get your six trucks across in an hour, we will have this operation done in three."

Escobar was silent for a long moment. "Nobody leaves this hotel. Nobody talks to anybody outside of this unit. Right now nobody knows what we're up to outside of this room except for a few other people that have way too much to lose if they screw up, so I cannot worry too much about them. But if we talk to the wrong waitress in the cantina we are screwed. Everybody wins here if we do what we are supposed to do. No talking to anybody! Is that clear?"

"Sí, Comandante!" They all replied in unison.

SUNDAY, MAY 4

Chapter 13

Magdalena had a restless night. Her hatred for the cartels and all they represented ate at her. She had felt and heard the gruesome effects of the cartels; good people turned to human garbage, the almost sacrificial exploitation of women by cartel kings, the raw effect it has had on her family. She would love to strike a blow at them, but she needed it to be such a blow that they would never forget. She imagined herself to be "the little lady that could and did."

Magda got up the next morning and put on her long chenille robe and fuzzy slippers. She shuffled into the kitchen where she found Cristina making coffee in her bra and panties.

"Good morning, mama, how did you sleep?"

"Like mierda in a blender," Magda responded, rubbing her eyes. "I want you to call your new *chile* and tell him to come over and tell us how we can help."

"Mama, yesterday you hated him; today you call him my new *chile* and want him to come back. What's going on with you? Are you trying to take him away from me, or what?"

"Chica, you heard what Max found out from Mr. Smith's computer. If there is something big that can be made to happen to

James Herrick

screw Docksneider and his cronies, but in a big way, I want a part of it, for all the suffering they have caused so many of us. I thought about it all night, and my mind is made up. And, chica – take him away from you? An old woman like me? That little *puta* dress you had on last night, I cannot compete with." Magdalena laughed at the thought and kissed her daughter on the cheek. "And these," she said, squeezing Cristina's bra just a little, "they skipped a generation. You got them from your abuela. I got my father's tetas and my mother's moustache. I can't compete with those either."

Cristina rolled her eyes and shook her head as Magda shuffled towards the stool by the kitchen counter and waited for the coffee to get done. "Mama, I love your boobies. They're so perfect and full. Mine are good for a man, but not so good for the woman who has to carry them all day."

Magda continued, "Anyway, mija, the only sex I want from that man is to give me more grand-babies. Maximino needs a brother and sister, too."

"Mama, you're a little bit crazy, but I love you. I want to help too, but I'm just scared for you."

The ladies talked about work and men and kids and drank the pot of coffee. Then Magda washed the cups and Cristina called Kelly.

Kelly had been trying to call Escobar at the hotel without any luck when Cristina's call came in. He answered, his voice a little tense and surprised. "Cristina…I'm glad you called. Look, I'm really sorry that I mentioned this whole investigation to you and your mom. I feel horrible about it, and I promise I'll never…"

"It's too late for that, Kelly. Mama wants to help…and so do I. But if you put her in a situation where she gets hurt or anything happens to Max, I swear I will kill you. Do you miss me? I miss you already. The dinner last night was so good…and so were the kisses. I touched myself in the shower this morning thinking about you."

Kelly marveled at the way Cristina could shift from terminator to fairy princess to slutty temptress in a single breath.

He mumbled softly near the phone, "I'm not sure if you want to stab me, paint my toenails, or ride the pony…"

"What's that, Kelly? I couldn't hear you."

"Uh, um…oh, nothing. I was just wondering if maybe I should come over."

"Well, you're the Herbert Hoover running this show. What do you need to do?"

Kelly was confused for a moment. "I think you mean J. Edgar Hoover, baby."

"Oh, sorry…baby." Cristina liked the sound of this new term of endearment.

"Look, I just got out of a meeting about this. I have to shit, shower, and shave…uh, I mean I have to wash my face and get my notes together. Can I come by in about 45 minutes?"

"Sure. We'll see you then…my *chile*."

* * * *

Kelly pulled up to Cristina's house. He closed up the laptop and put it under the seat. He was not sure how this would go. He knew he had to isolate these women from the danger, but he still needed Magda's help. She was the insider at the warehouse. He had to talk to her to find out just what she did know and what more she could do or find out. He was counting on her to place a tracking device and a microphone in strategic places.

He was about to knock on the door when it opened. Cristina was standing there in shorts and a halter-top with a stern look on her face.

"Come in," she told him.

Kelly walked in without saying a word. He began to wonder how serious Cristina was when she said she would kill him if any of her family got hurt.

Magda was standing in the living room in a brightly patterned

89

housedress and slippers.

Kelly just started talking. "Ms. Chavez, thank you for considering this. First, there is no way I am going to ask you to do anything that will put you in danger. And if you think that something I ask will put you in danger, please don't do it. This mission is about saving lives, not losing them. Can we sit down?"

"Of course," she said.

"What I think I really need from you is information on how things work at the warehouse. Are you seeing anything different? What is it exactly that you do there? Do you have access to all files?"

"Docksneider and Valdéz have been acting strange lately. Actually, things have been very different – a whole different mood and lots of secrecy – every since Docksneider hired Valdéz on as a manager before Christmas. There have been some unusual men coming around too. Not the usual clients. These men are not Mexican. They are from someplace else, you know, like South America. I can tell by their accents. It's not Mexican, and it's not Central American. I don't have a lot of interaction with them, but they are around, and I can tell. Usually Docksneider and Valdéz don't care if I talk to the clients. It usually helps if I can talk to them and get a feel for what the contract is all about. But in this case, all the meetings have been behind closed doors. I think they might be from Colombia. I saw a file for the Colombian Military. It looks like we are processing some equipment for them. Usually I have more to do with these files, but this is one that Valdéz is handling personally. I have seen him do this before. It usually means he is up to something. Valdéz has the same accent as these other men."

"Do you have access to his office?" Kelly asked.

"Pretty much so," she said.

Kelly was thinking that one of the microphones should be in that office.

"Could you walk in there and put a cigarette lighter someplace where no one would see it?"

Magda thought for a few seconds. "Yes, of course; but why a lighter?"

"Well, it really isn't a lighter; it's a microphone, a bug; but it's about the size of a disposable lighter."

"You would want one in the conference room also. That's where a lot of the business takes place when they all get together; it's a bigger room."

Kelly was starting to think he might need to get another case of tracking devices. Each of the cases had only three tracking devices and three microphones.

Cristina was silent, just sitting and listening.

"You go back to work tomorrow?" Kelly asked Magda.

"Yes," she responded, "but I will go in this afternoon to check on the janitors. I usually go in to see if things are taken care of. If I don't, things do not get done. I'll be there less than an hour."

Kelly was starting to see where Magda would be a great asset. He just needed to figure out what was going on and how to get it done.

"Do you think you could plant them then?"

"Yes," she responded.

"Now, if this even looks like it's getting dangerous, don't do it...wait...it doesn't have to happen right away."

Kelly opened the case and pulled out the remaining microphones and handed them to her.

"You turn them on by pushing this sliding switch, here, up."

"Okay, I see"

"Well, This is about all I have right now. I better go. Can I come by or call later on to see how things went?"

Magda nodded her head. "Of course."

Kelly closed up the case and got up slowly. "Thank you, Magda...Magdalena. If we take them down, it will be because of your help." He hugged her, and he could feel her tremble slightly as she squeezed him back. "Just relax. You can change your mind any time."

He turned towards Cristina and saw a look of concern he had not seen before. He was using them for his operation, and he knew it. He told himself he would make this right.

Cristina walked out with him to the gate. "If anything happens to her…"

"I know. I remember. Look, I'll call the whole thing off right now if you want me to."

Cristina shook her head, and her demeanor changed in an instant. "You're more interested in my mother than me," she pouted, pushing out her lower lip and placing her hand on Kelly's chest.

"Oh! That hurts! I know I'm asking a tremendous thing of you all, but…come on!" Kelly sensed that she was just looking for reassurance. "My concern for your mother is personal and real, but because I care for her like family now. Not because of intimate feelings, sweetheart. My only romantic interest is in you."

He held her tightly, and Cristina could feel something growing behind his zipper. She rocked her hips and belly against his crotch. "Are you sure that's not for her?"

Kelly stepped back and took her face in his hands. He smiled and looked deeply into her honey-brown eyes. "You're the only girl in the world for me."

She grabbed his belt buckle and pulled him in. "Nobody gets hurt, right? Including you!"

"If this thing even looks like it's going to go sour, I'll stop and just let it go."

Kelly's thought process had gone from an operational mode straight to a sexual one.

Cristina lightly pushed him back, turned away, and started walking toward the house.

If Kelly had a tail it would be wagging right now, as he watched her full, round bottom sway sensually with every step she took.

"Good. I'll see you later today," she said over her shoulder and then disappeared into the house without another glance.

Chapter 14

Escobar and Docksneider stood outside the warehouse and surveyed the situation.

"We'll need more vehicles, probably five or six," Escobar said as he re-lit his cigar stub.

"I have some trucks in the yard," Docksneider replied. "We can rent whatever else we need."

"I have a team of 20 men, so I'll need enough vehicles to haul them here. We'll also need some non-descript looking vehicles to do surveillance. We need to get that started right now."

"They can use the trucks for surveillance for now," said Escobar as Valdéz and several others came out the front door to join them. "Miguél, get them the keys to the trucks."

Escobar motioned for two of his men to go with Valdéz.

"Those two will get started on surveillance of the area. Pancho, you and Benito start checking out the equipment that has come in. The rest of the equipment will arrive today?"

"The trucker is in town already waiting to deliver. He will be here soon. Let's go get the rest of the vehicles."

"I need to go back by the hotel to pick up more men to drive them. The men here will keep checking the bridge system."

"I'll meet you over at the rental agency in about 45 minutes."

* * * *

Kelly was driving to the Intel office to pick up more tracking cases. He had the laptop open and saw that the Jeep was on the move again. As he pulled into the office parking lot it looked like the Jeep was heading back to the hotel. He closed up the laptop and hurried into the office. The building appeared deserted. He had to punch in the security code to de-activate the security system, which was always armed after hours and on weekends. At the receptionist desk he could see the equipment room keys where Grace had left them on Friday. He hurried down the hall to the equipment room and started thinking that it was going to be difficult to monitor all of these venues at the same time. Next to the tracking systems were several other cases marked *Recording Equipment*.

How convenient, Kelly thought to himself. He hauled all this equipment out to his Jeep, locked up the office, and headed out. He flipped open the laptop and saw that the Jeep Cherokee was still at the hotel, so he headed to his house and dropped off the equipment.

From there, he headed towards the hotel. As he reached the end of his street he saw that the Cherokee was on the move again. The Cherokee's direction of travel was East, so Kelly started in that direction, not moving too fast so that he could get an idea of where it was going. The Cherokee turned on McPherson Road and headed North. Kelly had just come to a stop light at McPherson several blocks North of the Cherokee. He turned onto McPherson going South, thinking he might see them. The Cherokee made a turn on Alexander Drive, going East again.

Hmm, Convention Center? Airport? Where are they going? Kelly thought to himself.

* * * *

Magda figured she would go to the warehouse early just to get things over with. As she pulled up to the main gate of the warehouse she could see that it was open...unusual for a Sunday. There were a couple of men in the yard looking at some cargo on a flatbed tractor-trailer. Alongside the tractor-trailer were a couple boats painted up to look military. She could also see that Miguel Valdéz's car was parked out front. She knew something was up.

Magda parked next to Valdéz's car and got out. She nodded at the men checking out the cargo. They acknowledged her but went back to their business. Entering the lobby of the office, she got past the security door with her key and headed toward her desk to see if anything new was on it.

The warehouse employed about eight office people and about the same number of warehouse men. Magda was third in charge, after Docksneider and Valdéz, with an equivalent in the warehouse and yard. Magda had known the yard manager, Pedro, for many years. He was a simple man with a wife and four daughters. They were about the same age, and every so often Pedro tried to convince Magda to be his mistress. Overweight and slovenly, he had no appeal to Magda.

Magda walked through the office area to do her inspection. Docksneider's office was open, and she saw her opportunity. There was a large Greek Nude statue near the corner of the office. The figure was standing on its tiptoes with both feet together. She walked over and placed the microphone behind the feet. She casually looked around at the carpet and started to walk out when Valdéz walked in.

"What are you doing here?" he demanded.

She looked down her nose at him and said "What am I doing here? What are you doing here? I always come in on Sunday to inspect the janitorial work. This is highly unusual that Mr. Docksneider's office is open like this on a Sunday."

Taken aback by her quick and terse response, Miguel retorted, "We're working on a rush order. Jerrod had to step out for a minute."

Magda noticed that he used Docksneider's first name to insinuate a familiarity with him that she did not have or want.

"I'll finish up my walk through and be out of here." Magda walked passed him and headed over to the conference room. Inside there was a twelve foot mahogany conference table with a teleconference phone in the center. At the left side was a coffee service bar with overhead cabinets. Magda always inspected this area, as it was typically a mess. But today everything was in order. On the other side of the room was a window looking out over the yard. A narrow side table was under the window with a fake potted plant. Magda walked over, activated the microphone, and placed it in the planter behind a leaf.

Feeling confident she had accomplished what she wanted to, she went back to her desk, picked up her purse, and headed out. As she was leaving she and turned to Valdéz, who was across the room at his desk.

"Mr. Valdéz, I'm leaving. I will see you tomorrow."

"Not tomorrow...we have all been given the day off for the holiday, No one is to be here," Valdéz responded.

"Tuesday, then."

Valdéz despised her. She acted too entitled and assumed too much power for his patriarchal taste. She demanded to know things that she didn't need to know and always tried to talk to clients. He preferred working with people of lesser intelligence who put in their time, asked no questions, and then went home. He was suspicious and feared that that she might get in the way. After all, this was all about him. He was the one that planned all of this. He brought all the people together. He didn't have the money or the political pull, but it was his attention to detail and his overall scheme that brought all the pieces together for this ingenious crime. He was the mastermind. And if she got in the way, he would have to deal with her.

Chapter 15

Kelly was in the airport parking lot watching three minivans and another Jeep Cherokee drive off. He saw a blue BMW depart as well when his cell phone went off.

"Hello."

"Mr. Smith, this is Sabrina from Enterprise Car Rental."

"Hey, Sabrina, how are you?"

"Mr. Smith, you asked me to call you if I saw anything else happen. Well, I just rented four vehicles to Mr. Docksneider, and the men that are driving them are all pretty strange looking. They're not from around here. They all have temporary International Driving Permits."

"Oh, okay. Well, could I get the description and plate numbers of the vehicles and any other information?"

"Yes, sir, I have it written down for you."

"Great, can I come by later? What time do you get off?"

"Yes, sir. I get off at 5."

"We'll be there. Sabrina…thanks. You're the best."

Kelly pretty much had a good visual on the vehicles, but the license plate numbers and designated drivers would be a great help.

He was going to need more help keeping track of all these vehicles. Hopefully, they would all be traveling together.

He fell in behind the minivans to see where they were going and followed them back to the hotel. He waited until the drivers had all left and then put tracking devices on the three vehicles. He could see from the laptop that the Cherokee went over to the warehouse then back to the hotel. His task complete, Kelly headed for home.

It was already 1:00 o'clock in the afternoon. He knew he was going to need some help tracking all the vehicles, so he stopped by Ruben's before going home.

"Daddy, Kelly's here!" Chuy said excitedly, as the two walked into the living room.

Ruben was on the couch in front of the TV, and Sylvia had just handed him a plate of steaming hot food, fresh from the griddle. It smelled delicious.

When Sylvia saw Kelly, she took the plate back from Ruben and handed it to Kelly with a half-hug and a kiss on the cheek. "It's about time you stopped by again! Sit down! This time you're going to eat, and I'm not taking 'no' for an answer. She took his arm and pulled him to the couch next to Ruben.

"Sit down partner...or, former partner. The Cowboys are down by six."

Kelly sat, and Ruben gazed longingly at the steaming hotcakes topped with two over-easy eggs and a couple of large chorizos on the side. His fork was still pointing upward in his right hand, and he handed it over to Kelly. Ruben forgot about the game and watched intently as Kelly cut the cakes and brought the forkful to his mouth.

"Buddy, I need some help," Kelly said quietly while he was still chewing. "Damn, this is good...Can you come over when we're done eating?"

"Uh, what's up?"

"I can't explain here. Too many little ears. Can you come over?"

"Yeah...ten minutes to halftime. If I get my breakfast pretty soon, we can go then. It better be worth missing the second half of the game, bro." But Ruben knew by the way Kelly was asking that it must be serious. "I got something I need to ask you later too."

Sylvia stood in the kitchen doorway with another steaming plate of deliciousness. "Chuy, can you bring this plate to your Daddy, please?"

"But, Mom," Ruben, Jr. chimed in excitedly from the recliner, "You said that I got the next plate!"

Ruben looked as though his life were being threatened. "After me! The next plate *after me,* Junior!" He turned his body halfway around and extended his hand toward his wife.

Sylvia shot Ruben a disapproving glance and put one fist on her hip. "Of course, you're right, sweetie. Bring this to your brother, Chuy. Is it okay if Daddy gets the next plate?"

Chuy turned and saw the pleading eyes of his father, and he nodded and pouted at the same time.

Five minutes later Ruben's stomach was rumbling, and he noticed that the plate of food was still on the side table next to his older son, still untouched as the boy rooted his team on.

Eventually, Ruben got his breakfast and the duo went to Kelly's house.

"What the hell do you have here?" asked Ruben, looking at the laptop and recording equipment on the coffee table and cases of equipment on the floor.

Kelly explained the whole situation. Ruben just sat and listened.

"Wow; heavy, dude. Are you sure you really want to jump into this mess? That's what law enforcement is for," Ruben said.

"I can't let this happen in my backyard, and...and we might be targets too."

Ruben shrugged and nodded his begrudging agreement.

"So, Ruben, you said you had something to ask me about too.

What's up?"

Ruben furrowed his brow in thought for a moment. "Oh…yeah," he said, leaning in with a very serious look on his face, "uh, how far did you get with Cristina? Did you get a chance to play with those big, brown boobies?"

"Geez, Ruben, this is serious!"

"Okay…okay. Just curious. What do you need me to do?"

"I can't handle all these monitors and follow all these people. Can you take one of them?"

"Yeah. You know, man, this is pretty serious. Maybe you ought to call your buddy at DEA."

"I will. I just haven't got around to it yet."

"I think you're gonna need more help than just me and Cristina's mom."

"Yeah, I just don't know who to trust."

"I think you're in the perfect place over at Intel to find people. Bird is a good guy. He doesn't like the Deputy either. I think if you went to him he would work with you; just don't get him in trouble. And Grace, well, as long as you tickle her twat once in a while, she can suck good information out of anybody…if you know what I mean.."

Ruben scrunched one eye and tilted his head for inspiration. "There are a couple of other guys there, young guys, that I think we can trust. One kid, Rick Buenavista, they call him 'Pretty Boy.' The women just fall all over the guy. One day we were processing a bunch of Brazilian women, supermodel types. They all huddled around his computer terminal and were flirting with him. The rest of us were just sitting there kinda like, 'Hey over here ladies; we got work to do.' He knows how to be discreet; he has to. And he has a degree in security stuff."

"Can you get a hold of him?"

Ruben pulled out his cell phone, and hit a speed dial number.

"He coaches baseball. My oldest is on his team. Lots of single moms...gold mine for the kid. 'Hey, Ricky, how's it going? ...Cool, cool...Hey, I have something I really need to show you. Can you come over right now? Cool. I'm at Kelly Smith's house. His address is 703 Lindenwood...Yeah, hurry.' He's on his way. You know, why don't you call your buddy with DEA? At least get this off your chest, and give him a chance to muster up whatever he can, Kelly. This sounds huge."

"Yeah, let me do that right now. Turn the TV on, and get us a beer until Buenavista shows up."

As Ruben went for the beer, Kelly called his old classmate, Ben Blackwell. Kelly was on the phone explaining the situation for about twenty minutes while Blackwell said very little. Blackwell finally gave his assessment:

"Whew...Man, you are so not going by the book...illegal entry, illegal eavesdropping, the whole bit. First of all, Escobar and an entourage of seven are here as guests of the United States military on official business for the Colombian Army. Some non-arms-related purchase of used equipment to help them fight the cartels in the jungle. That's why the DEA is in the loop. But if what you say is correct, he has a lot more than seven cohorts with him, and this would be a perfect cover for some major shenanigans."

"Is there anything at all you guys can do, Ben?"

"There's no way we can drop into this, and it's all so all-of-a-sudden. Being in Houston doesn't help either. Look, be careful, buddy; you've been through hell and back already. Don't let those raw nerves suck you into a shit hole full of alligators."

"I'm not, this isn't any kind of personal vendetta, Ben. This is some real shit that just dropped into my lap."

"I know, I know...I'm just saying. Our office still talks about what happened. There's a lot of pissed off people up here. I'm not going to leave you hanging like General Custer on this if at all possible, but I have to think it through and maybe make a phone call or two to see if we can do anything. I'll call our office in Laredo and see what can be done. Be careful. We'll talk later."

Kelly hung up, disappointed but not discouraged. He had a connection in the National Guard that he could tap too. It was always difficult to get official help on a mission that started as an individual or vigilante action, so maybe a personal, off-the-reservation appeal to the boys with the toys would work better. The Guard had a small fleet of helicopters for rescue and recovery operations, and most of them could be armed for attack as well.

There was a knock at the door. Kelly saw Buenavista through the spy hole and let him in.

"Ricky, thanks for coming over. I saw you at the office on Friday, right? You were working on your computer."

"Yes, Sir," he responded in a respectful military fashion, standing erect and rigid in his dress jeans, cowboy boots, and camou T-shirt. Ricky was 27 years old, single, 5'10", 175 pounds with an athletic figure and a chiseled face that women would turn their heads for. He had been in the patrol for about five years, so he was still kind of new.

"Yes, sir, anything I can do to help."

"Relax, relax," Kelly said as Ruben handed the young man a cold beer. He was used to the way his heroic and tragic reputation intimidated young agents, and he wanted to put him at ease. "Come on in; let's explain."

Kelly ran down the whole scheme for about 40 minutes and then passed Ricky the laptop for the minivans.

"Mr. Smith, I'm right there," said Ricky. "I'll be a part of this. This looks huge. And I just want you to know, most of us at the station will do anything for you. You're a legend."

"Well, thanks, kid; but what I need now is smarts, courage, and discretion. This is way out of bounds, what we're doing. You cannot tell anyone what's going on...nobody – and that includes girlfriends and family. Do you understand? This could ruin your career if things go bad, or worse: You could get killed."

"Yes, sir. I understand completely. And like I said, most of the station, including me, will do anything for you. We want those bastards. They hurt one of our own. What do you want me to do right now?"

"Okay, go to the airport and get that info from Sabrina; try not to be too charming, then come back. Let me send you my cell number. You send me yours so we have communication. I'll call Sabrina to let her know you are coming. You have a laptop and know how it works; keep monitoring it. Make sure it's set to receive trackers number 4, 5, and 6. Call as soon as you see movement."

Ricky left. Ruben and Kelly sat for a moment in silence looking at each other, wondering what was next. A few moments later Kelly's cell phone rang.

"Hello."

"Hi, it's Cristina."

Not sure if he should be flirty or serious, Kelly responded in a casual voice. "Hey, what's going on?"

"Did you like my dress last night?"

"Oh, yeah. I kept wondering what was underneath it."

"Nothing," she said. "Mama wants to talk to you."

Kelly was off guard at this point. She just teased him and then went straight to being serious. Magda took the line.

"Mr. Smith, Magda. I went to the office already and put the microphones in."

Kelly's mind was still on the little black dress. "Oh, Okay,"

Glancing over to his laptop, Kelly noticed that there was an audio icon at the top of the screen that wasn't there before.

"Yes, I can see it."

Kelly went over and found the volume on the laptop and turned it up. There was a low hum.

"It looks good. We're up and running. It was no problem doing that?"

"No, not at all. When I arrived some men were there looking at a shipment in the yard. Nobody should be there on a Sunday. The equipment looked like military equipment. There were a couple of strange looking boats with it. They were small, and the men called them 'skiffs.' Valdéz was also there, and he said that Docksneider had been there also. I found his door open."

"Wow. That sounds interesting. Things must be coming down soon. Well, okay. At this point I just need to keep monitoring. Thank you."

"They told me not to come around tomorrow at all, so maybe that's when something will happen. Cristina wants to talk to you again."

Kelly's mind was reeling, wondering what she was going to say this time.

"Are you going to come by tonight?"

"I'll try. I want to see what you're wearing. You're taking great pleasure in teasing me, aren't you?"

"Yep. I'll see you tonight." She clicked off the phone.

Kelly stood there looking at the phone and shaking his head.

Chapter 16

Ricky Buenavista arrived at the airport terminal and went to the rental car counter. Sabrina was on duty. As he approached he could see her head shift to the side and her eyes narrow. She bit her lower lip as she looked him up and down.

Rick thought to himself, *Well, there go the clothes again. She just undressed me with her eyes; seen it a million times. But this girl is kind of cute, and maybe sweet too.*

"Hi, Sabrina, my name is Rick. Mr. Smith called to let you know I was coming." He pulled out his badge and credentials to identify himself.

Sabrina's was trying to figure out some way to keep him talking. She didn't want this to be a brief encounter.

"Well, I'll need to examine your credentials a little more closely, Mr....?"

"Buenavista, but call me Rick."

She nodded and stuck her hand out expecting him to hand over the wallet. He handed it over, and she acted as if she was really checking things over.

"I guess this really is you, isn't it?"

"Yes, ma'am, in the flesh."

"Let me just check over the information I have here to make sure it's correct and complete. Do you always work with Mr. Smith? He seems like a nice man."

"Yeah, I do. He's the boss. So have you worked here long?"

"Almost a year, and I'll be around five days a week." She handed him the information. "You should come around sometimes. We get a lot of creepy guys, and it feels good to have a real law enforcement agent close by."

"I better get going; this is important. I'll see you, ma'am."

"Sabrina," she said with a smile, and flashing her eyelashes demurely.

Rick had fallen under her spell a little too, which was unusual for this ladies man. "Well, if you ever feel like you're in danger, Sabrina, just give me a call." He wrote his personal cell phone number on the back of his card and handed it to her.

"Ma'am," he said with a tip of his hat and a nod.

"Bye."

Rick made a mental note to check back with that one. She was cute, and he knew she would be putty in his hands – if he didn't get wrapped too tightly around her little finger first.

He got back to his car and saw that the tracking device showed the vehicles on the move. He called Kelly to let him know.

"Hey, this is Rick. I have the information, and my vehicles are moving. Do you want me to follow?"

"Yeah, mine is moving too. I think they are going back over to the warehouse. Can you go over and check it out? It's right at the site of the new bridge. Don't approach anybody; just look from the outside."

"10-4. I'm *en route*."

Rick knew the area. It was an older warehouse subdivision right in front of the Rio Grande River. The area was pretty run down. The new bridge construction was almost right next door to Docksneider's warehouse. As a matter of fact, some of the land cleared for the construction was backed right up to his property.

Rick pulled into the parking lot of the warehouse across the street. He could see the front of Docksneider's warehouse yard, where the military equipment was located, and the front of the building. Several minivans, two Jeep Cherokees, a blue BMW, and a little economy sedan that he didn't know the make of were parked there. He pulled out his binoculars and checked the plates on the vans and compared them to the list Sabrina gave him. They all matched. Kelly had told him about the BMW, so he didn't pay much attention to it. He scanned the economy sedan and got the plate number, EBD-243, and called it in to Kelly.

"Hey, I'm here and so are the rental vehicles and Beemer. There's another vehicle here. I have the plate. Do you want me to run it with radio?"

"No! Don't you do it. That will raise suspicion back at radio. Give it to me. They won't question it if I do it."

Rick thought to himself, *smart old bastard*. "Stand by for the plate: ECHO BRAVO DELTA, 2-4-3."

"Got It. I'll call it in right away. I'll let you know."

Rick looked at his watch: 5:10. He watched as two pickup trucks pulled into the yard. They parked next to the rest of the vehicles, and the drivers went inside. He got the plate numbers as they pulled in. Rick had one more set of tracking and listening devices that he wanted to attach to one of those trucks. He kept scanning with his binoculars to see if there was anyone else in the yard. Nobody was around, so he took the tracking device and microphone and got out of the car.

He walked across the street at a diagonal to the corner of the yard on the street side that had 6-foot high chain link fencing. There were Oleander bushes inside of the fence going along the front of the property. At the property corner, the fence post was bent, making for an easy entrance into the yard. The bushes also went along the side of the property making for good cover.

Rick was full of nervous excitement. He knew this was dangerous and risky. Working his way along the side of the property and keeping an eye open on the front door, he arrived at the edge of the building. This section had no windows. The trucks were parked about twelve yards in front of him. He was sure that he was safely concealed.

When he walked out across the front of the building he would be completely exposed. He took one last look and walked briskly across the front of the build towards the trucks. As he got nearer he could see that the nearest truck had its window open. He tried the door and found it was unlocked. It was obvious that the truck belonged to the warehouse – it was not very clean and there was paper work with the warehouse logo on it. He dropped the microphone in the door side pocket and gently closed the door. Then he took the tracking device and put it under the top edge of the bed of the truck. As he attached it he heard the solid clunk of the device's magnet holding it in place. He turned around and made his way back to the corner of the building, back along the side of the property, and back across the street to his vehicle.

He reported his progress back to Kelly on his phone.

"Kid! You're taking chances we don't need!"

"Yes, sir, I know…but nobody saw me, and we need to know where and what all of them are doing."

Kelly knew that what Rick had done was right, but he was still concerned.

"Okay, okay…you're right; but geez. I think we're good for now. Why don't you pull out to a safe distance. Maybe go and get some dinner and come back after dark."

"10-4. I'll glass the place from down the street for a while first."

Rick pulled out of the parking lot and went up the street to the corner. There was a convenience store across the street. Rick made his way into the convenience store parking lot and positioned himself so that he could still see down the street to the warehouse. He sat and waited. It was about a 5:30 in the afternoon.

Chapter 17

Inside the warehouse the brain trust was having a powwow in Docksneider's office. Kelly could hear and identify them all – Docksneider, Valdéz, Escobar, and Chavarria – but he was having trouble with the Colombian accent and some of the colloquialisms and slang. Chavarria spoke no English, while Docksneider spoke little Spanish.

Ruben was much more fluent in Spanish, but he was asleep on the couch. Kelly was able to figure out that they were waiting for the rest of the group to return from doing surveillance of the area. With Ricky in place, Kelly figured this was a good time to go over to Cristina's house. He packed up his equipment and headed over there.

"Stay by your phone, partner," Kelly said to his slumbering friend.

Ruben returned a salute of acknowledgment without ever opening his eyes.

Kelly kept monitoring the conversation in his car. Chavarria had left, and they proceeded in English for Docksneider. The product left Colombia ten days ago. It had traveled through Venezuela to a port in Caraballeda where the trucks were loaded onto a ship. The ship and trucks were owned by the same company, Cartagena SVA, and were of Mexican registry. The owner was a man named Jorge Sorios. The company was about three years old and worked this same route all the time. Up to this point the company had been concentrating on shipping coffee in order to establish credibility and contacts at both the Venezuelan and Mexican ports. The Customs officials at both ports enjoyed the generous "tips" the ship's Captain gave them.

Once at the Mexican port the trucks changed to Mexican plates. The trucks rolled right off the ship and headed directly for Laredo. Once near Laredo, they changed plates again to show Texas registry. This matched with what Carlos had told him outside the Roundup.

*   *   *   *

Kelly arrived at Cristina's house and grabbed his monitoring device. As he was walking up the sidewalk Cristina opened the door and framed herself in the door way with her hands on her hips. Her curly black hair was thrown enticingly over one shoulder, and she was wearing red stiletto heels, black spandex yoga pants, a red mini-dress that didn't quite cover her buttocks, and a button-down strapless bustier top that could barely contain her ample breasts. Kelly's mouth dropped open and he shook his head.

"Hi, Kelly. I just got back from church. I had a lot of confessions to make," she said with a sultry smile. "I wish I had one more."

"I bet the poor priest is still trembling in the confessional. You look…Wow! Can we go out sometime?"

"I'll think about it. Come on in."

She turned sideways and crowded the doorway so that he would have to brush against her breasts when he went inside – and Kelly took his time getting past her.

"Oh, sorry. I hope you're alright. I hope I didn't hurt you," she said, taking a deep breath to expand her chest as far as possible.

"Bad, bad girl. Back to the confessional. Maybe you can still catch the priest." Kelly wanted to take her right there in the entryway, but discretion got the better of him. "If you're trying to tempt me and drive me crazy, you're doing a damn good job, little lady. You win; I'm all yours."

"I'm not sure I want you."

"I don't think I've seen you dressed like that at work."

"Too much attention."

"Really? You get nothing but attention every minute you're at the Roundup."

Kelly set up the laptop by the stairs and plugged it in, as Cristina had done for him before. Max seemed very interested in the electronic equipment and watched his every move. Kelly plugged in the recording module and then headed for the comfort of the couch in the living room.

Max peeked into the living room, but Kelly was facing the other way, so he plugged in his headphones and sat on the little stool by the table.

The rest of the Colombian group had arrived, and everybody was in the conference room. As soon as somebody started speaking an icon appeared on the laptop indicating which microphone was activating so they knew which room they were in.

Magda came into the living room. "Hello, Kelly. How are you? Can I get you anything?"

"'Umm, sure, how about a cold glass of water...real cold?"

Magda nodded and disappeared into the kitchen as an orange sun began to blaze blindingly though the window on the west side of the house. Cristina got up and adjusted the blinds.

"Mija," Magda called to her daughter. A moment later Cristina returned with Kelly's water as he heard meat begin to sizzle on the stove in the kitchen.

"She's going to make some tacos for us – just the quick kind with crunchy shells from the store," Cristina said.

"I really shouldn't..." Kelly said, as the aroma began to reach his nostrils, "...but I will."

Cristina saw Max by the stairs, but didn't really pay attention to what he was doing. She scooted Kelly over to the end of the couch so that they would be out of Max's line of sight, and she snuggled up next to her man. "It's nice having you in my house with my family," she cooed as she ran her fingers through Kelly's hair. "I could get used to this, Mr. Smith."

"We'll get used to it together, pretty lady," Kelly said with powerful eye contact before stealing a kiss. "I'm not letting you get away."

* * * *

Meanwhile, as Max listened, a very important meeting was about to begin, this time in the big conference room.

The rest of the team spoke little if any English, so the meeting was in Spanish.

Escobar opened the meeting. "Okay, let's get this going. The trucks are on the ground in Mexico and are rolling this way. Four of them have already arrived at the staging site across the river. The rest will be here tonight. Mr. Valdéz, what can you tell us? Where is the rest of the equipment we need on our side of the river?"

"The trucker called about an hour ago. He is in town," Valdéz said. "He would like to deliver now so that he can get out of Laredo. He said he could get here soon. That should complete our equipment delivery issue."

"Good, good. Mr. Docksneider...anything?" said Escobar.

"My friends on the other side tell me that they have already raised tensions down river. Some squatters were publicly mutilated yesterday. They will continue on into the night. There will be chaos by the time we need to start our operation. My friend on this side of the river tells me not to worry, that the river will be clear and so will the highway with the checkpoint closed. They will be too busy responding to the chaos."

"You better be right, Cock-biter." Escobar said with a threatening tone. "But the chaos to the South may not be enough if our peasants there do not perform well. We cannot depend on cheap labor alone. What do you have to the North, Miguel?"

"Sir, the plan is complete. The bridge will be closed after dark for the Mexican holiday tomorrow. Deputy Marín has taken care of it. And the decoys have been hired to speed across the closed port bridge on our command, which will occupy any other available border agents."

"How do you know they will comply?"

"Sir, their families are already being held hostage in a warehouse across the river. The wives are pretty young women, and the children are small. These two men will choose one thousand American dollars over a dead family and certain death for themselves. There will be a delivery truck from a commercial bakery and a rented SUV. The second will be dispatched after the first one has attracted much pursuit."

"And what are they carrying?"

"Why...nothing, Sir. Only the driver."

"Fool! If they are caught the authorities will know it is only a decoy and look elsewhere for the real activity. Fill the truck with Mexicans – young ones so that the bleeding-heart Americans will take much time to give them special care..."

"But, Sir, we have no children to put..."

"Idiot! Find them on the street! Pull them from homes and hospitals and schools! Have you no brain, or is it courage you lack?"

"Sí, commandante. It will be done."

"And put a few kilos of the weed or powder in the other car. And my surveillance team...what do you have?"

A nervous voice responded: "Captain, we think the best thing for us to do is remove the fence off the back of the yard here and move the equipment straight down to the landing. This is only a few hundred meters, and we can avoid going through the construction entrance. If we do this, we minimize our exposure. We never really even have to go out on the street. They have security guards after hours, but they are of no consequence. They can easily be removed."

Docksneider chimed in. "I don't like this idea. This makes it look too much like I am involved. I'm already at great risk."

The nervous surveillance team member responded: "But, Sir, you are already very exposed, and with much risk comes great reward. This is an old saying we have, but the other thing is that we can make this look like a theft from your yard. The thieves came in the back way and cleaned you out."

There was a long pause as Docksneider seemed to consider this idea, then the nervous man spoke again.

"Captain, there is another option. If the construction site is open we can leave directly from there and head towards Corpus Christi where the Sorios ship is waiting to load the pontoon bridges for transport to Colombia through Venezuela."

"Chavarria, what do you have?" Escobar moved things along.

"When the last piece of equipment gets here tonight, we'll inspect it and we'll be ready. The bridge construction already has pylons in the river. We can secure off of them, and it will be much faster to erect the pontoon bridge."

Escobar seemed satisfied. "Okay, I think that is it. Wait for the rest of the equipment to arrive out in the warehouse. Mr. Docksneider and I have some other details to discuss."

* * * *

Cristina smiled and put her head on Kelly's shoulder. "I was attracted to the handsome shy Clark Kent at the bar, but this confident Superman guy makes a girl swoon and give up her heart, Kelly. And her body too."

She drew herself very close to Kelly and brushed her hand slowly across his zipper. Kelly responded with a hand to her cheek, which he slowly pulled down toward her breast. Quickly, Cristina grabbed his wrist and stopped him before he had reached his goal.

She looked at Kelly and said, "Those are for the man I will marry." Then, with her eyes still locked on his, she guided his hand to the warm, damp crotch of her barely-there yoga pants. "But let us see if you can make my kitty purr." She left his probing hand to explore as he wished and pulled his head in for a deep, hot kiss.

Kelly's deft fingers found the magic mound at the apex of her warm spot and began to massage the pleasure button with firm circular strokes. Cristina responded with delicate but powerful thrusts as she lost herself and began to moan. The sounds got louder and higher pitched with each thrust of her hips.

"Ahhh...*ahhhh*..."

"Tacos!" Magda announced.

Cristina looked up suddenly and saw Magda's face. "...choo!" she said, trying to cover up her titillation by pretending to finish a sneeze.

Magda just rolled her eyes as she carried a platter of a dozen tacos into the living room and placed them on the coffee table. "Max, come and eat now!"

The couple jolted to upright positions and groggily returned to reality, a bit disheveled, from their steamy love bubble.

Magda shook her head. "My goodness, I have teenagers again. Such uncontrollable kissing and such is only for two kinds of people: the young and inexperienced who are eager to chase their raging hormones and touch something they have never touched before – and those experienced in the ways of the world who have become very busy falling in love after a long loneliness, and have a ravenous appetite for affection, like a wolf swallowing a deer."

"Mama..." said Cristina as she handed a taco to her man, "...we were just talking."

"Yes, of course you were, my dear. And that was really just an 'ahh-choo.' Max, put this towel over your lap and eat carefully."

"Yes, abuela. I have never been allowed to eat in the living room before. It's nice."

"So, what were you doing, my son?" Cristina said as she

crunched into her taco.

Max looked at her and then looked away with a shrug. "Listening."

Kelly perked up. "To my laptop?" He looked at Max and then at Cristina with concern.

"It's okay, Kelly," Cristina said. "He is the one who told us about the drug plan when you left after our spaghetti dinner yesterday. That is why Mama decided to help you."

Kelly was a little stunned. "So...what did you hear today?"

"Well, there will be something like a riot to the South and they will close the bridge in the North after dark. Some vehicles will come across. And..."

"Good job, Max. That's just what we had figured out. They will distract us in the South and bring the big trucks across the North bridge."

"But that's not..."

"Did they say when this will happen, Max?"

"When the bridge is closed, after dark. But..."

"Well...I better get back on this – right after I have another taco." Kelly pushed the remainder of his second taco into his mouth and grabbed another.

"Take more, Kelly. We are small women and a child; we cannot eat them all," Magda insisted.

Kelly nodded his willingness to oblige. He was pleased to hear Magda call him "Kelly" again.

"Mr. Kelly, Mr. Kelly..." Max pleaded.

"Max, please, just let the man eat now, okay? Please?"

"But, Mama..."

"Max!" scolded Magda sternly. "You must never question your mother. Now not another word." Her glare of intimidation was a look that Max understood well. To speak now would have its consequences.

Max felt like he might burst from holding back the information he knew. Kelly had it wrong. The trucks on the bridge to the North were just a distraction too. The real cargo would pass somewhere else, on a pontoon bridge. But he knew that he must hold his tongue.

"Max, bring Mr. Smith's laptop over here so he can listen, and then take a taco up to your room and play or read," Cristina said.

The boy obeyed. He unplugged his mother' phone from the laptop, which had been recording while he was in the living room, and brought the base unit to the coffee table where they all could hear it. He stopped briefly in front of Kelly and looked at his grandmother. She looked back at Max and shook her head. Then he went upstairs, grabbing the phone from the side table on his way.

*   *   *   *

Rick Buenavista munched on an egg salad sandwich from the convenience store and called Kelly.

"You still in the area?"

"Yes, sir. I don't know if I told you this, but that warehouse yard looks like a National Guard Armory with all that equipment, and another truck loaded with more equipment just like it just turned down the road to the warehouse. What now, Boss?"

"Stick around until the activity dies down; see if you can figure out what's happening there and what the equipment is. It's probably just the old military equipment the Columbian army is buying, and has nothing to do with the drug run – other than bringing Escobar and company here. Then you better get home and get some sleep; you have to work tomorrow."

"No work tomorrow, Sir. Deputy Marín declared a holiday for all departments and details for Cinco de Mayo. Just a skeleton crew on the border. I'll stick here until the lights go out and then catch a few zees at home, freshen up, and be back after breakfast."

Kelly shook his head. "The bastard Deputy is leaving things wide open for the bad guys. Anyway, Escobar is here on official business with our military to buy some equipment for the Colombian Army. See if you can figure out what it is without getting too close. It's probably unrelated to the smuggling operation, but it just gives them an excuse to be here to oversee the clandestine operation. It looks like things will be coming down tomorrow night, so I'll need you well rested. We're going to need to meet with Bird and put this on the table at some time too." Kelly just sat there in the Chavez living room, which he had transformed into a war room, with the mother and daughter looking at him incredulously.

Cristina couldn't hold in her reaction to this unfolding operation any longer. "Kelly, this is crazy! What are they thinking? Mama, all that military stuff didn't make you suspicious?"

"I guess it did. I just didn't think. It always came in at night. I never saw it come in." said Magda, shaking her head with her hand to her cheek. "Diós mio. They told me it was an inter-government transaction. I just never put things together. I'm sorry."

"Cristina, most of this stuff just arrived yesterday and today, and it's part of a real government transaction. It probably has nothing to do directly with the drug operation. Hell...we wouldn't know all the details of their drug deal if it wasn't for Magda," Kelly said in support of the distraught mother. Kelly sat between the women. He put his arm around Cristina and his hand on Magda's shoulder. "If we get this guy, it will be because of the devices you planted, Magda."

Magda smiled as one tear streamed down her cheek. It made her feel good to be defended and comforted by this powerful leader of men. Cristina rolled her eyes as her mother put her head on Kelly's shoulder and sobbed.

"I need to call somebody else," Kelly said, as he switched back into operational mode. He flipped open his cell phone and speed dialed his friend at DEA.

"Hey, you are not going to believe this, Ben." Kelly went into detail about what has transpired since he last spoke to Ben Blackwell.

"Wow, Okay. This thing just went through the roof. How do you want to work this? You know we'll screw it up if we take over. You already have the inside track."

"I'll need assets at the ready – helicopters, SWAT teams. I can get that if I call our SWAT Command. I'm sure they'll jump if I call. I just got to be careful. They won't come into the Sector without notifying the Chief and the Deputy. Maybe if you guys called and made secrecy and location disclosure a last minute thing, stress the urgency, make it sound like it is out of country to distract them."

"Okay, Kelly. I'm back on it. I'll make the calls and make something happen. This is huge."

Kelly called Rick. "Hey, can you upload your pictures of the equipment and email them to me?"

"Sure, as soon as I get back to the house I'll do it. What's your email address?"

"Deadman walking at Mailbag dot com. All one word.

"Ouhh, man, you really need to change that. Later."

Kelly started packing up his equipment, but then changed his mind. Magda walked out of the room, and Cristina was still sitting next to Kelly.

"Other than the fact that you're neck-deep in the kind of trouble that can kill you, you really are a nice man, aren't you, Mr. Kelly Smith? Your people really respect you. I can tell by the way that kid, Rick, talks to you. I could overhear the phone conversations."

"What can I say? I've been around."

"So, what's next?"

"What's next?" Kelly put one hand on Cristina's thigh and the other on her cheek as he leaned in with his face only inches from hers. "That's up to you."

Cristina grabbed his shirt collar and pulled him in for a long, passionate kiss. "I like this confident, take-charge man a lot better than the little boy that visits me at the club," she said, as she went in for another kiss.

"Alright! Enough of that." Magda demanded as she rose to her feet and smacked Kelly on the shoulder that was still damp with her tears.

"Mr. Smith, you better go home before the house burns down."

"Yes, ma'am. Cristina, I'm going to leave this unit here to keep recording any meetings these guys have. I have the master base unit monitor at home. Just make sure it stays charged and powered up, if you can." Kelly grabbed his stuff and took one step towards the door.

"What's this? No hug for Mama?" Magda said to Kelly.

Kelly and Cristina looked at each other in shocked amazement, and Cristina nodded her head toward her mother twice. Kelly understood the signal that he'd better jump at this rare opportunity.

"Yes, ma'am," said Kelly as he bent down to embraced the petite woman.

She hugged him tightly for a brief moment and then turned toward her daughter. "Afuera! Afuera! Besarlo!"

"Mama!"

Magda walked towards the kitchen, then stopped and turned to her wide-eyed daughter again. "Cuando encuentras un hombre de verdad, debes hacer lo que sea para ganarlo y mantenerlo." Then she walked away.

"Did she say what I think she said?" asked Kelly.

"She wants me to go outside and kiss you."

"Well…a girl should obey her mother, you know."

"And her heart," she said with shy smile as she took Kelly's hand and walked outside onto the small porch.

"What was that last part she said?" Kelly asked.

"Nothing," Cristina lied. "Just that she had some things to do before she went to bed." She had never heard words like those from her mother before: *When you find a real man, you have to do whatever it takes to win him and keep him.* She was still stunned and lost in thought as they went out onto the porch.

It was 8:15 and the sun had just set, with a bit of a red glow still remaining on the horizon.

"I'll see you tomorrow?" Kelly asked as he closed the door behind them. Then he faced her and put his hands on her waist as he guided her to the enclosed side of the porch.

"Mmm hmm," she said, nuzzling her face against Kelly's chest. "And everyday after that, if I can help it."

Kelly's heart began to beat harder, and he pulled her tender and voluptuous body close. They kissed in the waning moonlight of a very small sliver of a crescent moon, much more tenderly this time, and they both seemed to sense that everything had changed in this moment. It was a new beginning for both of them.

Magda peered clandestinely from behind the drapery in the living room window. Cristina was holding Kelly's face in her hands, and Kelly was awkwardly playing with the top button on the overflowing bodice of Cristina's dress. He was being very careful not to overstep a gentlemanly boundary, but his mind was locked on the double-D prize only inches away.

Like lightning, Cristina's hand went into the pocket of her mini dress and grabbed the small stiletto switchblade, which she pulled out and clicked open all in one seamless motion. She held the glistening blade close to her face as she locked gazes with the stunned and petrified Kelly Smith.

"Ah...I..." Kelly tried to speak. He released the button and moved his hand slowly to her shoulder. *Man, I really blew it this time. She said the next time she pulled it out she would use it.* Kelly knew of Cristina's legendary blade-handling abilities from the Roundup. He'd seen her stick a fly to the bar with one quick jab of her blade, and he had heard stories of "handsy" patrons learning to respect her the hard way. "Cristina..."

"Shhht," said Cristina curtly, her eyes still locked on his. Without ever averting her gaze, she grabbed the top of her dress with one hand and, with the deftness of a ninja, sliced the button off with a quick whoosh of the blade, which was closed and back in her pocket one second later. She gently grabbed Kelly's wrist and guided his hand from her shoulder to the black satin bra beneath her dress, the destination of Kelly's wildest dreams.

Magda's smile turned to an approving chuckle. Then she walked away, applauding and mumbling praises to her daughter in Spanish.

The next kiss seemed to last forever, with passions flaring as Kelly explored the wonderland of Cristina's bosom. The fiery filly could feel Kelly's growing manhood pressed against her belly, and she writhed slowly from side to side, stimulating their passions even further as she moaned a soft and gentle whimper of vulnerable delight.

Their soaring bubble of otherworldly passions was burst by two short, loud raps on the door behind them and Magda's voice calling, "Cristina, I need you here now."

Chapter 18

Kelly tried to shake off the distracting affects of his intimate encounter as he walked into his silent house and turned on the lights. He flipped on the TV for background noise. Kelly was coming to terms with the fact that he now clearly loved his amazing Latina sweetheart. Thoughts of her had taken over his mind, crowding out the important job he had to do. Feelings for her rushed through his veins and weakened his body. He could still detect the scent of her skin and hair on his shirt and he breathed it in deeply. And, putting his hand to his face, he smelled a subtle hint of the epitome of her feminine mystique that he had fondled through her yoga pants.

There was a note on the couch from Ruben: *I'm home if you need me.*

Instead of sitting down, Kelly marched into the bathroom, threw his shirt in the hamper outside the door, and stepped into the shower. He liked the water very hot. He wiped the steam off the little round mirror mounted in the shower and saw his face with several days of ugly stubble. "I think a shave is in order," he said, soaping his face and grabbing his razor. This was the start of the final day of action, and he wanted to be fresh and ready. He cleaned up extra well, put on deodorant and one spray of the cologne that had lasted him for a couple of years now. *Poor Cristina*, he thought as he brushed his teeth and gargled. *She put up with my stank body and stank breath all weekend.*

He put on a fresh shirt and some clean sweatpants and then put on his shoulder holster for good measure.

"Time for some work," he told himself, with a vigorous shaking of his head and a couple of slaps to his face. "Escobar..."

He returned to the couch, flipped on his base unit monitor, and put on the headset to listen.

* * * *

There was silence at the Chavez home. Cristina had been sitting curled up in her chair with a faraway look and an occasional tear. Her mother looked at her daughter above her reading glasses with compassion as she knitted in empathetic silence. She could sense every feeling and every thought that her daughter was experiencing.

Without a word, Magda got up from her seat on the sofa and went upstairs. A few moments later she returned and laid some of Cristina's things on the couch. First she laid out a beautiful red satin robe. On top of it she laid a fancy white lace bra and white thong panties.

Cristina gave her mother a puzzled look as Magda pulled her up from her chair. She held her daughter's wrists and looked at her with a slight nod.

"Go," Magda said softly with an encouraging smile.

Cristina's eyes welled up with tears, and she hugged her mother tightly. Then she gathered the clothing her mother had laid out and ran up the stairs.

Magda made a sign of the cross and looked up with her hands folded prayerfully. Then she did three fist-to-the-heart *mea culpas* and returned to her knitting.

* * * *

Kelly heard Docksneider's voice as the others left him alone with Escobar and Valdéz. "Let's go to my office."

In his office Docksneider opened up a bar cabinet and offered him a drink. "Okay, now, what about the money? When will Cartagena arrive?"

"He will arrive in the afternoon tomorrow," said Escobar.

"And he'll have the money?"

"He will be with us. As soon as the trucks are past the checkpoint, you get your money. Good for you. I do not get mine until it arrives in San Antonio."

"My friend, the Deputy, will want his as soon as the trailers are past the checkpoint too," Docksneider said.

Then Valdéz spoke. "The Cartagena group is getting a great deal here. Each tractor that comes across the bridge will be pulling about 40,000 pounds or 18,000 kilos of cocaine – and there will be six tractors. Cocaine is going for $15,000 a kilo. Total value of all this cargo, if we can get it all across, is about 1.6 billion dollars. Not million gentlemen, but billion. Give or take 20 million. We're costing them about 6% on this side of the border. That includes all that equipment out in the yard plus our payoffs. Considering this is the most difficult and most important part of the project, getting across the U.S. border, that's cheap."

Kelly took out his phone and accessed the calculator for a quick computation. "Holy fuck! That's a hundred million dollars these guys are sharing."

Before Kelly could put his phone away, a text came in. It was from Carlos, the kid from the Roundup parking lot.

There will be a red flare at sunset tomorrow. When the green flare goes up, they will all cross the river.

"Sounds like a job for Tom Bird," Kelly said to himself, as he continued to listen.

Chavarria knocked on the door and entered without waiting. "The rest of the equipment has arrived."

Valdéz nodded.

"You men process this quickly. We don't want any more people seeing you than necessary. Leave three men you can trust to watch things overnight, and we will all meet back here at noon tomorrow. The day we have all been waiting for is almost upon us."

*   *   *   *

Just as the voices all stopped, Kelly took off his headphones and heard a soft rapping at his front door. He grabbed his sidearm from the his shoulder holster and crept silently towards the door. He leaned on the wall next to the door, and then three more raps came rapidly. He knew that Ruben would just walk right in and bang or holler if the door was locked.

"Kelly...it's me!" a gentle voice whispered.

Kelly flipped on the porch light and looked through the spy hole. He saw no one but heard three taps on the window. He opened the door slowly with one hand and his gun in the other.

"Well, it's about time," Cristina whined as she pushed the door open the rest of the way and walked inside. She was wearing the satin robe, which she took off to reveal her white lace bra and matching thong panties. "We have some unfinished business," she said as Kelly holstered his pistol. Then she stepped closer and unzipped his trousers and unbuckled his belt. She climbed onto him for a kiss as he flailed with one hand to turn out the lights and bolt the door.

"You keep taking me half way there, and it's driving me crazy," said Cristina softly. "Let's go now." She took his hand and looked at Kelly. He nodded towards to doorway on the right.

Kelly's heart began to race, and he could feel it beating in his chest and in the arteries of his neck and upper arms.

They paused by the edge of the bed.

"Do you want some wine, or beer, or whiskey?" Kelly asked in the darkness.

Cristina's younger eyes had already adjusted, and she looked into Kelly's tense face and sensed his nervousness.

"No. I am not nervous; I am ready. My heart has made me ready, Kelly." She stroked his smooth face, and her cool confidence helped to settle him down.

Kelly grabbed a nightlight from his side table drawer and plugged it into the wall. "Sorry…it's the closest I've got to candles. Sarah used to like a little light at night." Kelly embraced his woman and kissed her lips. "Cristina…I'm ready too, thanks to you. I've dated some women, but I've never brought them to my own bed, and I've never loved anyone until now…not since…"

"Shhh," Cristina said as she grabbed the bottom of his T-shirt and lifted it over his head and arms, with some help from her man. She stroked his face again. "You shaved…and you smell good…for a change." The she added with a smile, "I thought I might have to hose you down first."

"Sorry. I didn't realize how disgusting I was until I got home." He embraced and kissed her one more time, and then they sat on the bed. "Cristina…"

"Not now…just love me."

"…I have to tell you first. You are not just a night of pleasure for me. This means everything, your being here with me this way. I love you…and I need you. I thought that the joy in life was all behind me, but you have changed all that."

Cristina reached behind her back and unsnapped her bra. She tossed it on the floor and pulled Kelly back on the bed with her. "No more talking."

Kelly marveled at her breasts; they were so large while still being firm with almost no sag. The chest-to-chest, skin-on-skin experience exhilarated him. They kissed and caressed each others' bodies for several minutes, and then Cristina sat up. She reached into the front of her thong panties and pulled out a condom, which she extended toward Kelly.

"Now," she said. "We have had three days of foreplay. I can wait no longer." She slipped her panties off and tossed them next to her bra.

Kelly tried to squelch a chuckle as he took the condom and smiled at Cristina, but part of the laugh came out. The beauty looked worried when Kelly threw the condom on the floor and then reached across her and into his drawer. His large hand and arm came back with an over-sized condom packet the size of the bar coasters Cristina used at the Roundup. It read *Magnum XXXL*.

"Open it," Kelly said, as he got up on his knees and pulled down his sweatpants.

Cristina gradually looked up from his exposed penis, her eyes getting wider and her jaw dropping more and more, until she was looking into Kelly's eyes. "Diós mio!" she said, making the sign of the cross. "I...I...I am just a small woman, Kelly."

The condom fell from her limp hand onto the bed. Kelly opened it and set it on the tip of his erect penis, and nodded at Cristina. She began to unroll it down the length of his rod with both hands.

"I cannot get my fingers all the way around this," she said.

"It's the only one I've got, baby; you're going to have to work with it."

Kelly sat and took his pants all the way off. Then he embraced his girl and rolled on top of her, supporting his weight with his knees and elbows. He slid his hand to her crotch, which was very wet. He massaged her clitoris for a while as she writhed in receptive pleasure, grinding on his manly hand. Kelly put in one finger and then two to prepare her for the girth of his joystick. He rolled his fingers around inside of her and then inserted a third finger very slowly and gently. Finally, he whispered in her ear, "Put it in," and kissed her face repeatedly.

Cristina's throbbing love tunnel ferociously accepted Kelly's huge man part without any problem. She moaned loudly as she took it all. Then her whole body shook and she let out an impassioned scream as she climaxed on the first stroke.

Kelly held her tenderly, making short, slow thrusts. But this woman wanted more. Her hips thrust back enthusiastically, urging Kelly to pump harder and faster. Her erotic moans and animal passion were exciting Kelly too much, but his only goal was to satisfy the woman that he loved. He made a few circular grinds to regain control, and then he let loose with a flurry of long and deep thrusts. Cristina wrapped her arms and legs around him and thrust with all her might, biting his shoulder and digging her trimmed nails into his back. She tensed up every muscle in her body and held still as she urged her lover, "Go! Go! Go!"

Then, from the depths of her soul, a low growl began to emerge, gradually growing into a bellow and then a loud and long holler. Cristina quivered and shuddered as she began to experience multiple, rolling orgasms for the first time in her life. One, then another, then another. This had become an out-of-body experience for the little Latina.

When the trembling began to subside, she pressed her shoulder against Kelly, signaling him that she wanted to roll over and get on top. She was in no mood for Kelly's slow and gentle movements, and her adrenaline quickly had her in the upper position. She bounced like a cowgirl on a bronco and then leaned forward to put her breast on Kelly's mouth. "Bite it," she commanded. "Harder!" The girl writhed on his erect penis and then sat up for her grand finale, collapsing in a limp, sweaty heap on her man.

Kelly rolled her onto her back, without ever losing his connection, and then thrust a dozen times or so until his right leg began shaking and he had his release.

The exhausted couple lay side-by-side on their backs and panted for oxygen as sweat rolled off them everywhere. Kelly removed his condom and set in on the floor. Their eyes were wide as they looked at each other, neither of them having ever experienced this level of intense lovemaking before in their lives. Their smiles grew as they looked with wonder at each other, until they both broke out into rollicking laughter.

Cristina covered her face and kicked her feet, and Kelly rolled onto his side to embrace his woman. He pulled the sheet over them and cuddled with his soulmate as they drifted off into a much-needed and blissful slumber.

Chapter 19

Meanwhile, Docksneider and Escobar followed Valdéz, out of range of the surveillance equipment.

Valdéz walked out into the yard as the tractor-trailer was maneuvering around to park the trailer next to the rest of the pontoon bridge. Valdéz was in front of the tractor and gave the driver a thumbs-up to let him know he was parking in the right place.

Buenavista had parked a little further down the street and sneaked up to the warehouse. He had his camera this time, and from the corner of the warehouse he was snapping pictures wildly.

The tractor had stopped where it needed to be. The driver got down with a clipboard and walked toward Valdéz. Valdéz and the driver shook hands.

"Thanks for letting me deliver tonight. I didn't want to stay any longer than I had to," said the driver.

"No problem," said Valdéz. "The client is anxious to see his equipment. They will be here early tomorrow."

"If you will just sign the manifest and invoice, I will unhook and be on my way."

Valdéz scribbled his signature hurriedly and handed the clipboard back to the driver. The driver pulled the paper work apart and gave the original to Valdéz.

"Thanks." He turned and went about unhooking the trailer from the tractor. When he finished, he got back in the truck and left.

Valdéz went back inside. A few minutes later some men were coming out the front door headed for the equipment.

Total inventory was 12 Heavy Expanded Mobility Tactical Trucks, 12 trailers, 4 boats, 18 bridging pontoons, and accessory equipment. Total cost was about 12.5 million dollars. This cost was covered by the Colombian government and the US Government as a gift in support of drug interdiction programs.

*   *   *   *

The mobile bridging system was called a ribbon bridge. It was made up of a three-fold section that unfolds when you put it in the water. Rounded up with motorized skiffs, cabled together, and strung across the water, the bridge would be complete.

The ribbon bridge was constructed out of modular aluminum-alloy. It was a floating bridge system consisting of interior units and ramp bays at the entrance and exit that were transported, launched, and retrieved by a transporter/launcher vehicle. Bridge bays, which are carried in a folded position, automatically open upon entering the water to form a 22-foot section of bridge. Under ideal conditions with slower river current speeds, the M1 Abrams tank, which weighs even more than a loaded semi, can cross the ribbon bridge.

Ribbon equipment was designed for use, primarily river crossing, where no permanent bridge exists and numerous crossings were needed. Because ribbon bridges and rafts were significantly faster to construct with fewer personnel than other floating bridges, they were used extensively by the military with great success. Site considerations were of primary importance when ribbon equipment was to be used for rafting or bridging operations. Both the launch sites and actual bridge or raft sites had to be considered.

Ribbon bridges could be emplaced during daylight hours at the rate of 600 feet per hour. Assembly times increase by 50 percent when construction is at night. These times are also based upon the use of an experienced bridge crew for bridge construction under ideal conditions.

The velocity of the river's current can impact significantly upon all float-bridging operations. Ribbon equipment can be used in currents of 0 to 10 FPS. Rafting and bridging operations can become quite difficult in currents greater than 5 FPS unless the boat operators and bridge crewmen have experience working in swift currents.

The ribbon bridge was a floating, modular asset with an integral superstructure and floating supports. Individual bays were joined to form rafts or bridges in support of river crossing operations. Ribbon bridges and rafts provide a military with a reliable and responsive means for crossing rivers, lakes, and other potential water crossings. All of these men had been trained by the US military and were very experienced in using this equipment. Colombia was crisscrossed with numerous rivers in very undeveloped areas. This equipment expanded their reach immensely.

American units were deployed to Colombia in the late 90s and early 2000s to assist in the war on drugs and to test out the bridging equipment. The Colombian Military was, of course, attached. At the end of the tour the equipment was left there, the rationale being that it was cheaper to leave it than transport it.

Monday

CINCO de MAYO

Chapter 20

The morning sun was just beginning to light up the warm, dry Laredo sky and burn off the dew. Kelly stood over his sleeping beauty and smiled.

"Juice?" he asked, waking her with a kiss.

Cristina squirmed under the crumpled sheet that barely covered her naked body. She tossed one way and then the other as she struggled to open her eyes. She finally pried one eyelid open and was completely disoriented. Then she sprang up to a sitting position, holding the sheet against her bosom. She looked at Kelly and relaxed while she took in a large waking breath. She dropped the sheet to expose her perfect body, stretched with one arm and reached for the glass that Kelly was extending towards her with the other.

"Good morning, sleepy lady," Kelly said, sitting next to her.

"What time is it?"

"Seven."

"What!" she said, trying to scramble out of bed. "I have to get Max off to school."

"Settle down, sweetheart," Kelly said with a hand to her shoulder and a gentle kiss on the cheek. "No school today. Cinco de Mayo."

"Are you sure?"

"I checked in with Magda. No school. Docksneider gave her the day off too, of course, so he can pull off his big scheme. Max is still sleeping, and you'll be home before he wakes up. I was thinking I could pick up some warm *pan dulce* at the bakery and meet you back at your place as soon, as you're ready to go."

Cristina was impressed with her man, and feeling very good this morning. "That sounds perfect..." she said, "...like you." She gave Kelly a little smooch and jumped out of bed, pulling him up with her. The rising sun in the window backlit the perfect silhouette of the cowboy and his waitress, inches apart as they gazed into each others' eyes, her hands on his neck and his at his sides. Then she squeezed him tightly. "Mmm. I could get used to this."

Kelly slapped her on the bare butt and pointed her towards the shower. "There's a towel in there for you."

"Yes, sir," she said. She paused in the doorway and turned to face Kelly with the morning sun lighting up her magnificent hourglass figure. "So, how many times did we...you know?"

Kelly smiled and chuckled. "Well, from my end, we had two pretty good sessions, counting the one in the middle of the night," he said. "Not sure if you were awake for that one. But for you...I'd say about six or seven."

"Cristina laughed and shrugged. "What can I say? I'm a needy girl...and it's been a few years." Then she walked towards Kelly. She locked eyes with him, stroked his crotch and put both hands on his neck. "Kelly...I think I never knew what lovemaking really was until last night."

Kelly smiled and stroked her face. He was very tempted to pull her onto the bed for another round of passion. Instead, he broke the mood and turned her towards the door. "Shower! Or we won't get out of here till noon."

*   *   *   *

Kelly rapped twice on the front door and then let himself into the Chavez home, carrying a box from the bakery.

"Mijo! Max!" Cristina hollered up the stairs as she took the box and gave Kelly a hug. "We have warm *pan dulce* from Enrico's Bakery. Mr. Smith brought it for us. Wake up! Come down now!"

She listened to see if she could hear him moving. Finally, a small, tired voice replied: "Okay, Mama. I'm coming. Does it have nuts?"

Cristina looked at Kelly with concern, and he shook his head.

"I don't like nuts."

"No, Max. It's the kind you like."

Magda looked at the rapt eye contact and unstoppable smiles the lovebirds shared, and felt a warm glow of contentment come over her. She knew now that she was right to send her daughter to seal their bond of love. Their faces were only inches apart and their conversation never stopped as they basked in their private love bubble, oblivious to the world around them.

Magda turned up the volume on the TV as the Mexican station showed hundreds of people on the riverbank near Hipódromo; and riots, fights, and fires were beginning to overtake the area.

"Kelly, I think it is starting," she said.

Just then the newscast was interrupted with a breaking news report. Franklin Basham, Governor of Texas, was speaking to the people of Texas and Mexico. The text of his speech was shown in Spanish subtitles at the bottom of the screen. After wishing everyone a happy Cinco de Mayo, he got to the point of his impromptu address:

"We are getting reports of huge crowds gathering along the river near Nuevo Laredo. Celebration is fine, but there are also reports of violence, gunfire, and rocket-propelled grenades, some of which have made their way across the river onto American soil. This is unacceptable.

"I must issue a warning to those gathered on the riverbank: Any mass crossing will be seen as an invasion of the sovereign State of Texas and the United States of America. As such, it will be met with military resistance. Continued cross-border gun and grenade fire will make any crossing an armed invasion and an act of war. And it will be dealt with as such."

Gunfire and violence dwindled and disappeared over the next hour as the news spread, but the small settlement of Hipódromo continued to swell, with hundreds more arriving every hour, almost like Mecca during the Haj.

* * * *

Back at the warehouse, Valdéz and his crew were wrapping up a final inventory and inspection of the equipment and getting each piece in the proper order for a smooth deployment tonight. One of the surveillance team members stayed back to drive to the hotel and send the rest of the team down to the warehouse.

Docksneider and Escobar were at a coffee shop on Water Street between the warehouse and the hotel.

"I saw that little prick again when I was waiting for you," said Escobar.

"Who's that?" asked Docksneider between sips of his hot, black coffee.

"That cowboy we saw the other night at the saloon. Border Agent, Kelly Smith. He went into the bakery across the street."

"So what? There are a million cowboys here. This is Texas."

"This one cost me tens of millions in Colombia three years ago. He knows I'm in town, and he will do what he can to derail my plans. He must die before the sun goes down tonight," Escobar said pensively as he stared out the window into his daydream.

"Let it go," advised Docksneider. "Why complicate things? That will only attract more attention."

"No! This has to be done. Smith cost us millions and set us back years. I will not be satisfied until he suffers a slow and painful death, which he will know is a gift from me. Nobody fucks with Hector Escobar and lives to tell about it."

"It will bring suspicion right down on us. Didn't you already kill his wife? She was pregnant, you know."

"That's a little bonus I wasn't aware of. But this will happen. We will get away with this. Let them be suspicious! America is falling apart anyway. They don't have the muscle or the stomach to push their way around like they used to. It seems that even their president wears women's panties and bows to the weakest and most cowardly these days. Their land border needs to be compromised hard. We will get away with this. Besides, who trained us to do this, but the Americans! They do this every time. They did it with that Muslim guy, Bin Laden; the Panamanian President, Manuel Noriega. They build people up to their own advantage, then those people see the hypocrisy and turn on them. Why not us? Smith has to die."

Docksneider said nothing. He saw Escobar's words as the ranting of a madman – a madman he was in bed with.

"Besides this is no concern of yours, Cock-biter," said Escobar. "If your friends in Mexico have done what they are supposed to do, our operation will go forward as planned."

Escobar threw a 50-dollar bill on the table for the two cups of coffee and went outside to his car, leaving Docksneider alone at the table. Kelly hadn't noticed the Jeep Cherokee on the street on his trip to the bakery, as his head was still in the clouds. The Colonel nodded to Octavio, the driver and head of Escobar's personal security team, and he pulled away from the curb.

"Hotel. I have a job for you and your men." Escobar explained his intention to kill Kelly Smith.

Octavio, unlike Docksneider, saw Escobar as a military operative that planned an operation and saw it through. He believed that Escobar was invincible and would succeed. He did not care if this Smith person was collateral damage. He didn't know him, except as another expendable pawn in his boss's game. Then his mind turned back to the mission. He had to tell Escobar his thoughts.

"Captain, may I speak freely?"

Escobar was surprised. Octavio was a trusted accomplice and specialist, but he was not a partner or planner. It was risky for mid-level underlings to have an opinion. "What is it?"

"Captain, as we were saying in the meeting last night, taking the equipment and the product through the back side of the warehouse yard is the quickest, easiest way. The sooner the trucks and equipment are off the riverbanks and not on public streets is the best. Anyway, it will look suspicious for the equipment to be coming out of the construction site. I really feel this is the best procedure. This man, Docksneider, has to be getting big money for his part in this. He needs to accept the risk."

"Yes, I saw that. Docksneider is not a military person. He does not understand how an operation like this can go. If all the other elements go as they should – the riot, the pontoon bridge, the closure of the checkpoint, and the decoy smugglers on the North Bridge – we should have no problem. That is how we shall proceed. Docksneider will not be able to stop us. Do we have the weapons?"

"Yes, Sir. Valdéz just confirmed that our Colombian contacts in Houston brought them by this morning while you were here. And Cartagena will be here with the money this afternoon. What about this other detail we need to take care of...this old history you spoke of? How should we handle that?"

"It cannot happen too long before the main plan begins so there is no time for them to trace a car or shell casings or anything to us, our hotel, or the warehouse. But it must happen before dark. The real job begins at sunset. I need a team of men that can go in quietly, execute the target cleanly, and get out. We don't need the rest of the group knowing what is going on."

"I need Pato and Gerardo. That is my team."

Escobar flipped open his cell phone and hit a speed dial number.

"Chavarria, send Pato and Gerardo to my room. Tell them to wait for me there. I have a special project for them."

"Si, Comandante. Anything else?"

"I'll let you know." Escobar clicked off the cell phone. For Escobar, ordering an execution was no different from ordering takeout.

Chapter 21

Chavarria had been around enough to know that this operation was not going to be just a simple matter of putting up a pontoon ribbon bridge, letting several trucks go across, disassembling it, and going home. He had his team. He knew his team; they were like family, worked together well, and had each other's backs. But there were several men, including the ones who had just been summoned, who were not part of the team. He could see they were more casual, unruly, and uncivilized mercenary creatures who cared only about themselves. They had a cunning look about them that he did not trust. They didn't blend well with the rest of Escobar's disciplined and mission-minded gang of military thugs.

Chavarria walked over to Pato, who was lying down, asleep on the floor in the same hotel room, and kicked his foot.

"Hey, go get your cutthroat friend, Gerardo, and go to the Captain's room. Wait in the hallway until he arrives. You have work to do."

"Yeah, okay," Pato said with an annoyed sneer. He was groggy and sat up slowly.

"Move it! Arriba!" Chavarria demanded. Conveying the sense of urgency to the hired gun sometimes required a bit of prodding and physical intimidation.

147

Pato nodded twice and got up quickly. He grabbed his bag and went to the other room to get Gerardo.

As they were walking to Escobar's room Gerardo asked, "What's up? I'm tired of sitting around looking at trucks."

"It's showtime; I just don't know what the story is. We'll find out soon."

They walked up to Escobar's room and sat by the door.

Moments later, Octavio and Escobar arrived. Octavio opened the door for his leader and then addressed the two men harshly. "Get in here!"

Escobar was standing near a table by the window. He had a map of the city and a Google Earth printout of Kelly's residence on a table. There was a suitcase with three silenced AK 47s, three silenced Walther PKs, and a half-dozen hand grenades.

"You've been planning this for some time, it appears, Comandante," said Octavio.

Escobar didn't respond directly or bother with greetings or formalities for the new arrivals. "Here's the reconnaissance information. A guy named Kelly Smith lives at this address. He needs to be taken out. This might not be an easy target. He has been hit before and survived, so he is probably always expecting something to happen. He's also a Border Patrol agent."

"Ahh, so he will be armed," said Octavio.

"Yes. He has been watched for some time now, but he keeps a very low profile. He is a creature of habit, but we cannot count on that. With his past he could have some very dynamic assets available to him."

Octavio glanced at the rest of his team. He saw no outward reservations from them. He knew his men. Difficult targets actually make their mission more interesting. The cartel paid for this team to go to Israel and learn assassination tactics from the Mossad.

This was not their first difficult target. It wasn't really that difficult. Once you get used to killing people, you just need to figure out how to get up close enough to your target to execute the mission efficiently. Some targets take more planning. Some targets just need to be taken out.

"He drives a Jeep. If the Jeep is there, so is he. Don't shoot him unless you have to. Too much noise. Stabbing is much more personal, slow, and painful too. Take one of the rentals. Go have lunch, do your reconnaissance, and figure out your plan for a smooth daylight operation. Smith is out eating baked goods right now. Just wait until 7 p.m. The Lieutenant will call you. The sun will be getting low, and I don't want his body to be discovered before our plan is complete, which will be an hour or so after darkness falls."

Briefed on their mission, the three assassins gathered their information and equipment and left the room.

"Chavarria, get your men and let's get back to the warehouse," Escobar said as he walked toward the door. "You will be my driver today while Octavio leads the assassination team."

Chavarria and his men prepared the final details for the operation when they got back to the warehouse.

* * * *

Kelly made it back to his house and opened his email, looking for the photos from Rick. He attached the photos and the audio recording of the meeting at the warehouse and sent them to Ben. The laptop was open next to him, tracking his prey. But he had no time for checking all of his recordings. Besides, he was sure he understood Escobar's plan completely.

Rick Buenavista was back in place surveilling the warehouse activity and monitoring the movement of the minivans on his tracker. He was monitoring Docksneider's office while Escobar and Octavio were in the Cherokee discussing the plan to assassinate Kelly, and Kelly was busy eating pan dulce with Cristina and her family while it was recording on his device. No one heard the assassination plot take shape in the Jeep Cherokee.

Kelly called Rick to see what was happening there.

"Sir, they're lining up all of the military equipment behind the warehouse. Not sure what it is, but there are some small boats, probably for drug interdiction in Colombia. It looks like they have a small shipment of weapons that arrived today too, but it's not marked with U.S. military insignias like the other shipments. The minivan looks like it's still at the hotel. Should I check in over there?"

"No, stay there. I'm sure they will come your way soon enough. The hotel poses no threat."

"10-4, Boss"

*　　*　　*　　*

With all of Escobar's ducks in a row, Kelly knew his plan was set, so he pulled out his cell phone and called Senator Cuellar.

"Sir, this is Kelly Smith. We need a favor. Can you call the Governor and have some National Guard Blackhawks and attack helicopters come this way?"

"Kelly, don't joke around like this."

"I'm not joking, sir. Let me explain. I have solid information that a country other than Mexico is ready to make a significant incursion into the United States by illegally breaching our borders and bringing in over 1.6 billion dollars worth of cocaine. It's going to happen around sunset. I have pictures and recorded conversations."

Kelly explained the whole situation to the Senator, and the Senator agreed to try his best to help, telling Kelly that this was the Governor's call.

A couple of minutes later Kelly's phone rang. "Hello?"

"Kelly Smith?"

"This Kelly."

"Kelly, This is Governor Franklin Basham. I just got off the phone with Senator Cuellar. What the hell is happening down there?"

"Governor, if Senator Cuellar told you what I told him, we are going to need back up down here very soon. The cartel is bringing truckloads of drugs across the Rio Grande tonight. I can't run it through Border Patrol because our Deputy is in on this and has closed the North Bridge and the I-35 checkpoint to let the trucks pass without any inspection. As you already know, we have a riot ready to explode across the river to the South, which is part of this drug operation. That is strictly to cause a diversion and keep all the agents and law enforcement busy, and it's getting out of hand. The hired Mexican thugs are still shooting a few rocket-propelled grenades over to our side so we don't lose interest."

"What the hell! Are you sure? I warned them about that in my speech this morning."

"Yes sir, I just saw it on the TV."

"Okay, Kelly, if your deputy is in on this who can we trust? What do you want?"

"Governor, how about a half-dozen gunship helicopters? It wouldn't hurt to scramble some helo units to back up your military threat anyway. They could fly along the river a couple times as a show of force, and then come back up and head straight West on Highway 20 to 69W, towards the World Trade Bridge at low altitude looking for the trucks.

"There will be six big rigs with armed escorts, so we could use your best; some men or commanders with special ops backgrounds would be the best. There's potential for a lot of gunfire, so make sure they are all prepared for a real battle – no green kids that are going to get themselves shot up. Give them my phone number, because I might need to direct some of them to help out back at the riot area south of town too, Sir."

"Son, you had better be right on this. You better not be making a fool out of me. I'm trusting you because the Senator told me about your valiant history in Colombia. I'm on it, but this better not turn out to be a personal revenge play."

"Sir, have one of your people call our radio room to confirm the extent of the riot and that the checkpoint is closed."

"Don't worry, son; they're already on it. You didn't think I'd scramble helicopters without verification, did you? You'll get a call in a few minutes, and you will need to coordinate Go Time with the commander."

The governor clicked off his phone and immediately called his National Guard contact.

Chapter 22

Magda was nervously pacing as the minutes ticked slowly by. It was late afternoon, and she couldn't just stay home and wait for things to happen any longer. She really wanted to go back to the warehouse to see what was going on, but the thought terrified her. It was Cinco de Mayo, but she didn't feel much like celebrating. The TV news showed more and more people swarming to the riverbank on the Mexican side, and violence and small disturbances were breaking out everywhere. There was an ominous feeling of dread that she could no longer bear. She was going to the warehouse. Valdéz had told her to stay away, but what could one little afternoon trip hurt?

"Cristina, I'm going out for a few minutes. I'll take the rust bucket in case you and Max need the good car for something," she said in a determined and authoritative tone, the way Cristina heard her speak when she was at the office barking out orders.

"You better not be going to your work. It is very dangerous there, and you might screw up all of Kelly's hard work."

"It is none of your concern where I'm going. You can prepare supper tonight – something nice for the holiday." She opened the door and without looking back, said, "I love you," and closed the door firmly behind her.

Mama doesn't say "I love you" when she's going to the store, Cristina thought. She felt an ache of concern in the pit of her stomach.

*   *   *   *

Buenavista observed a Hispanic lady in her 50s pull into the warehouse yard and walk towards the building. He called to relay the information Kelly, but got his voice mail.

He left a message for Kelly and described the woman he had observed. "She's walking into a snake pit in there, Kelly. Let's hope they turn her around and send her home," Rick said with obvious concern, and hung up.

Halfway to the building Magda was approached by Chavarria. He was suspicious and anxious about an outsider walking into the middle of the operation.

"Señora, what are you doing here? This is a company holiday. Everyone was told to stay away."

"I work here. What are you doing here?" she said, trying the same bulldog approach she had used on Valdéz on Saturday when she planted the devices. But this military chief would not be so dismissive.

Chavarria radioed Escobar and informed him. "Captain, there is a woman trying to go inside. She says she works here."

Escobar and Docksneider were in the office and could both hear the report.

"Magdalena Chavez," Docksneider told Escobar. "She checks on the janitors on her days off."

Valdéz was just entering the office and looked at Escobar. "I told her very specifically the other day, and in my most persuasive voice, that she should not come around at all today."

Escobar squinted one eye to capture a thought as he put his hand on his chin and looked at Docksneider. "Didn't you tell me that our waitress at that bar last week was the daughter of your employee?"

"That's right. Why?"

"And wasn't that Border Agent cowboy I mentioned to you spending a lot of time with her at the bar?"

"Yeah, but all the guys in the bar like Cristina," Docksneider said.

"But from what I saw, she liked him back." Escobar exhaled and nodded slightly. "So if Kelly Smith is fucking her daughter, maybe she is more than just an exemplary employee coming to work on her day off. We can take no chances."

Escobar pressed the talk button on his radio and called back to Chavarria, who still had Magda detained outside.

"Guillermo, bring the lady to the conference room, immediately."

"Diez-Cuatro, Comandante."

Escobar got up and nodded his head toward the door, and they all followed him to the conference room.

"Your boss and mine both want to see you inside," Chavarria told her, grabbing her arm and escorting her roughly through the entrance and to the conference room.

Magda was thinking that perhaps she did make a mistake in going to the warehouse, and with all of the activity and strange equipment around her she sensed that she was in serious trouble. She was desperately trying to think of a story for being there that they would believe, and she knew she had to contact Cristina.

Escobar looked at the warehouse owner with a very matter-of-fact attitude. "She knows too much. We need to get rid of her. That she is here is suspicious enough."

"Somebody will notice she is gone," Docksneider said, feeling a little protective of the woman who had done so much for his business. He knew her family; he liked her, and didn't want to see harm come to her – definitely not the kind of harm Escobar had in mind.

"By the time anyone notices it will be too late. We will be long gone. We can make her disappear so nobody knows she was even here. I will have one of the men take her car to a nearby store and leave it. It will look like she disappeared there. Her body will be at the bottom of the river…way down river. The fish will take care of her."

"Let's get her in here and find out what she knows first."

"Of course! But the outcome will be the same."

As Magda and Chavarria entered the office area of the warehouse, Magda began to worry more, and she coolly removed her cell phone from her purse and hit the speed dial for her daughter. Then she put the phone back into her bag and palmed a tube of lipstick. Cristina's phone rang and she answered, seeing that it was her mother from the caller ID.

"Yes, Mother."

Cristina heard no response but could hear some background noise.

Entering the conference room Docksneider asked in a conciliatory manner:

"Ms. Chavez, you know Mr. Escobar from your visit here on Saturday. What are you doing here, again, on a holiday weekend? I gave you an extra day off so you would not have to be here today."

"I left my lipstick last week. I came to pick it up."

"All this way to pick up lipstick? You could not have waited until tomorrow when you come to work?"

"I am going out tonight to celebrate Cinco de Mayo, and I need my good, red lipstick. And this place is only five minutes from my house."

Escobar arose with a sinister smile. "Well…we cannot have a lady go out without her lipstick! Let us go find your good, red lipstick. Shall we?" he asked, extending his arm towards the door with a slight bow in a faux gentlemanly manner.

They all exited the conference room to Ms. Chavez' desk. She rummaged through the top drawer in an attempt to make it look like she was looking for her lipstick. She let the tube in her palm roll into the drawer.

"Here it is," she said, reaching for the tube in the drawer. "See?" she said holding up the tube a little too high, allowing Escobar to see the colored sticker on the bottom.

"I still do not believe that you came all this way for lipstick," said Escobar with a villainous smile.

"Then you must not know women very well, Mr. Escobar."

"Oh, but I do, Ms. Chavez! I know how they hide lies behind their pretty faces, and I know how stupid men never learn," Escobar said, snatching the tube from her hand. He removed the cap and twisted it to reveal a pale pink shade of lipstick inside. "I guess the color faded over the weekend, hmmm? I know when I am being lied to, Ms. Chavez! Chavarria, take her and lock her in a safe side room in the warehouse, one of those small secure rooms with locks for precious cargo...like our lovely...Magdalena, isn't it? We will decide how to dispose of her later. So sorry, ma'am. It does not please me to kill a lovely woman like you. I would much rather fuck you than kill you, but time and money prevent me from choosing that option."

Chavarria nodded to one of his men who grasped her upper arm tightly, took a ring of keys from the wall in the hallway, and led her away.

Cristina overheard the whole conversation and knew she had to do something. She was overcome, first by fear and dread and then by power and determination. Nothing would stop her from saving her mother.

She tried to call Kelly, but got only his voice mail. "Kelly! Call me!" She grabbed her purse and her keys and headed for the base of the stairs by the front door.

"Max! Come here quickly!"

Max was already on his way down the stairs with headphones on and carrying the laptop. He had something to tell her too. "Yes, Mama?"

"I'm taking you to your Tia Belinda's house."

"Why Mama?"

"Don't ask why. I have to go somewhere. It's important."

The boy recognized the serious "game face" on his mother and knew that she was on an important mission. "Mama, is it because the bad men have grandma at the warehouse? Or is it because they are sending three men tonight to kill Mr. Kelly?"

Cristina's blood ran cold as she learned of this new threat to the man she now couldn't live without. Her mother, her lover...her whole world could be incinerated into meaningless ashes before the sun went down tonight. But she did not yield to fear or helplessness. Now, more than ever, she became an unstoppable force with a mission that could not fail.

Beyond denial now, she didn't question Max on the veracity of his story about Kelly. After all, he knew about her mother too. "What time are they going after Kelly?" she asked.

"Seven," Max said.

She looked at her watch. "We have less than two hours to save your grandmother and warn Kelly."

"Mama, I have to go with you."

"Max, it's dangerous and you're just a child. I..."

"I will listen so I can tell you where the men are. You can park a block away where I'll be safe. And I can keep trying to get a hold of Mr. Kelly," Max said in a cool and confident tone.

Cristina couldn't believe it, but everything Max said made sense, so they got in the car and drove toward the warehouse.

* * * *

Escobar and his group were standing outside the open door to the conference room. He explained the situation to his henchmen, and told them to take Magda's car to the grocery store up the road and park so it looked like she had parked it there to go shopping, and then dispose of Magda later upon his command.

"Chavarria, you come with me," Escobar said. "We will meet Cartagena. He has arrived at the hotel. Then we will all come back here for our final meeting before our perfectly crafted year-long master plan begins to play out."

"Colonel, if you are coming right back, I can go with Chavarria to pick him up for you," Valdéz offered.

"Miguel, when a man is bringing you 1.6 billion dollars, you do not send a surrogate to fetch him," Escobar responded, somewhat condescendingly.

"Of course, jefe," Miguel said, with a slight bow of his head.

"Besides, I want to see all the money myself, which will mostly remain there at the hotel under armed guard until the trucks have successfully passed the checkpoint."

"I'm coming along for that ride too," Docksneider said. "It will be dark in an hour or so, and I want to make sure that money is real before truckloads of your contraband start coming through my warehouse yard. And this is the man who will pay me and that I will be waiting in the hotel room with once you have left for Corpus Christi. I want him to see me with you, as a member of your trusted inner circle, Hector."

Escobar nodded in agreement. "Miguel, you stay here and run point for Octavio and his team, the bridge crew, and be my eyes and ears here. When you can spare a couple of men and a vehicle, take care of the old woman and send her to the fishes, but not before the trucks have crossed. The bridge team is about ready to go, so make sure things are in order and every man knows his job before dark."

"The woman is in Safe Room Number One by the double-wide bay door on the far end of the dock," said Chavarria in Spanish. "She is not tied, but she's harmless. The keys are on the wall outside the office door – the key ring with the white rabbit's foot."

Valdéz nodded his understanding.

Chapter 23

Kelly had been busy for several hours working out the logistics for covering the riot site and getting forces ready to meet the trucks when they came across the North Bridge. He hadn't paid any attention to incoming calls because he was on outgoing calls the whole time. He hadn't had time to monitor the audio from the warehouse either.

Fortunately, however, Rick was able to hear the whole conversation that just went down on the conference room microphone that Magda had planted. The voices were distant and hard to hear, but he got it all – the English and the Spanish.

Now I know exactly where the woman is and where the keys are, and most of the honchos are gone. Maybe I can fit in with the Mexican workers and break her loose before they get rid of her.

Just then his phone whistled with an incoming text.

"I hope to hell that's Kelly," he said to himself.

But it wasn't. He didn't recognize the number, but he knew the name when he read the text:

Hi, Agent Buenavista, it's Sabrina from Enterprise. Remember me? I'm just having a long and lonely night at work and was wondering if you would care to join me for a cocktail when I get off at 9. I hope I'm not being too forward. ☺

Rick smiled. He had thought of her often since they met at the airport rental car location. He texted her back:

It's Rick. How could I forget a girl with a smile like yours? Would love to join you, Sabrina, but I am sitting in my old red pickup truck keeping an eye on some of your rental cars at a warehouse on the river. Busy night. Rain check?

Sabrina remembered the Import/Export company that had rented the cars and looked up the address. It really was by the river, but so were most warehouses. She texted back:

It's okay. I just thought you might be interested.

Rick didn't waste any time in responding.

I'm very interested. Tomorrow. 7. Dinner. Wear a dress. ☺ I'll be in touch. Got to go.

Rick had a little spring in his step now and hatched his plan to free Magda. He was in Intel, and like so many young agents was spending his money on things that would generally be useless, but in this case, he had a small disguise kit in his car that he had bought when he was assigned to the Intelligence Unit. He put on a wide moustache and a very convincing scar on his cheek, tied a red bandana around his forehead, and put on a black baseball cap with a fake braided pony tail in the back and got out of his car.

The heavy equipment was all on the riverbank now, 50 yards from the warehouse dock, and the crew of men was all there too. The sun was sitting on top of the horizon. It would be dark enough soon, and there would be no moon tonight. He watched from a distance as a man in a white suit and Panama hat emerged from the back of the warehouse and walked towards the action by the river. He recognized the voice as Miguel Valdéz.

Valdéz stopped halfway and hollered towards the crew. "Manuel, Antonio, Enrique! Begin in ten minutes. The first truck must start to cross 45 minutes after you begin. Each truck has only 10 minutes to cross. Oh, what the hell. Just start now. Better early than late." He headed slowly back toward the warehouse and then turned around and watched the final preparations.

This is my chance to get inside the front door and grab the keys, Rick thought. He walked along the street in the opposite direction for a block and then crossed the street and double back toward the front of the warehouse. He could see Valdéz turn and start walking toward the back end of the warehouse again.

He got deep enough into the yard to screen himself from Valdéz and the crew and ran for the front door. It was unlocked. He looked around for offices and followed a hallway behind the reception area. *Bingo.* He saw Docksneider's office with a key board next to the door, grabbed the rabbit's foot, and headed back out the front just as he heard Valdéz whistling his way in from the warehouse area at the end of the hallway. Rick wanted to go around the warehouse on the outside the other away, away from the street and farther from the work crew. It was swampy and filled with debris that Docksneider had had his crew discard there, and it was quite the obstacle course.

* * * *

It was almost 7 o'clock, and Kelly finally had things as ready as possible to take down Escobar's drug operation. The TV was reporting an enormous crowd and increasing violence across the river, but Kelly knew he had to get going soon to meet the trucks on the north side of town.

He looked at his phone and saw the message icon flashing, so he called his voice mail. First he got Rick's message about the Hispanic woman that Escobar's gang had detained at the warehouse and brought inside. He knew at once that it had to be Magda.

Why the heck would she go there today? he thought.

He was very worried and hoped the next message would be the all-clear. Instead, he heard Cristina's desperate plea for him to call her. His heart sank as he called her number and prepared for the worst.

"Kelly, where are you?" she blurted anxiously when she answered his call.

"Home. Where's Magda? Is she all right?"

"I'm going to get her now. But you have to get out of the house now! Three men are coming to kill you! Get out now!"

"What? How…?"

"Max was listening. Get out!"

"When are they coming? Do you know?"

"Seven o'clock – in 5 minutes! Kelly, get out of there now!"

"I'll be fine here. Thanks – and thank Max for me. I've got to deal with this and then we'll get your mother together. Wait for me!"

Kelly peered through his blinds and saw a car across the street with three men in it.

"Too late to run," he said.

He immediately texted Ruben and started to prepare for an attack.

Ruben read his incoming text:

Chicken stew… my house… blue

Ruben dropped everything. "Gotta go!" he said to Sylvia, and was out the door in seconds flat. He knew that Kelly needed assistance and that he had to approach cautiously and without any fanfare or noise.

Kelly knew the killers would wait for their signal and begin at seven sharp. He closed the shades to make it as dark inside as possible in the pre-dusk hour, left the lights and TV on, and turned on the shower and the radio in the bathroom. Then he unlocked the back door in the kitchen, leaving it slightly ajar, and headed for his closet in the bedroom. He had a small arsenal there, along with night vision goggles and a vest.

Kelly locked himself in his closet, put the two-by-six plank across the door into the steel brackets, and plugged the night light into the outlet above the bulb, which he unscrewed enough so that it wouldn't light. He felt to make sure that his service pistol was safely stowed out of sight beneath his belt at the base of his back. Then he unsnapped two hasps on the back wall of his small closet, which opened into his nicely loaded arsenal. He had taken the back half of the kitchen pantry and repurposed it as an armory after his wife was killed. He used to keep his toys in a locked cabinet in the garage, but this would be much more convenient in a time of dire need, like tonight, and he could also access it from the kitchen side.

He pulled out a Mossberg pistol gripped, nine round, twelve-gauge shotgun, a bandoleer of shotgun shells, and a .40 caliber Glock with several high capacity clips. He also pulled out a Mini 14 carbine with a high-powered scope attached. There was a 30-round ammo clip inserted into the receiver part of the weapon and another 30-round clip taped to this clip facing down.

"Okay, Rambo," he said to himself, "I think we're ready."

His nervous tension was gradually turning into fervent and steady anticipation. This would be a first and long-awaited step in avenging the cold-blooded murder of his wife and unborn child. "Come on, boys. You know that little surprise party you've got planned? The surprise is going to be on you." He snapped a clip into his Glock and called his partner.

Ruben was just pulling up two houses away and already saw the car with the three assassins when his phone rang. It was Kelly.

"Did you get out of there yet? Who are these guys in the car?" Ruben asked.

"They're just some, you know, assassins Escobar sent to kill me. And I'm not leaving. I'm fine. I'm in my panic room."

"Panic room? You got a living room, tiny kitchen, and a bedroom. I hope you're not talking about your bathroom, because the door doesn't even latch on that, dude."

"Okay, I guess it's my 'panic closet' in my bedroom. I'm barricaded in with weapons, and I already put on my vest. I've got a full array of toys including every type of grenade, tear gas...you name it."

"Geez, bro, that's great stuff to have, but you shoulda gotten out when you had the chance. What's to stop them from shooting your brains out through the closet door, huh?"

"I'm covered, Rube. I've got a crib mattress stuffed with old flack jackets mounted on the inside of the door."

"Oh…well…that ought to extend your life by 20 or 30 seconds, I guess. The driver is on the phone now. I think they're getting ready to move. What's your plan?"

"Uh…"

"You do have a plan, don't you?"

"Ya, ya, sure. Of course. When they come in, you sneak around the neighbor's house to my shed out back. When I give you the signal, pull the lever down on the fuse box and kill the lights. I've got all the blinds closed, and I never get much light in here anyway. It should be dark enough, and I'll add a little fog if I have to. Got your night eyes?"

"I'm way ahead of you partner," Ruben said, just securing the band to his head and pointing the goggles upward for now. One guy is out of the car, but the others haven't moved yet."

"Three of them, right?"

"Roger that."

Ruben had put his vest on, loaded his pistol-grip shotgun, and checked the clip on his sidearm. "Hey, I have an idea. It may be a little complicated for you, but listen closely so you don't miss any details. Why don't you call the police and tell them you have a home invasion in progress? Let the Police come in and deal with all the shit, and we'll sit back and watch."

Kelly shook his head in disagreement and responded. "No, no, bad idea, won't work."

"Why, Gringo? Why? Because a Mexican thought of it? Is that it?"

Kelly rolled his eyes. "No, that's not it. You always gotta throw the race card, man."

"It's not the race card; it's an ethnicity card."

"The reason it's no good is because I didn't think of it – and because these assassins will leave a pile of cops in a bloody heap in the middle of my living room, and three or four families will have kids without fathers. We'll call the cops in time for the cleanup so we can take down the drug trucks."

"Pinche Cabrón. What's this 'we' stuff, former partner? I'm not sure if it's the mess in your living room or the dead cops that bother you more. Okay, we'll do it your way. But I like my idea better because it keeps me out of a bunch of shit. They're on the move, bro. I'll be around back in a minute. Keep me posted."

The others got out of the Jeep Wrangler and walked up Kelly's driveway and paused.

"Okay. You're going to lose me for a minute, because I'm going to call it in now."

"Sure, steal my idea and call it your own. We can use a little help."

"Once they're inside we'll communicate by text. Silence your phone."

*   *   *   *

Escobar's entire team gathered in the conference room back at Docksneider's warehouse shortly before 7:00 p.m. for the final briefing. Cartagena, a slender businessman in a grey suit, fedora, and dark glasses was seated on a very large, green military shipping case, which might usually hold half a dozen bazookas. Today, it was filled with twenty million dollars in cash for Escobar's pawns and henchmen.

There were three large caskets of cash in Escobar's getaway car under guard back at the hotel. The getaway car was a hearse he had hijacked from a funeral home in Mexico and used to pick up the caskets at the airport. Behind Cartagena stood two huge goons, each with two vicious pit bulls on leashes.

"Miguel, tell Octavio and his team it is time to kill Mr. Smith." Then, the Colonel, in full dress uniform, addressed the meeting.

"I want the riots to start getting out of hand right now so that The Border Agents will all be on high alert down there, and we can deploy the bridge without any worries."

"They are calling it the Tejano Woodstock, Comandante. Many more people than we expected," Valdéz reported proudly.

"Don't be so pleased, Miguel. We did not want it so big that it will attract the attention of the governor and his state militia. But at least it will keep their focus away from our little plan. Just remember – no one crosses the river until I give the signal. Then, when the bridge is complete, you will send everyone across all at once," he said pointing to Valdéz, "and, Chavarria, you will send the first decoy truck across the North Bridge."

"It is ready as we speak, Comandante, filled with a dozen children."

Escobar nodded and continued. "That is when we will bring our shipment across the pontoon bridge right here, behind the warehouse. The six semi trucks are loaded and ready to move. The second decoy truck will run the north bridge the minute the first one is caught...or ten minutes after it departs. We are already tuned in to the scanners to keep us updated. Then the drugs will pass the checkpoint, and my official Colombian military entourage will head for Corpus Christi while the bridge is taken down and loaded onto the military flatbeds, which will meet us there. And in just a few hours you will each receive your agreed share of the money. Mr. Cartagena..."

Escobar nodded at the businessman, and his goons, with much effort, lifted the huge military case onto the conference table and opened it. There were smiles and much excitement all around as they beheld the 2,000 bundles of American cash, each containing ten-thousand dollars in one-hundred dollar bills.

"Any questions?" Escobar asked.

*   *   *   *

The three hired assassins stopped at the corner of the house and reviewed their plan as Ruben scurried through the neighbor's yard two houses down. Octavio had his Walther PK and Pato and Gerardo had their assault rifles and handguns checked, loaded, and ready. Escobar didn't want gunfire if possible, so they had Tasers and knives ready as well. They looked at all of their weapons and laughed about how easy it was going to be to take down one man by surprise with their wealth of weaponry.

The 911 operator answered. "Laredo Police Department; how may I help you?"

"Yes, Ma'am this is Border Patrol Agent Kelly. I'm inside my house, and there is going to be a home invasion here in a minute or two. I'm at 703 Lindenwood. Can you send somebody over to get these guys? You better send an ambulance too; I'm pretty sure there will be plenty of bloodshed."

"Sir, this is not funny. Are you sure about this? You sound like you're ordering a salami sandwich, not waiting to be attacked."

"Ma'am, I'm sorry about the lack of panic in my voice, but I'm with Border Patrol, and this isn't the first time I've been invaded; I'm experienced and I'm prepared. Please send somebody over, preferably two or three squads, I can hear them kicking down the door now. These guys are armed and dangerous, so tell your guys to approach silently, wear vests, and be careful...and don't shoot me or Ruben."

"Mr. Kelly, units have been dispatched. They are on the way. Most of our units are south of town for the possible riot, so it may take several minutes. Please stay on the line and do not engage the perpetrators."

"I've got to go, ma'am."

Kelly heard the men in the living room and slowly removed the barricade and exited the closet with his goggles on his head. He set the shotgun quietly by the door for insurance, slung the carbine over his shoulder on a strap, and put his hand on his Glock. He stood behind the door of his bedroom and texted Ruben.

Are you by the box?

Ready.

Kelly listened to the men in the living room.

"Let's just plug him through the shower curtain. Nobody will hear. We're inside and we've got silencers," Pato said.

Octavio wasn't so sure; he believed in following orders. "Let's just wait for him to come out," he said. We'll greet him with Tasers and many stabbings and leave him naked and dead in his own house."

"Maybe we can bring his head back for the Captain," Gerardo added.

Remind me to buy Max a car and pay for his college education, Kelly thought to himself.

"Good idea," said Octavio. "That might be worth a bonus from our little dictator. See if you can find a plastic bag in the kitchen."

One guy leaving the room...now's the time.

Kelly put his goggles in position and texted the order:

Come in the back and get the guy in the kitchen. Lights out now.

Ruben pulled the switch, and the house became dark and silent except for the sound of the shower. It was somewhat dark, but Kelly thought a smokescreen would help, and his goggles would see right through it. The door creaked slightly as Kelly stepped into the living room. He pulled a flash bang grenade from his tactical vest, held it for one second, and then lobbed it into the room. He plugged his ears and turned his eyes away. Before it hit the floor, it exploded with a deafening bang, a blinding light, and a percussive shock wave that disoriented the killers.

With his gun raised and night eyes on, he saw Octavio dive for the floor and cover his head. Pato raised his gun and fired off target in the direction of the creaking door, stunned and blinded from the powerful grenade. Kelly tapped him once in the forehead and once in the heart. He fell in a lifeless heap. He fixed his sights on the team leader, cowering in front of his couch with his arms extended.

"Don't kill me!" he whimpered.

Then Kelly heard an errant shot from a silenced Walther PK and then a blast from Ruben's pistol-grip 12-gauge shotgun followed by the thud of a falling body.

"All clear, buddy," Kelly shouted to his partner, his gun trained on Octavio. "Get your cuffs ready for this scumbag, unless you'd rather just shoot him."

"No, no, Señor! I am not a bad man like the others. I did not shoot," said Octavio in a nervous voice.

"Well, that's true," said Kelly. "Only a good man would bother to get a nice clean plastic bag to put my head in. Shoot him, Igor," he said with a wink to Ruben.

"No, *no!...* "

"Right away, Dr. Frankenstein." Ruben shot once above the prone assassin into the couch with his handgun, and Octavio thought he was a goner.

"Hey! That's my couch, man! Easy."

Ruben shrugged. "Insurance will cover it...or you've got a sentimental memento of a special night to remember. Hey, I could've used my 12-gauge again."

"Yeah, what's with using a shotgun in my kitchen, man? A little WMD happy, are we?"

Ruben cuffed the third killer and sat him on the couch, and Kelly sat next to him. "WMD? You just set off a grenade in your living room, bro. Besides, you needed a new refrigerator. Now you don't have to open the door to reach inside." Then he narrowed his eyes with a grimace and looked at Kelly. "Igor? What the fuck?"

* * * *

The riot started to boil over well down river from the new bridge site. Mexican officials could be heard on the scanners saying that the violence had erupted much more severely than usual.

Escobar's scouts had been roaming the bridge site for several hours looking for Border Patrol units patrolling the area. The Mexican contacts with the trucks on the other side of the river from the bridge construction had been keeping all activity in that area down to make it look like the area was calm so that BP agents would divert their attention to other areas.

Days prior to this the scouts had been using sophisticated jamming equipment to interrupt Border Patrol communications equipment on an intermittent basis in order to instill a sense of doubt in the Border Patrol communications operators.

The violence in the Hipódromo area could be heard on the U.S. side; gunfire was sporadic and intense, and full automatic weapons could be heard. An occasional explosion was also heard from Rocket Propelled Grenades and hand grenades.

Right about that time an RPG hit about ten yards in front of the Supervisor's vehicle.

Border Patrol Deputy Marín directed all personnel to the riot location, ordering the checkpoint closed so that personnel could go to the location and ordered all other assets and resources to concentrate on the riot location. He justified this with his concern that he had information that this riot was going to be one of the biggest and most violent and that it potentially could spill over into the US, therefore all available assets were needed to concentrate on the riot.

Back at the warehouse Escobar and his group were listening in on the Border Patrol radio traffic hearing all units deployed up river. Escobar picked up his radio:

"Recon Units 1, 2 and 3, command; Recon units 1, 2 and 3, command; how does it look?"

"Command, Unit 1 all clear, all clear."

"Command, Unit 2 all clear, all clear."

"Command, Unit 3 all clear, all clear."

"Recon Units, 10-4, Break; Bridging unit, command; Bridging

unit, command; proceed with ribbon deployment; repeat: proceed with ribbon deployment."

"Command, Bridge unit, 10-4, the ribbon is already being deployed."

Escobar shot Valdéz a confused and wicked glance.

"I had them begin when I saw your car arriving, Sir…in case we ran into any snags."

Escobar nodded his head toward the door, and everyone filed in behind him and headed for the riverbank.

Chavarria was in the warehouse yard with his men standing by to move the equipment into place and deploy the remainder of the ribbon bridge. Chavarria walked out towards his men, circling his arm above his head and gave a sharp whistle. His men immediately mounted up in the trucks and started the engines. One by one the remaining trucks moved out in an organized manner typical of a well-orchestrated military operation. The trucks started pulling out the backside of the warehouse yard, circling back and through the new bridge project.

The first truck, sent by Valdéz earlier, had already deployed a small skiff boat, and the next truck had just unloaded the first piece of bridging. Once the bridging was in the water it automatically unfolded. The skiff pulled up to it, and two men jumped up onto the bridging piece to secure the foldable section while the skiff pushed the bridging into place. Once the bridging was pushed into place the men on the bridging secured the piece to the pylons of the new bridge construction. This wasn't the usual practice but was an advantage to securing the ribbon bridge that the crew used. This process would repeat itself nine more times.

In ten minutes, the second piece of bridge was in place. Two more skiffs and eight more pieces of bridging were unloaded. The remaining pieces were put in place within thirty-five minutes. A total of ten bridge sections were deployed, spanning a total of 300 feet across the river. The pieces at the shore were ramped to allow vehicle entry on and off the bridge, and the first truck was driven up to shore, with the other five lining up behind it.

Escobar saw a lantern waved back and forth three times on the other side of the bridge. Chavarria signaled back with three flashes of his flashlight, and the first truck slowly drove onto the bridge.

Escobar nodded to Valdéz and Chavarria. The time had come. Valdéz called his contact in Hipódromo, and Chavarria called his man at the North Bridge. The signals were given for the riot and the decoy port runners to begin.

Escobar signaled the drivers to come and get them. He, Docksneider, Cartagena, and their entourage headed back to the hotel. There they would follow the progress of their caper and prepare their getaway to Corpus Christi. Chavarria would follow after the trucks had successfully crossed the bridge, escorting Cartagena and the hearse full of money to the ship, perhaps a half hour behind Escobar, along with the bridge convoy.

* * * *

Kelly put his arm around Octavio and smiled at him. "Now, Mr. Killer, you're going to call Escobar and tell him that Kelly Smith is dead." He pulled Octavio's phone from his pocket, looked through his contacts, and speed dialed #1. "And tell him you have my head in a bag. If you're not convincing enough, I think your buddy in the kitchen found a nice bag we can use for your head."

Octavio nodded and spoke into the phone that Kelly held to his ear. "It is done, jefe. The Border Agent is dead. Yes...yes...I'm sure. Yes, the big blond cowboy."

Kelly silently reminded him about the head in the bag, and Octavio nodded.

"Sí, comandante. I have his head in a bag for you."

Kelly could hear Escobar laughing.

"Shall I bring it to you at the hotel? Okay...okay, then. See you soon."

Kelly hung up the phone and saw the spinning lights outside.

"What will you do with me now?" the assassin asked, a little fearful of the answer.

"Not a thing." Kelly said as he got up and walked towards the door. "But these nice men here might have some plans for you."

Kelly opened the door with his badge in front of him, and soon his house was flooded with police officers carrying flashlights. Kelly recognized the lead officer, Cantu, and told him to radio one of his men outside to flip on the breaker box switch out back, and soon the lights were back on, along with the TV and bathroom radio.

"Careful, everybody. This is a crime scene. We'll need photos, markers, and a forensic team to bag the evidence. Two bodies. Take this live one out. Kelly...glad to see you got the better of this exchange."

"So am I, Cantu."

"We'll need to get a statement from you, so just have a seat. This may take a while."

"Sure thing, officer," Kelly said. He looked at Ruben and nodded his head toward the door. Ruben acknowledged with a slight upward nod and slowly edged his way to the front to make his getaway.

"Just let me turn off the shower and the radio in there," he said. "No one was in that room, so there's no evidence in there. Gonna drain the dragon while I'm in there too."

Kelly went into the bathroom and quickly went out the window and around to Ruben's car. He didn't have time to make a statement right now. He had a damsel in distress and a drug bust to take care of.

Ruben took his time getting through the growing team of cops in front of the house, so Kelly was already waiting in the passenger's seat, trying to get a hold of Cristina on the phone, when his partner arrived.

"That was fast. Where to?" asked Ruben.

"Just a sec. I'm not sure if I should go to the warehouse or the

North Bridge."

He got no answer from Cristina. Her phone was on the seat of the car, and Max was inside the store looking at comic books. So he called Rick Buenavista.

"Rick – what's going on there? Cristina's mother…"

"I've got her, Mr. Smith. She was in a lock-down room in the warehouse, and we're sneaking back towards my truck now. Waiting for the activity outside here to clear."

"That's a relief. So, have you got it handled? If you need help, I'm on my way."

"I've got Mrs. Chavez, Kelly. Go catch the bad guys. I just heard them say the first truck is starting to cross right now."

"Roger that. Bye. Ruben, let's go up to the North Bridge." Kelly dialed up the squadron commander for the helo team and gave them the "Go" signal.

Chapter 24

Several miles downstream nearly two thousand men, women, and children hired by the Colombians had gathered, many of them carrying torches. And several thousand more who had heard of a major event gathered there as well. A flare gun sent up a red flare, and a shrill whistle was sounded. The crowd became almost silent and stepped toward the shore and into the water. Dozens of inner tubes, small fishing boats, inflatable rafts, and other types of flotation devices were pushed, pulled, and tossed into the river. Some had their babies and toddlers in Styrofoam coolers. Most were preparing to walk and swim across the dark murky water.

Several minutes later, a green flare went up, and all hell broke loose. The mob began to holler and cheer and move quickly through the water toward the American shore. Surely this was the single biggest breach of the border ever attempted.

* * * *

On the north end of town, the driver of the donut truck sat near the west end of the bridge with his motor running. His phone rang, and he shushed the frightened and excited children. It was time. He drove out of the shadows onto the roadway, turned his lights off, and put the accelerator to the floor. He was scared, but he knew that his family's lives depended on him doing this right now. All he knew was that he should speed across the bridge and drive straight ahead on the highway. When police pursued him, he should give them a good chase and go as fast and far as he could. In a few seconds he was across the bridge, and a big smile grew on his face as he realized he was in America, and there were no cops in sight.

* * * *

"...Three...two...one...Light 'em up!" ordered Tom Bird, standing on the American side of the river across from the riots. As he barked the command into his walkie-talkie, 20 men 40 yards apart touched their torches to the half-mile-long pile of logs soaked in fuel oil in front of them. Then they ran and lit the pile about every 10 yards until a wall of flames and nauseating black smoke rose along the riverbank. A line of searchlights was turned on from the top of the bank, blinding the eyes of the on-rushing mob, which stopped in its tracks. Rounds of military machinegun fire were let loose into the air, and an amplified bullhorn announced in Spanish that no one would be crossing the river tonight.

They also announced that a popular Tejano band was setting up in the village on the Mexican side, and one hundred kegs of beer were being provided, compliments of the US Border Patrol. They were wished a happy Cinco de Mayo, and a huge cheer went up from the crowd, which turned tail and settled in for a great fiesta.

* * * *

"Well, it makes no difference," said Escobar as he sat in the plush hotel room and listened to the news on the scanner. He dialed up Chavarria on his cell phone as he continued speaking to the men in the hotel room. He had changed out of his military uniform and was now wearing a more comfortable yellow suit. "They will be occupied there for hours, and our mischief team will continue to fire RPGs and such. One of our loaded trucks is already across the pontoon bridge, and the second one is on its way. Even though we can just cross one at a time, we will finish in another 45 minutes."

Chavarria answered, and Escobar now addressed him. "The riot may not be working as expected, and there will not be hundreds of people rushing into the U.S. top keep law enforcement busy. Can we move the trucks across any faster?"

"Sir, no we cannot. The bridge is very narrow and hard for the drivers to see in the dark. And the river is very rough tonight. We cannot afford to lose a truck," Chavarria responded.

"Very well. Just make sure each truck is checked thoroughly so we know the Mexicans on the other side did not try any funny business."

"They would not dare pilfer our cargo, Sir. Each truck has been chained and sealed with a tag and pull strip that would have to be broken to open the doors. I personally inspected them yesterday and signed the seals."

"Still, take the time to check the underbellies and every surface for cutting or welding."

"Sir, that will slow us down in dispatching the trucks."

"Well, we have to wait long enough to make sure that the checkpoint has been closed and the agents have been dispatched to the riot scene anyway. Just send the first three trucks out from there together so that there will be plenty of armed guards for better security, and then come to the hotel and tell them to send the next three together as well."

Chavarria's military instinct told him that this was not a good idea, but Escobar was his commander. "Sí, Comandante."

James Herrick

Chapter 25

While Kelly was busy foiling the assassination plot, Cristina was embroiled in an effort to rescue her mother. Max told her to drop him off at the convenience store. He knew from the recordings that they had dropped Magda's car there, and sure enough there it was, unlocked with the keys in the ignition. She got him some Laffy Taffy and iced tea from the store and gave him her cell phone too.

"Take my phone. Call Kelly or the police if you see anything. Stay in this car, and run in the store if anybody comes. Do you hear me?" She gave him a twenty-dollar bill and a tight hug and headed for the warehouse in her car.

By the time Cristina got to the warehouse all of the action seemed to be on the riverbank, and the building appeared nearly deserted, except for a few fancy cars, a black van, and several thugs with assault rifles parked near the front door.

She waited around the corner and watched for a chance to get into the building without being seen. All of her fear and adrenaline had turned into a steely determination that transformed her into a calm but desperate woman who would do anything to get her mother back. Nothing would stand in her way.

Finally after many long minutes she heard a whistle from the riverbank and saw a man in a military uniform waving for the men by the cars to come. The drivers and body guards all drove down to pick up the men in a slow caravan, and Cristina made her break for the office, walking briskly but not running.

Escobar and Cartagena left for the hotel with their entourages while Chavarria barked orders to the crew to get the trucks across. Well-armed representatives for Cartagena were waiting to board each truck as it came across the floating bridge to escort the expensive cargo, and a Jeep with two heavily armed military men was assigned to lead each truck for protection and to guarantee there would be no rogue actions of drivers trying to hijack the load.

The first truck had been examined and was just being cleared to pull ahead and wait for the second truck. Satisfied that things were going according to plan, the overlords were heading back to the hotel to prepare for their departure.

Valdéz took the opportunity to head back inside to get a snack from the vending machine in the reception area.

Cristina made it inside the office area without being noticed. With no real plan in mind, just a sense of calm rage and wanting to find her mother, she called out.

"Hello? Mama?"

No one answered.

Cristina called out again. "Hello! Is anybody here? Mother, are you here?" *Oh...Max said she's locked in a room by the loading dock...I have to find the key...*

The door from the warehouse opened and closed as Miguel Valdéz returned from the deployment area on the river. Cristina heard the door and his carefree whistling, and she waited to confront him. He was startled to find somebody else in the office, and his whistling ended abruptly. Cristina sometimes stopped in to visit her mother at work, so she and Miguel knew each other vaguely.

Caught off guard, Valdéz addressed her angrily. "What are you doing here? We're closed." Valdéz continued through the hallway, past the conference room and Docksneider's office, and approached

Cristina. She was standing in a Lara Croft pose, clad in black slacks and top, in the reception area between her mother's and Valdéz's desks.

Cristina was not intimidated by this imposing figure and stared into his beady eyes. "I'm looking for my mother. Where is she?"

Valdéz was a little nervous. First Magda showed up unexpectedly and now her daughter, both right in the middle of their secret and very criminal operation. Valdéz responded with more harsh language, hoping it would scare the petite girl away.

"She's not here. Now you must go! We're closed! Leave!"

Cristina was having none of it. She knew he was lying, and her rage began to build with every word this fat troll uttered. Her gaze remained steady and undeterred – even threatening – and her breathing began to take on the feral cadence of a wolf loading oxygen before attacking its prey. Her chest and abdomen heaved in and out. Finally, she spoke in a fierce but measured tone.

"You're lying! She's here; tell me where she is!"

Valdéz hesitated for a moment, taken aback by the brashness of her accusation. "She's not here. I don't know where she is. Please leave now!"

Her breathing became faster as her rage soared, and the little rationality she had remaining left her. She was possessed by a vengeful soul that had only one directive: save her mother. She could hold it back no longer.

"Liar!"

Valdéz was incredulous at her fearlessness and froze as she took three quick steps forward and kicked him squarely in the crotch with the full force of her muscular legs. When he bent forward in pain, she grabbed his ears and pulled his face into her swiftly rising and powerful knee.

She dug her nails into his face from both sides and pulled him upright with great strength from her rushing adrenaline and brought his bloody face close to hers.

"Would you like to lie to me again, Mr. Valdéz...Sir?"

She was in a wild state and did not have the patience to wait for his reply. She wanted her mother, and she wanted her now.

With her nails in still his face, she stomped his toes with her boot heel, but Valdéz did not respond. Then she faced him directly and sneered.

"Let's see if you are really even a man."

She kneed him three times in the balls, each time harder than the last, and tears began to roll down his bloody face.

 But she was still not satisfied. She wanted to hear him scream in excruciating pain. She let go and he collapsed to his knees and then face-first to the floor. Blood began to slowly flow from his ears and nose. She knew she had him completely subdued and wanted to continue to abuse him. She was furious, but she caught herself. She needed him to tell her where her mother was.

She was trembling with energy to punish him more, but tried to control her breathing and become more rational. Instinctively, she pulled the small pocketknife from her pocket and opened the razor sharp blade. She inserted it into his nostril, ripping it open. She had seen this in a movie and thought it would really get his attention. It did.

The man was now a sniveling, whimpering pile of blood, tears, snot, and sweat.

"This is just a little knife, and I'm just a little girl. But you're going to tell me everything I want to know."

Valdéz was too distraught to talk or even think.

Cristina stopped and thought. She pulled his belt out of his pants and rolled him over on his side. She strapped his hands together with the belt to incapacitate him further. Then she rolled him onto his back and pulled him to a sitting position.

"I am *so* not done with you!" She slammed her fist into his nose. Blood spurted even more. She was enraged, pissed, and enjoying the pain she was inflicting upon him. She pocketed the knife and started unfastening his pants, striking him in the face and abdomen at the same time to keep him subdued and flat on his back. Her rage was intense as she grabbed the cuffs of his pant legs and pulled his trousers completely off. She used her knife to cut through each side of his huge white underpants and pulled them off from the front like removing a diaper from a baby.

He was so incapacitated from the assault that he could not defend himself. Her rage was abrupt and so sudden that it caught him off guard. With his pants off and genitals exposed she found the knife again and grabbed his balls, clenching them firmly.

He groaned loudly.

"What kind of man doesn't like a pretty girl playing with his balls, Mr. Valdéz? Don't you think I'm pretty? Or maybe you don't like girls, like the other maricones around here."

She took the knife and very slowly ran it along the base of his ball sack below one of his testicles; then she squeezed them again and punched him in the stomach. She noticed that he was trying to get his hands free from the belt behind his back, so she grabbed his left hand, and stabbed it through the palm with the knife. Then she did the same thing to the other hand, causing him enough pain in his hands that he couldn't try to use them for defense.

He was terrified, in extreme pain, and not sure if he would live much longer.

She pulled off his necktie and tied it tightly around the middle of his limp penis.

"I don't want you to bleed to death when I cut your cock off," she said. "After all, I'm a nice girl, you know."

The man's eyes grew wide and he shook his head nervously. "I'll tell you! I'll tell you!" he said in an almost inaudible voice with no breath behind it.

But Cristina was not listening.

"I wonder what would happen if you got excited with this tourniquet around your tiny little dick. If you didn't stink so much maybe I would lick it and find out." She looked around and found a *World's Greatest Boss* trophy on his desk. It had a three-inch figure of a man standing on a four-inch cylindrical post.

She held it, stroking the head of the figurine with her finger. "I think you are the kind of guy who would like a man in your ass. Let's see if this excites you." He tried to resist as she grabbed his buttock and rolled him on his side, but he didn't have the strength. "You should clean your asshole a little better," she said and shoved it in up to the post. Then putting her shoulder into it, she said, "This is for my mother," and pushed it in all the way to the wooden base.

"Where is she!" she screamed at him. She had the knife near his head. Her rage intimidated him.

"I'm not letting you die until you tell me! You're going to suffer until you tell me, so tell me."

He was too stunned and shocked to answer.

Sitting on one of his thighs, she round-housed his other thigh with the knife and then did it again for good measure.

He was screaming like a little girl.

"Stop! Please! Don't hurt me anymore!"

She was so enraged that she had to struggle to control herself. But she knew she would have to settle down in order to save her mother.

* * * *

The donut truck sped along I-69W without any problem as the driver approached the spaghetti junction where it met I-35 and

Highways 83, 59, and 20 in a mind-boggling twist of ramps and overpasses.

"Qué dirección?" the sweating driver asked aloud.

"Norte! Norte! Siempre Norte!" replied one of the children as the others giggled at the obvious answer.

"Sí, como no!" he said as he moved to the right lane. He was going much faster than the few other cars on the road.

Suddenly two Blackhawk helicopters rose above the tangled ramps in front of him, and the driver's eyes grew wide with fear as they shined a spotlight on his vehicle and barked commands from their bullhorns. He slowed down and pulled to a stop on the side of the road as the helicopters hovered over him with armed soldiers pointing machine guns at him. He raised his arms as the children fled in every direction.

"Hellfire! There are no big rigs here. Just this mule running a car full of kids. Send the cops or border agents to clean this up, and let's get the hell outa here! Get me command," said the pilot of Helo 1.

* * * *

Cristina saw his cell phone and grabbed it. She was in a savage state. She tapped in Kelly's number. As the phone rang she backhanded Valdéz and held the knife to his throat, drawing a slight amount of blood.

Kelly answered in a terse tone: "Hello? Who is this?"

"Kelly, this is Cristina. I have Valdéz. They have my mother."

The menacing tone of her voice echoed through the phone.

"Cristina, don't worry. Everything is okay. What going on?" he asked.

"They have Mom."

Cristina's rage reached through the phone in a way that made Kelly realize he had better be calm and careful with the person on the other end. "Just settle down, Cristina. Everything is under control now. Rick…"

Cristina put the phone down and then punched Valdéz multiple times in the top of his thigh where she had just stabbed him.

His screams caused Kelly to pull the phone away from his ear.

Cristina retrieved the phone.

"They have my mom." She set the phone down and began to beat Valdéz with her fists, and he screamed loudly in agony.

"Cristina…Cristina…Rick has her…she's okay…she's been rescued!" Kelly kept hollering into the phone, but Cristina was not listening. "Cristina…!"

She grabbed Valdéz by the hair. "Where is she?" Her eyes and facial expressions were menacing and the abuse so profound that he could say nothing but what he knew to be the truth.

"Room number one by the dock. The key with the white rabbit's foot," he said looking toward the board of keys by the first door in the hallway. Then he passed out.

Kelly wanted to call the police, but he was already on the run from Cantu and the cops at his house. He couldn't risk being tied up at the police station now. Not tonight. He kept calling Cristina's name.

Valdéz roused slightly as Cristina looked over the key rack a few steps away. He was in serious shock but coherent enough to know that he needed a hospital…but if things did not go the way this woman wanted he was never going to get medical attention. He began to wonder if this was all worth it.

"Can I have some water?" he asked.

Cristina walked back and bent over to slap his face full force.

"No, fucker! You don't get shit! There is no key on the rack for room number one and no white rabbit's foot." She opened her blade again and knelt beside him. "I guess if I had a tiny cock like that I might risk it for a lie too. You have so little to lose. But this is going to hurt…"

"I swear!" he said with all the breath he could muster. "The men must have the key outside, but they will not take her until I tell them. She is still here."

Near hysterics now, Cristina heard Kelly's pleading voice from the cell phone on the floor, and she picked it up: "Get my mother...do you hear me? Don't worry about me; I don't need help."

"Cristina, we have your mother. A Border Agent, Rick Buenavista, has her, and they should be outside in his truck by now. Stop before you kill that guy and end up in prison!" Cristina...talk to me!"

It was like Kelly had just performed an exorcism on her, and the demon spirit that had possessed her vanished. She slowly returned to reality. "Oh, okay, sweetie. So you have her? She's okay?"

"Yes, Rick has her, and she's fine. How about you?"

"Me, well of course I'm fine. Why? Oh...my goodness this man is lying on the floor bleeding. His hands are tied and his pants are off. Oh...I think I did this. He wouldn't tell me where my mother was."

"Baby, just don't touch him. Wait there for me. I gotta stop the trucks, and then I'll be there."

*　*　*　*

Outside, the fourth truck was being checked, and the first three were ready to be dispatched. Two more to go. Each truck would pass the checkpoint and then disperse to a site outside of the city where half a dozen smaller trucks were waiting to offload the cargo and take it to 36 different cities where it would be difficult to trace and could be quickly sold.

"Send the first three trucks," ordered Chavarria.

Chapter 26

Carlos had been watching from the Mexican shore for some time, waiting to cross for his 9 o'clock shift at the Roundup. It was quite dark now, on the black water with no moon. He would have to swim underneath the pontoon bridge to get to safely to the other side in time for work. He could hear men's voices on the other side of the bushes and trees, where the trucks had been staged for the crossing, and he crawled closer on his hands and knees to get a look at the action.

He heard one man shouting in Spanish, "Number 5 is halfway across; get the last truck in place. Hurry, hurry, hurry! There's free beer and music in the plaza. Let's finish this up. Five thousand dollars is waiting for each of us there. Faster!"

He saw a black van nearby with the side door open and many weapons inside and on the ground. No one was looking. He snapped the big red rubber band on his wrist for good luck and thought about the brother he had lost to the drug lords. Then he walked casually over to the van, grabbed three grenades, and stuck them in the plastic bag with his dry work clothes. He saw some glow sticks that the men were using to direct the trucks and shed a little light in the dark night, so he grabbed a handful of those too. He had to cross the river now.

Carlos cut a small hollow reed from the shore for a breathing tube, just in case, and walked into the river up to his chest, 50 feet from the bridge. He took a deep breath and began his swim under the water. The sides of the bridge were lighted so the drivers could see the edges, so Carlos knew he would have to stay submerged until he got well past the bridge. But the current was brisk and working against him. He didn't want to use the breathing tube near the lighted bridge and wasn't sure if he could make it, but he knew his life depended on it. He struggled fiercely against the current, his lungs burning from the lack of air, with only his determination keeping him from giving up. At last he felt a pontoon from the bridge. He pulled himself past it and came up for air underneath the bridge. He could feel fish all around him, but it was pitch dark between the pontoons. He heard the final truck beginning its slow ride over the bridge and pulled a glow stick from his pants and snapped it for illumination.

In the eerie green light he hatched a plan. Pulling the grenades from the plastic bag he wedged one between a pontoon and the roadway above it and he held another grenade in his hand. There was a crushed soda can floating nearby, which held the grenade up nicely. Then he waited for the truck to be directly above him.

* * * *

On both shores there were smiles and laughter as the final truck reached the middle of the bridge. A big payday was coming up soon for everybody. Suddenly there was a loud fiery blast right under the truck followed immediately by another. The bridge rocked and listed severely to one side as flames rose beneath the trailer. The cab of the truck was still on a solid footing, and the men encouraged the driver, "Drive! Drive!"

The powered wheels spun and slid to the side, making little progress as the pontoon section below the trailer twisted and offered no support.

From the Mexican side, a searchlight was aimed at the water on each side of the bridge. One of the men shouted excitedly and pointed to a reed sticking up above the water and moving briskly downstream. Machine gunfire followed, and the reed stopped and fell sideways in a small red pool.

One of the Mexicans was dispatched to get the intruder and see who had sabotaged their mission. He reached into the water and pulled something up, holding it over his head.

"A fish, Jefe. It is a fish."

The fish had a red rubber band around it holding the reed to its body.

*　*　*　*

Well past the new bridge construction upstream from the action, Carlos walked onto the American shore and looked back as the final truck – and more than $250 million in illegal drugs – slid into the dark, uncaring river while the silent men looked on with stunned faces and fearful eyes. The fourth and fifth trucks were quickly sent on their way with three escorts.

Carlos changed into his dry clothes at the river's edge, but he still had a very long walk ahead of him to the Roundup, so he stopped at the convenience store for a soda. The cashier was also a "commuting" Mexican boy and knew Carlos from his frequent visits to the store.

Carlos recognized the car in front of the store, as Cristina often drove that one to work, so he walked up and looked inside. If he could get a ride from her, that would save him a lot of time.

Max was sitting on the passenger's side with his earphones in place. He could hear bits and pieces of his mother's conversation with Valdéz from the microphone in the nearby office. He couldn't understand most of the conversation, but he could tell that his mother was very angry and in control of the situation.

Carlos had never met Max, but he rapped on the driver's window and, with a big smile, motioned to Max to roll it down.

"Good evening. Is this Miss Cristina's car?"

Max didn't know why the young man with wet hair was asking, but his instincts told him that it was okay. "She's my mom, yeah."

"Oh! Your mother! Your mama is very…"

"Yeah, yeah, I know. She's real pretty."

"No! Well, yes of course, Miss Cristina is very pretty. But she is so nice and gives me five or ten dollars and a plate of food almost every day when she works."

Max perked his head up. "Are you Carlos?"

He nodded, and Max pushed the door open for him to get in. Carlos looked at him, wondering if he should get in with his bag of wet clothes, and he was still a little wet himself. "It's okay. This is the old car; get in." Max handed him a can of iced tea and began to introduce himself. "I'm…"

"Max. You're Max. You look just like she said. What are you doing? Is your mama coming out of the store soon?"

"Oh, she's not here. She's at the warehouse where my grandma works."

"Oh, no…not the warehouse over there," Carlos said, pointing in the direction of Docksneider's place.

"It's okay. Mr. Kelly should be coming to help her."

"He is not there? The trucks are already across and three trucks just left and will be on the highway soon!"

"I would try calling him again, but my phone is dead, and he wasn't answering before anyway. I really hope he listened to all the recordings and found out that the trucks are crossing here."

"Here…use my phone." Carlos found his last text to Kelly, pushed the "call" button, and handed the phone to Max. Tell me what you know about what's going on, and I will drive us over there."

"You can drive?"

"Well, not really, but the customers at the bar ask me to park their cars sometimes, so I have done it in the parking lot many times. Sometimes they give me two dollars!"

Max had the phone on speaker when Kelly finally answered.

"Carlos? I'm kind of busy right now…"

"Mr. Kelly. It's Max…and Carlos too. Are you almost at the

warehouse? The trucks are already across the river and probably getting on the freeway right now. And my mama and grandma need you too. Why aren't you here?"

"And I blew up the pontoon bridge and sunk one of the trucks, Mr. Kelly, but five of the trucks made it across. Big red trailers with yellow trucks pulling them."

"Hold on a second guys...I got a call from the governor coming in." Kelly was confused. *Pontoon bridge?*

"What's that, Governor? Donuts? And Kids? Sir, sir... Send those copters due South on I-35. Tell them to look for a convoy of six – or maybe five red semis with yellow tractors coming towards them. They probably got a lot of armed escorts on board and leading the parade as well."

It all started to gel in Kelly's mind. *Puente pontón – pontoon bridge.* He smacked himself in the forehead. *How did I miss that? It's almost the same word!*

"Yes, sir. Sorry, sir. I guess I fell for one of their decoys. No, sir, there's no chance of an error. What? Uh...the intel came from...my people on site sir. I'm in phone communication with them now. They had visual on the trucks as they left the departure point on the river. Escobar set up a military pontoon bridge by the site of the new international bridge construction site. Yes sir. Yes. I'll explain the whole thing as soon as we take care of business. Bye."

Kelly got back on line with the boys. "Guys...stay away from that area. I'll be there in..." he looked at Rueben who held up four fingers, "...five or ten minutes."

"Oh, ye of little faith," said Ruben with a grimace.

Kelly put the cherry on Ruben's roof and hit the siren. "Okay, Batman, do your thing."

Ruben was glowing with adrenaline-fueled excitement and did a high-speed U-turn. "How was that for a 'Bat-turn,' buddy?"

"Just get us there in one piece," Kelly said. He spotted the tracker base unit he had given to Ruben, flipped it open, and tuned the audio for Escobar's Cherokee. "Let's see if we can find out what the Colonel is up to. It looks like he's on the move too…probably leaving town."

* * * *

Escobar was just leaving the hotel, heading to Highway 59 for his Corpus Christi getaway.

"Everything is loaded up, Colonel. They just left the warehouse with the bridge equipment," Chavarria said into the phone as he headed back to the hotel.

"How is that possible?" asked Escobar. "That is too fast to take down the bridge and load it and the skiffs onto the trucks."

"Uh, Sir…" Chavarria paused, afraid to relay the news to his hot-headed chief.

"What is it?" Escobar said in a slow and cautious tone. Then he yelled it: *"What is it, Guillermo?"*

"Sir, there was an explosion, and the last truck was lost into the river. Three of the bridge segments sank and could not be salvaged, and two more were twisted so badly we could not disengage them. Half of the men ran off, and the others loaded the remaining pieces hurriedly and then fled into Mexico. A dozen men are remaining to clean up the yard."

"Ahhhhrrrgghhhh! That fucking Kelly Smith. He did this!" screamed Escobar. "Each truck is worth more than 250 million dollars. Motherfuck…Cocksuck…shit…piss!"

"Yes, Sir. But the first three trucks have made it past the checkpoint, and the other two should be there soon," Chavarria told the Colonel, hoping it would reassure him about the success of the mission. "And the bridging convoy has all the official U.S. paperwork to get it safely on the ship in Corpus."

Highway 59 was just a few miles from the warehouse. Keeping the convoy together, following all the traffic laws, passing through the city, and going down the highway to Corpus Christi would be no problem.

The convoy lumbered through the city as if nothing had happened. All was in order. The route to Corpus Christi had been laid out with all the proper paperwork, stamped and approved by the Department of Defense, State Department, and Immigration to pass through any checkpoint without problems.

With so many other crises going on at the same time, this one thing would go off unnoticed.

Chapter 27

The first half of the drug convoy made it onto Interstate 35 and was past the closed checkpoint. They radioed their progress as ordered to Escobar in the Cherokee and to Chavarria and Cartagena, who were at the hotel with Docksneider.

"Looks like it is time to get paid, Señor Cartagena," Docksneider said.

"Do not be so anxious, Mr. – what is it he calls you? – Cock-biter. There are still three more trucks to report," Cartagena responded nonchalantly, as Chavarria smirked just a bit.

"Well, give me half now for the first three trucks so I can pay the Deputy," Docksneider insisted.

"Let me think about that. No." said Cartagena.

* * * *

The first three rigs were being escorted by a Jeep Cherokee and two Wranglers with heavily armed men. The Cherokee with three men was in front. A Jeep Wrangler with no top took up the rear of the convoy with four men. Each tractor had a driver and an armed guard. As they topped the hill north of the checkpoint two Blackhawk helicopters rose up from the down side of the hill. The Wrangler swerved all over the highway, frightened by the looming attack aircraft and began to slow down.

"Speed up, you fools!" shouted, Santiago, the commander in the lead Cherokee, into the walkie-talkie. The convoy responded and hit the gas, but the loaded trucks could not accelerate quickly.

"Sir, these are attack helicopters armed with missiles and perhaps .50 caliber machine guns. They will destroy us if we try to flee," responded the armed military escort in the lead truck.

"You didn't sign up for a picnic. Now, floor it! Besides, there are no skilled pilots or real soldiers in this town, and they will not fire into traffic. These weekend warriors will probably flee as soon as we fire on them. You have a gun, now use it! All of you!"

The lead commander opened the sunroof and stood up. He took aim and fired a long clip of ammo at the helicopter in front, but the armor deflected most of the small caliber rounds.

"Ésteban, give me that grenade launcher! What the hell...I wasn't expecting helicopters and heavy artillery. Tell truck number 2 to take the next exit and go East, and tell number 3 to take the second exit and go West. We have to split up; it's our only chance to get some of the cargo through."

Other traffic moved to the side, and the speeding convoy pressed on at high speed.

The pilot in Apache 1 radioed the team commander in the Blackhawk behind him. "Blackhawk One Command, this is Apache 1. The lead Jeep has engaged us with small machinegun fire. It looks like he's preparing to hit us with an RPG. Please advise."

"Apache 1, this is command. Use your M134 Mini Gattling to fire on the shooter now. I'll try to clear traffic in case we have to take out the vehicle. They're not going to get away, and we don't need any collateral damage."

"Roger that."

Apache 1 circled back as the Cherokee and first truck went under an overpass. He fell in behind the second truck at practically zero altitude as it prepared to take the exit and followed it under the overpass, while the third truck had fallen far behind. The Mexican driver was not familiar with American cloverleaf exits and entered the 25 mph ramp doing 85. Truck number 2 flipped, rolled, and bounced for a city block. Fifteen thousand one-kilo bags of cocaine spilled from the wreckage while passers-by came to gather as much of the booty as they could. One man crawled slowly from the cab as small flames began to erupt from the fuel tank.

The crash diverted the attention of Santiago as Apache 1 rose up over truck number 1 from the rear and dropped its nose toward the Cherokee. As the wide-eyed commander turned to see the copter, he tried to swing his weapon toward the Apache, but it was too late. Dozens of rounds blew the head off the commander and other passengers, but the pilot aimed away from the driver.

"Pull over, or we'll blow you halfway to hell!" announced the pilot to the truck and its escort. "Missiles are locked onto both vehicles, and there is a roadblock ahead."

A few more rounds to the semi trailer was all the convincing they needed. The Cherokee slowed to a stop, and the driver came out with his hands up. The truck buckled and lurched as the momentum of the heavy trailer pushed the braking cab forward. The driver and guard in the truck threw open the doors and ran in opposite directions, firing towards the helicopter as they ran for cover. The driver ran across the median and shot his handgun at an oncoming motorist, who stopped her car for fear of being killed. The thug opened the door, pulled out the driver and shot her three times, then he jumped in the car and sped away. The armed guard disappeared into the neighborhood.

Accompanying the two Apaches were three Blackhawk helicopters with soldiers ready to hit the ground. One of them was already securing the site of the truck crash. Another of the Blackhawks flew ahead, directing traffic to the sides of the freeway, while the third took up a position at the front of the third truck and its escort vehicle. The other Apache positioned itself along the side of it.

The passenger in the Wrangler lifted his weapon and took a shot at the Apache. A sniper in the Apache aimed in on the shooter with the M134 Mini and took out his torso and the seat back where the shooter had been sitting. The driver, recognizing he was outgunned, pulled the Wrangler off onto the shoulder of the highway, across the grassy area separating the highway and access road, and hit the brush line. He abandoned the vehicle and absconded into the brush. The rig saw the gunplay, radioed the information to the home base at the warehouse, and pulled the rig over into the brush as well.

The Captain in Apache 1 that made the first shot radioed to the other aircraft.

" Apache 2, Blackhawk 1, 2, and 3, this is Apache 1. We're gonna land and secure the lead truck. Blackhawk 3, keep us covered. Apache 2 and Blackhawk 2, secure the overturned truck and cargo, and Blackhawk One Command, maybe you can move in front of the runners and dust 'em out. See if you can force them back towards the highway."

"Apache 1, roger; Blackhawk 3 has you covered."

"Apache 2 here. Roger that."

"Blackhawk 2 here. Roger that."

"Blackhawk One Command here. Roger that. You've got the lead."

* * * *

Kelly turned off the light and siren. Then he pushed his seat all the way back, put the seat into the full reclining position, and handed his phone to Ruben.

"Here. Just a sec…when we get to the red light take a picture of this," he said as he got onto his hands and knees, facing the back of the car.

He pulled his pants down to his knees and reached between his legs to put his middle finger in front of the crack of his full moon.

"Have you lost your mind!" Ruben hollered as he pulled to a stop for the traffic signal. "What the hell are you doing? Turn on the light and siren so I can go."

"Just take the picture. It's for Escobar."

Ruben clicked a couple of snapshots while the dog in the car to the left eagerly put his paws on the window, and a little boy on the other side tapped his mother on the shoulder and pointed.

Ruben flipped the siren back on and went through the red light.

"Dude, if you really want him to cry, you should turn around and send him a picture of that armadillo you call a cock."

*   *   *   *

"I don't like this," said Escobar. "If they knew about the bridge, they know about the trucks. I've got a very bad feeling." Just then his cell phone rang.

"Bueno, dígame!"

The voice at the other end of the phone was frantic.

"Colonel, it's Javier! The convoy has been captured! Helicopters came in, many of them, and shot my vehicle. They had bigger guns, so we had to abandon and run. The first three trucks are captured, but I don't know about the rest. I'm still hiding in the brush, and the helicopters are flying around trying to bury us in dust from their rotor blades."

"*Chinga mi madre!* Where are you?" Escobar shouted.

"We're a few miles past the checkpoint; we got past there with no problem. It was closed just like you said it would be, but these helicopters with soldiers attacked us. We had no choice."

"That Fucking Kelly Smith! I know he's behind this! That bastard better be dead!"

"I don't know, Señor," Javier said into phone, thinking Escobar was really talking to him.

"Not you, idiota! I was thinking to myself. I need to think! You stay hidden; try to escape and get home. There is nothing we can do for you at this point. You are on your own. If you die, you die." Escobar hung up immediately.

"The Gringos have captured the convoy. They did it with a helicopter team. They made it past the checkpoint, and the helicopters came in and attacked them. All the men abandoned the trucks and ran. This is bad, very bad. Nothing we can do. Keep moving."

Escobar screamed, bashing his fist on the dashboard. "Son of a bitch! God damn it That cocksucking motherfucker! Fuck! Shit! Piss!"

A text message was coming in on Escobar's phone, and he opened it.

"Now what? The pool boy is fucking my wife and my daughter sucks cocks on the street?"

It was the picture of Kelly's ass and middle finger with the message: *I thought you might want something to kiss while you're getting your ass fucked in prison. Let's do lunch! – Kelly P.S. I think you left out "tits" and the "C" word.*

Then another text came in: *And your daughter sucks cocks almost as good as your wife!*

"That son of a bitch is listening to us right now!" he screamed furiously as he searched around and under his seat for the bug. He pulled out the device and yelled into it, "You're going to have a "C" word right between your legs when I get through with you, you smug little shit. You are nothing! You are dirt! Everyone who has ever said hello to you is going to be dead, Kelly Smith, and that includes that hot little whore you're fucking and that fat prick of a partner and his family. You want to play with Hector Escobar? You will see a blood bath like you've never seen before! Get ready, because I'm coming for you, fucker! The whole Colombian Army is coming for you!" Then he threw the listening device out the window.

The driver of the Cherokee and the other two men in the vehicle had wide eyes and were afraid to say anything. Finally the driver asked, "Colonel do you want me to pull over?"

Escobar paused for few moments to consider everything else that was going on, and then thought out loud. "I cannot go home to Colombia. They will kill me. My family will be dead within the hour. But at least I can track down Smith and his girlfriend and cut them to pieces. Take me to the warehouse, but first pull over here, and have the other car pull over too."

"Check inside and out for a tracking device," he said. "If they were listening they were probably tracking us too." Then he called Chavarria.

"The convoy is lost, but we still have work to do. Activate Plan B. I will be at the warehouse in 15 minutes. You find the other two trucks, and secure the money for us."

"Yes, Sir. I will take care of your exit strategy at once."

"Give me 15 minutes. Maybe 5 more to kill some people." Escobar's rage had turned to cold, calculated revenge.

"Sir, I have found the device," said the driver.

"Give it to the driver in the other car, and have him put it on a truck heading north at the next interchange."

Chapter 28

"Señor Cartagena," said Chavarria, "There has been a slight change in plans. We will be leaving now with the money."

"I think not," said Cartagena. "We will remain right here until we have heard…"

Those were Cartagena's last words. Chavarria shot him in the heart with his silenced weapon. The stunned goons clumsily reached for their weapons.

"The money is ours now. You two take as much as you can stuff in in your clothing and go," he said, pointing to the bazooka case they had used to keep everyone interested at the warehouse meeting.

"You won't be needing those," he said waving his pistol at their partially drawn weapons, which they threw on the floor. "And I'll be needing the keys to the hearse."

The large goons opened the case and began stuffing handfuls of bundled Benjamins into their clothing.

"The keys," repeated Chavarria, with his weapon still trained on the two. Docksneider sat nervously on the couch, fidgeting.

One of the bodyguards pulled some keys from his pocket and hurled them at Chavarria as he reached for another weapon. He had a bullet in his brain less than a second later and fell lifelessly over the case of money. Docksneider rose and walked further from the line of fire.

"Don't worry, Mr. Docksneider. I always hit my target." Then he turned his attention to the remaining bodyguard. "More for you," said Chavarria. "Pull him off before he bleeds all over the money."

The man pushed his dead partner to the floor. Then he removed his necktie and tied it around one of his own pant legs. He began taking the other man's stash and putting it down his pants.

"Let's not get greedy now. You have ten seconds to get out of the room or you will be dead. "You have the keys for the Jeep with your dogs. It's in the back. Then drive out the front entrance over there," he said pointing out the window," so I know you're gone. Throw your cell phone on the table. If you go near or approach the guards at the hearse, I will blow your head off." He patted the tripod-mounted .50 caliber machinegun by the window, overlooking the parking lot where the heavily guarded hearse was parked.

When the man left, Chavarria called the lead escort for the remaining two trucks. "It's time for Plan B," he said. "There are helicopters waiting for you on the freeway. They captured the first three trucks. Head for the rail yard by the park with the two trucks as we arranged for our backup plan. Don't tell Cartagena's men what's going on, and we will meet you there with the money in ten minutes."

Then he turned to a very nervous Docksneider. "The rest of the money here is yours. Take the case if you can carry it and drive me to the rail yard near Slaughter Park. My lieutenants are on their way to assassinate the guards out front, and they will follow with the rest of the money in the hearse. I'll leave the keys to the hearse at the front desk for them."

*　　*　　*　　*

The dynamic duo came screaming into the parking lot in front of Docksneider's warehouse without the siren or flashing lights and slid to a stop on the loose gravel. Both car doors opened before they were completely stopped, and Ruben and Kelly flew out.

"Sylvia and the kids are on their way to her mother's," said Ruben.

"He will be coming for me first. Be ready for anything."

"I'm loaded for bear, bro."

Carlos and Max got out of their vehicle, and Kelly quickly raised his arm, pointed firmly at the car, and looked at them with a no-nonsense look.

"Stay...In...The...Car."

They shrugged and went back to the car, and the two agents went into the office area of the warehouse.

"Cristina!" Kelly said breathlessly as he saw her.

She was sitting on her mother's desk, dangling her feet and filing her fingernails. She looked at Kelly and blew the nail dust from her fingertips. "Hello, Mr. Smith. Glad to see you finally decided to drop in. Where's my mother? You said one of your agents has her here."

"Ruben, see if you can spot Rick's red F150 on the street. They should be there."

"Yes, Boss," Ruben responded, a bit sarcastically, as he headed for the door, shaking his head and mumbling to himself: *So much for my time as Batman.*

"Help me!" A weak voice from the floor summoned their attention. "This girl almost killed me!"

"Oh, forgive my manners," said Cristina. "Kelly Smith, meet Miguél Valdéz, my mother's boss and a big fat criminal. Mr. Valdéz, meet Border Agent Kelly Smith, the man who is going to arrest you – and laugh at your tiny little cock."

"The truck is there," said Ruben as he reentered the office, "but nobody's in it. Should we be worried?"

Cristina jerked her head up and gave Kelly a very concerned look. He raised his palm towards her to signal her to keep her cool. Ruben followed Kelly's gaze to the floor and saw Valdéz lying on his side.

"Text him. Find out where he is."

"Why is this guy wearing a necktie on his pecker, and what's that little board on his ass?" Ruben asked.

Cristina looked away guiltily, hoping to deflect the question to Kelly.

"Take it out, please. And please remove the necktie," Valdéz pleaded in a weak and wispy voice.

Kelly and Ruben turned towards each other with a confused expression, and Kelly nodded at Ruben to check out the necktie and the piece of wood. Ruben put his fist backwards on his hips defiantly, raised his eyebrows, and shook his head slowly. Kelly rolled his eyes, shook his head, and got down on one knee to check out the situation.

"What the... Cristina, give me your knife," Kelly said, seeing that the tie was very tight, and he didn't want to get his hands too close.

She tossed it to him and he caught it.

"Be very careful, Señor. Please..." said Valdéz.

The end of the penis was very thin, cold, and purple now as Kelly cut through the tie. Valdéz let out a sigh of relief.

"Massage it a little to bring back the circulation. It needs blood, Señor!" One look at Kelly made it clear that that was not going to happen. "Or just take the belt off my hands so I can do it."

But Kelly's attention was already focused on the 4-inch square piece of wood attached to his butt cheeks with a brass nut in the center. Kelly poked at it, but it didn't move.

"Is this super glued, or what?" He looked at Cristina, but she only returned a guilty shrug.

"Take it out, Señor!" Valdéz insisted in a more demanding tone.

Kelly gave Ruben a quizzical look.

Ruben made an I *don't know* gesture, and then said, "Pull it."

Kelly pulled tentatively.

"Harder, Señor…*but slowly! Very slowly!"*

Gradually the cylindrical pedestal emerged from the Colombian's rectum, and then the male figure at the top of the trophy was revealed. Kelly and Ruben looked at the slightly bloody trophy in bewilderment, and then, in unison, looked at each other and then slowly turned towards Cristina as Kelly rose to his feet.

"What?" said Cristina. "Maybe he sat on it."

The baffled and panicked expressions of the two men stayed on her.

"Okay…I don't know…I don't remember. He took my mother. I had to do something, I guess. I don't know!"

Ruben took a step toward Kelly, put his hand on his shoulder, and whispered in his ear. "Dude – Do not piss off this girl."

"Señor…my hands," Valdéz said.

"Ruben, take that belt off his wrists," Kelly said.

Ruben almost tried to refuse again, but Kelly pointed to the trophy still in his hand to remind him of the disgusting task he had just done.

"Or, I could give it to Cristina and tell her you're holding her mother prisoner."

Ruben reluctantly went to help Valdéz.

"And help him put his pants on too," Kelly added.

"Helluva way to treat Batman," he muttered, and then looked at an incoming text on his phone. "Rick and Magda are at the back corner of the warehouse waiting for the stragglers on the river to clear out."

Chapter 29

"Blackhawk 1 Command, Base; Captain Boles, you need to send one of your units to back up to the local feds down on the river; they're taking heavy fire. They have explosions on our side coming from the other side. Do you copy?"

"Base, Blackhawk 1 Command; I copy. Need coordinates."

Boles' cell phone rang.

"This is Captain Boles."

"Captain Boles, this is Patrol Agent-In-Charge Bird with Laredo Sector Intelligence Unit. We have trouble on the Mexican side, downriver from downtown Laredo. Thousands of people. We stemmed the swimmers, but a goon squad of hired thugs is sending rocket-propelled grenades to our side from the Mexican side, setting fires, and shooting up the place, trying to force people on the Mexican side to cross over. They are slaughtering families over there to convince the others to storm the border. It's starting to work. We need some heavy back up. Can you go down and assist?"

"Wow! Real Cowboy stuff on the homeland. Bird, your Intel office has official cooperative liaison channels with Mexican Agents, don't you?"

"Yes, Sir. They have been on site all day and are the source of my info. But they have to be low profile, undercover, or they will be in danger."

"Can you get us an official invite to the party?"

"Yes, Sir. They are requesting a flyover, smoke, and flash bangs...but they don't want us to initiate mortal fire."

"As long as we can defend ourselves, that sounds like a party to me."

"I think you may want one of us on board to cover the legal justification, you know; you would be flying under DHS/CBP/Border Patrol authority with me on board."

"Where can I pick you up?"

"You guys know where our emergency hangar is by the Slaughter Park railroad yard. Head over there. You can refuel if you need to also."

"Understood. I'll send a gunship right away."

Boles clicked off his cell phone and clicked on his radio mic.

* * * *

"Okay, Martinez, this is what's happening. You're gonna take Apache 1 to the Border Patrol Hanger at Slaughter Park. A few of the hired guns on the Mexican side weren't interested in the beer and music we gave them, and they are lobbing grenades onto our side. Pick up Tom Bird from Intel. You're going to go in and scare the hell out of them and scour the fringe areas for any stray swimmers. Be smart – no casualties but lots of show. Do you understand? This is just a friendly show of force along with a smoke and a light show. *And don't cross the border unless or until Bird gets the go-ahead from Mexican authorities.* Do not engage except on command under any circumstances. We don't want an international incident."

"Sure, captain. This sounds like a real ride."

Boles sent the new plan out to the others. "All helo units, we have a change of plans. Unit 1 Apache has been redirected and is out of here."

Martinez headed due South down IH-35. He punched in the GPS coordinates to bring him in to meet his new passenger.

Boles continued: "Sergeant Stripes, the copters are going ahead of the bad guys and are going to try and dust them and any runners back towards us. You need to set your men up in a line and work in towards the helicopter and try to find and apprehend the bad guys; understand?"

"Good plan, Sir. We'll give a try."

*   *   *   *

"This must be it," Martinez thought to himself.

As he landed, the Agent turned off his headlights, closed the vehicle door, and trotted over to the helicopter. Bird opened the passenger side door of the helicopter.

"Captain Boles?"

"Nope...Captain Martinez. Boles was busy, so I'll have to do. Get in."

Bird didn't hesitate. He climbed in, strapped himself in, and extended his hand.

"Captain Martinez, Tom Bird, nice to meet you. Can we go now? My radio traffic says we're taking a lot of fire up river."

Bird pulled up an iPad and told Martinez the GPS coordinates and Martinez punched them in.

"You do have some fire power on this thing, right? I don't want to fly in and just be a target. I'd like to be able to fight back a bit if we have to."

"No worries, Mr. Bird. I have a Minigun shooting 6,000 rounds a minute, a 30 millimeter cannon, and a few stingray rockets. I think we can make an impression. Boles sent a box of toys for a light show too – some flash bangs and tear gas."

"Good."

As they approached the area, flashes of gunfire could be seen in the area along with a few explosions that looked like grenades. Structures were on fire, and trees were burning. Martinez wasn't too fazed by all this as he had seen real combat in Afghanistan and Iran. Bird, on the other hand, was shocked. This sort of thing didn't happen on the border of the United States. It looked like a real war right on our border.

They could see people swimming and floating across the river. Those that were floating were bringing weapons, some shooting as they floated across. Some return fire could be seen from the US side from the muzzle flash.

"Agent Bird, tell your people to get back right away; clear the area. I'm going to strafe this side of the river with the Minigun and a few cannon rounds. If that don't scare the North bounders back South, then we'll need a Marine battalion. I mean, this is an armed invasion, isn't it?"

"Sure looks like one to me. Standby." Bird keyed the radio mic and spoke. "Unit 226, unit 226, this is unit 099. Get your men on the river to back off a hundred yards immediately. Air support will attempt a radical dust-out maneuver. Repeat: All units back off immediately, back off immediately. It's going to get hot down there, real hot! You have 3 minutes. MOVE!"

When the three minutes were up, he launched a salvo of 30 millimeter cannon rounds down river along the US side. The rounds hit the water and shoreline, exploding in great balls of fire. He then proceeded to let loose with a volley from the Minigun along the same path. A couple of pontoon boats exploded. Others that were in the water started turning around and going South. He had not even moved from his position.

"If that's a Minigun, I'd hate to see what a Maxi can do," Bird quipped as he witnessed the power and destruction of the M134 Mini Gatling Gun.

Martinez started to fly the chopper downriver, sporadically shooting the Minigun and 30 millimeter cannon into the river, churning up the water. He was getting the result he wanted. All of the people in the river were turning back to Mexico. He had passed through the area of the riot and was now downriver and turning around for another sweep.

"I can't tell if the shooting has stopped from the Mexican side."

A light on Bird's radio indicated an incoming communication on the Mexican frequency. "Greetings, Tom Bird, and thank you. The militants are in retreat. No need to cross over. Mayday conditions are over, and Cinco de Mayo fiesta conditions have resumed!"

"Copy that."

"I'm gonna do one more pass just to make sure they understand." Martinez pushed his bird forward and started shooting a few more rounds. His speed was a little faster, just in case somebody on the other side got the idea to shoot an RPG at his bird.

Once he was through the hot spot he positioned the helicopter so that he could look into Mexico from the US side of the border, and he started scanning the area with his infrared equipment.

"It looks like a lot of foot and vehicular traffic working its way back deeper into Mexico. I think they got our message. I'm taking this birdie back to its nest, but first I better check with mission command."

"Drop me at my car back at Slaughter, if you don't mind, Lieutenant," Bird requested.

"No problem, Agent Bird."

Minutes later they were approaching the emergency hangar.

"Looks like something is going on up ahead, Agent Bird. Should we check it out?" Martinez asked.

Bird looked through his binoculars to the brightly lit area between the lines of railcars up ahead. "Negative. Let's get down before they see us. Maybe it's part of the drug run. I see a couple of semis and some smaller trucks."

"The semis are red and yellow, just like the ones we busted on the freeway, Sir," Martinez said as he descended for a landing near

Bird's car. "Looks like they're moving the load to smaller trucks, so they'll be there for a while. Let's call it in to Captain Boles and wait for some backup when they get the interstate cleaned up."

Chapter 30

A Jeep Cherokee turned into the warehouse yard at an urgent speed. The headlights bounced as the car found the gravel of Docksneider's parking lot, flooding Magda's old car with light.

"Get down!" Max said to Carlos. "That's the Jeep we've been tracking. It should be halfway to San Antonio by now."

The Jeep veered to the right and headed toward the back end of the warehouse. They heard the doors open, and some men got out.

"Your ride is one kilometer away across the river. It will be here less than one minute after it sees the flare, Colonel."

"Very well. I will go in the back. You pull closer to the front and kill anyone who comes out the door," said Escobar.

"But, Sir, Señor Valdéz is still here…"

"*Kill everyone. Everyone here must die.* Is that clear?"

"Of course, Sir. It will be done."

The car turned around and waited several yards from the front corner of the building.

"I've got and idea," said Max. He slid the switch on the dome light so it would not light when he opened the door. "Give my your iced tea can," he said, then he jumped out and ran stealthily over to

219

Ruben's car.

The windows were rolled down, so he reached in and grabbed the battery-powered megaphone from the backseat and sneaked into the bushes near the road. He smashed the top of the can in with a rock, set the megaphone to a low volume, and lay on his back. He held the can to the side of his mouth and aimed the megaphone straight up near the can.

"Kkkkkkkk...Chopper 1-9, this is Romeo. I've got eyes on the vehicle. What's your 20? Kkkkkkkk..."

Holding his nose to change his voice, Max continued: "Kkkkkkkk...Romeo, Chopper 1-9. I'm 300 feet above I-35 and Washington Avenue. I can spit on you from here. Kkkkkkkk..."

"Kkkkkkk... Roger that. I'm going to put a GPS marker on the vehicle for you with my tranq gun. Stand by, Kkkkkkkk..."

Max grabbed a small rock and got to his knees. He lobbed it high, and it came down right on the roof of the Cherokee.

"Kkkkkkkk...Reading your signal loud and clear, Romeo. Stinger missile is locked on the vehicle now. Delivery will be seven seconds from your command. Kkkkkkk..."

The car's headlights came on, and the wheels started to spin. It left the parking lot in a cloud of dust, pelting the other cars with stones and pebbles, and sped quickly away.

Carlos was pounding his feet and smacking his head like a bongo drum when Max got back in the car.

"Did you really just do that, Max?! Who are you...James Bond? That was amazing."

"Nah...Was It? It was a lot of fun, and I'm glad it worked."

"Max, you just saved the lives of everybody inside the building – Your mother, Mr. Kelly...and probably you and me too."

"Huh. You think so?" Max asked and Carlos nodded. "Got any more Skittles?"

* * * *

"Did you hear a car outside?" Kelly asked Cristina.

"It seems like," she said walking towards the window. "There's a lot of dust. Probably kids having fun. They come through here a lot. Mama's always complaining about it."

"Let's see if we can find the listening devices she planted," Kelly said. "Maybe I can return all the equipment back to the office without anyone knowing. Where is Docksneider's office?"

"First door," she said. "Second door is the conference room."

Cristina looked at Valdéz sitting in a desk chair in handcuffs shaking his head and cursing. She walked towards him and their eyes met.

"So, do you have a problem with something, Mr. Valdéz?" she asked, with a threatening look in her eye.

"No. No, Miss Cristina." He rubbed his bloody pant leg where she had stabbed him twice. "You don't have to worry about me. I will never try to hurt your mother. The only safe place for me now is an American prison. I was just thinking about how the great and detailed plans that we worked on for one year were ruined by one small woman."

"There are no small women," Cristina said, putting her face very close to his. "Only little men with small dicks."

Ruben walked over and escorted her away just as Kelly came out of the conference room.

"Got 'em. Let's see if we can find Rick and Magda," Kelly said.

"We can go through the warehouse to get to the back," Cristina said, pointing to the door at the end of the hallway. "Let me see one of those devices."

Kelly handed her one and put the other in his pocket.

"What about him?" asked Ruben.

Kelly tossed him his handcuffs. "He's already cuffed, so just attach him to the door or something – where he can't reach a phone or a drawer with a gun he might have stashed."

"Señor, I need a doctor!"

Kelly nodded. "Yeah...I'll call for an ambulance."

The threesome headed across the mostly vacant warehouse toward the open bay doors at the dock on the far end. There was no sign of activity on the riverbank, but they could see the corner of a semi trailer emerging from the middle of the river.

"Head toward the door on the end," said Ruben. "They should be by that corner, unless they already went to his truck."

They were 30 feet from the open bay door when a figure emerged from the corner and started to walk across the dock area.

"Rick?" hollered Ruben.

He stopped and nodded. "Yeah," Rick responded solemnly and continued along the dock to the second bay door.

"Where's my mother?" Cristina asked, anxiously.

Rick looked back over his shoulder to where he had come from.

"Your mother is right here."

It was Escobar. He emerged slowly from the shadowy corner with one arm around Magda's neck and a gun to her head. He stood in the doorway and took a step forward, changing his dark silhouette into the image of a broken and desperate man under the warehouse lights. He was sweating profusely and his eyes were wild. Magda looked angry but resolute.

"Throw your guns on the floor and kick them to me. Then come a little closer."

Kelly and Ruben dropped their guns and kicked them across the floor.

"Oh, come now. The great superhero Kelly Smith has more than one gun. Throw it!" Escobar commanded.

Kelly was wearing only a shirt and pants with nowhere to hide a gun. He held up his arms and turned all the way around, and then pulled up his pant legs. "That's it, Colonel. I can run to my car to get the other one if you'd like."

"Heh Heh. Very funny Mr. Smith."

"Give me my knife," Cristina whispered to him.

Kelly gave her a confused look.

"Give it!" she demanded, pinching the side of his abdomen.

Kelly turned towards her slightly so that his right pocket would not be seen by Escobar as he reached in quickly and palmed the small knife. Then he put his arm around Cristina with his hand flat against her belly. She put her hand on his, and the knife was surreptitiously exchanged.

"Come closer now." He pushed Magda to her knees and took a step back. I want you to feel the splatter of her blood and brain matter when I blow her brains out in front of you. Your little playmate will be next. Then the fat boy and the young agent. I will save you for last, Mr. Smith."

Escobar pulled a different gun from his pocket and stepped to the edge of the dock. He aimed it upward and pulled the trigger, sending a red flare up into the night sky.

"My ride is coming, so we will have to hurry. Say goodbye to mommy!"

"Hector," Kelly said in a calm tone, trying to create a human connection, "You don't want to do this."

"Heh heh heh...Oh, you are so wrong, Mr. Smith. You should have pulled the trigger when you had your gun to my throat three years ago. You Americans are so soft and cowardly. In the same position, I surely would have killed you without blinking an eye. And now I owe you the deaths of these people you care about, and you have earned your own death at my hand as well."

"Hector, you already killed my wife and my son who was not even born yet. I've paid for doing the right thing, and I've paid for letting you live."

Escobar's eyes grew even wilder and he became furious. "The

right thing? It was not the right thing for me or the people I love." He took a breath. "Does it surprise you, Mr. Smith, that there are people who love me and that I love? And thanks to you," he said, becoming very agitated again, "all of them are being killed right now as we speak! My parents...my wife...my two teenage boys...*and my 9-year-old daughter!*" With his final statement, he waved his gun high and fired a round, hitting a light in the middle of the warehouse, which sent sparks flying. His face was a sniveling mess of tears and sweat and deep anguish.

"I am truly sorry for that, Hector. That was never my intention. But it was your own deeds and ambitions that caused it."

Kelly took a breath and looked at Cristina. Her eyes were focused like a laser on Escobar, watching his every move. They were now separated from their antagonist by only about 12 feet.

"Perhaps we are not so different after all, Mr. Smith. Your idea of what is moral and what is evil is just upside down from mine. If not for you, I would have accomplished a great thing for my people tonight. But, unlike you, I will not be returning to a hero's welcome, Mr. Border Agent, Kelly Smith. I can never go home! My wounds will never heal. My life now can only be dedicated to your destruction and the little peace that will give me."

The rotor of a small chopper could be heard getting closer as it descended behind Escobar. The distraught and irrational Colonel swung his gun down, grasping it with both hands, and he aimed it at Magda's head a few feet in front of him.

"And now it is time for this woman to die!"

He leveled the gun and took aim, and Cristina made her move. With his focus away from them, she leaned forward on her left foot and threw her knife at Escobar with a swift and almost invisible movement. It stuck in his forehead right above his right eye. It seemed no more than a distraction for this man, like a pesky mosquito, as he was beyond the point of feeling pain. But it caused him to turn his head as he pulled the trigger, and the shot from his gun went harmlessly over Magda's head.

"Run, Mama!" Cristina screamed as she charged the Colonel. She took three running steps and then leaped with her knees tucked in and her feet aimed at his chest. Still in the air, she pulled the knife from his forehead and then kicked him hard in the chest with both feet. She used his chest as a springboard to do a back flip, and she landed on her feet right where her mother had been kneeling.

Escobar stumbled backwards towards the helicopter, which was now right at the edge of the dock with its landing skid even with the concrete. Ricky was charging from the left as Escobar blindly let a round go, hitting the young agent in the side of the abdomen and knocking him down. Cristina ran forward, giving Escobar a fist to the face, and then she slid her hand into his front pocket, but Kelly pulled her away and took cover behind a pallet of boxes with Magda.

"Good shot with the knife," Kelly said.

"Good?" Cristina answered. "I was aiming for his eye so it would go into his brain and kill him. But I missed by almost an inch, and now he is getting away."

Escobar stood on the runner, holding onto the copter with one hand and shooting wildly with the other, unloading curses and threats as the chopper started to rise. Ruben pulled a small derringer from his boot and took a shot, which bounced off the helicopter next to Escobar, and then they were above the roofline and out of sight.

"Ricky!" a female voice cried out from the darkness at the other end of the warehouse, and then she ran quickly towards him. It was Sabrina. She knelt beside him and the growing pool of blood around one side of his torso.

"Sabrina?" Rick said, lifting his head slightly. "What are you doing here?"

"Shhhh," she said, ripping off her blouse, folding it several times, and holding it against his wound. "Since you were busy, I thought I would bring sandwiches and a cocktail to you in your truck. But the only red truck out there was empty, so I came inside and followed the noise."

"Usually women don't tear their blouses off for me until after the cocktails," he joked, twinging in pain from the slightest bit of laughter.

Kelly, Cristina, and Ruben were walking toward Rick.

"Loaded for bear?" Kelly asked sarcastically looking at Ruben's tiny gun. "I thought that was a cigarette lighter."

"It shoots one bullet, usually within a few feet of your target," Ruben said, shrugging meekly. "And the bears in my neighborhood are small. How you doin', buddy?" Ruben asked, kneeling next to Buenavista.

A text came in on Kelly's phone:

Mr. Kelly – We can hear the man in the little helicopter on your tracker. We are following them East along the river. He said something about money and trucks at Slaughter Park rail yard. – Carlos

"Hear them?" Kelly said, a bit confused.

"I put one of those things in his pocket," Cristina said as she read the message on Kelly's phone. "Carlos? My Carlos from work?"

"Uh, yeah. I'll explain later. He was out front in your car with Max."

"What?!" Cristina said excitedly. "Max can't be here. We have to stop them, Kelly!"

"Settle down," said Kelly as his phone began to ring with an incoming call. "That's probably them now. I'll tell them to go home. Hello...Carlos?"

"No. This is Governor Franklin Basham. Agent Smith? Is that you?"

"Uh...Yes...Yes, Sir...Yes, Governor Basham. This is Kelly Smith."

Sabrina perked up and quickly turned toward the phone

conversation when she heard the governor's name. Ruben had found some shop towels and was wiping Rick's forehead.

"What the hell is going on there? The helicopter team captured three trucks, but you said there were six."

"Yes, Sir. There are six. One is here in the river behind the warehouse with parts of the pontoon bridge they were using. The other two trucks must have heard about the helicopters and took a detour. We just got some intel that indicates that the trucks and the money may be near Slaughter Park at the rail yards there, and the mastermind, Hector Escobar, is likely headed there now in a small chopper too. He just left the warehouse."

"Well, that squares with what Martinez and Bird told Special Ops Commander Boles a while ago. You must have a pretty good intel crew."

"The best, Sir. Sir, I request that you send us a helo unit to take us to Slaughter so we can wrap this up."

"Uhhh, Kelly, I don't know. We've already had some war zone activity on a major freeway with at least one civilian fatality. I don't know…"

"But, Sir, the rail yard is remote and away from…"

Sabrina jumped up and grabbed the phone from Kelly.

"Uncle Frankie?" she said into the phone.

There was a pause. "…Sabrina? What are you doing there?"

Kelly and Ruben looked at each other, confused and amazed.

"I was just…delivering a rental car across the street."

"Sabrina, you're in a dangerous place; you need to get…"

"Uncle Frankie, Agent Smith needs that helicopter right now. One of those small Apaches would be good enough…"

"Sabrina, an Apache can take out a small village in two minutes."

"Yeah, that should be good then. Uncle Frankie, these are the same guys who killed Auntie Felicia's son, Jeff; and she and my mom aren't going to be happy if you let them get away scot-free. And please send a Med-Evac helicopter to the warehouse here too. We've got an agent with a serious bullet wound and one of the bad guys in front that seems to be in pretty bad shape too. Okay...okay...kind of at the end of Eagle Pass Avenue, in back. They'll see the truck in the river by the new bridge construction...thank you, Uncle Frankie...okay, I will. Okay. Bye."

Sabrina handed the phone back to Kelly. "He said to tell you that your helicopter is on the way from I-35 now. There's already another Apache on the ground by the park there with a guy from your Intelligence Unit, and three Bluehawks will be over at the rail yard in about a half-hour too, after they finish up with something that's going on on the freeway. Oh...and he's already on his way, flying in from Austin. And he said that he'd better look like a hero in the morning, or you'll be the one facing the cameras to explain all this."

Kelly nodded. "Uncle Frankie?"

Sabrina smiled and shrugged.

"And if it goes well," Kelly said, "I'm sure Uncle Frankie will be happy to take all the curtain calls and all the glory."

"He's the governor," Sabrina said. Then she went back to attend Rick again, who was looking much better, as a helicopter could be heard approaching.

Chapter 31

Kelly could see Escobar's chopper between several rows of railcars up ahead through night vision binoculars as he rode in the Apache helicopter. The rotors on Escobar's chopper were still spinning, slowly winding to a halt. There were two vehicles, and the two red and yellow semis were nearby with a crew busily off-loading the cargo into a lineup of several small trucks of all shapes and sizes.

"Tell the other helo units to stay out of range of their ears and eyes for now, Sergeant..."

"Pierce," the pilot responded.

"...Sergeant Pierce. We don't want to have a war right here in the city. These guys look organized and probably have heavy artillery and shoulder-mounted SAMs ready to blow them out of the sky. Is there a commando team aboard the Blackhawks?"

"Roger than, Agent Smith," said Pierce as he relayed the request to Martinez and Bird in the other Apache and to Boles in the command Blackhawk unit. He listened to an incoming message.

"Captain Boles says the governor doesn't want us to take out any human targets. We can destroy equipment and trucks, but no people."

"That figures. All this political correctness on the battlefield gets a lot of our guys killed. Follow the bend and head down the river.

They'll think we're heading to the riot. Then double back at low altitude and drop me at the end of the rail yard."

*   *   *   *

Buenavista, Sabrina, and Valdéz were headed for County Hospital in the Med-Evac unit, and Magda drove the good car home. Cristina and Ruben were in Ruben's car heading toward the rail yard.

"I'll drop you at the softball field with the boys, and then I'll do some reconnaissance at the rail yard," Ruben said to Cristina.

She rolled her eyes. "Like that's going to happen. Just park next to these train cars. Kelly might need some help."

"But..."

"But what? I'm just a girl?" she asked, as she played with her knife in her right hand. "You never know when a girl might come in handy. Ask Valdéz and Escobar."

"Kelly will skin me alive if anything happens to you, Ma'am," Ruben said shaking his head.

"And I'll rip your balls off and shove them up your ass if you try to drop me off...Sir," she said with a sweet smile and a kiss to his cheek. "And call me Cristina."

Ruben reluctantly gave in to reality. "Just don't get hurt, and don't take any chances. There are plenty of soldiers and law enforcement units on their way."

Ruben turned out his lights and pulled up next to the tracks. There were long lines of railroad cars on ten sets of tracks, with a wide truck lane in the middle with five sets of tracks on each side. They parked on the outer edge near the river.

"It sounds like there's some activity down that way, towards the sewage plant," Ruben said as they got out of the car.

"Ya, I can see lights there too. Let's go," Cristina answered.

"Whoa," he said. He handed her a Kevlar vest. "Here, this is Kelly's."

Cristina hesitated.

"Put it on," Ruben told her firmly, with a no-nonsense look. "You might be a ninja, but bullets can still penetrate your skin. I'm putting mine on too." She complied as he slid into his vest and put his night vision goggles on his head. Then he put a new clip in his Glock and handed her the Walther PK that he took of the dead assassin in Kelly's kitchen.

"You ever used one of these before?" he asked her.

"Just aim and shoot, right?"

Ruben nodded, and she put it under her belt.

"And remember," he said. We're just here to look and report. No getting close, and no interacting with the bad guys. Comprendes, mamacita?" he said authoritatively.

"Sí, Papi," Cristina replied, with a submissive bat of her eyelashes.

They climbed over the hitches between the cars on three rows of trains, then headed quietly towards the action between two rows of railcars. Light from the trucks was shining between the railcars as they began to get very close. A few cars ahead they could see the shadow of a man standing on an empty flatbed shaking off the last few drops of urine, so they stopped and waited.

Cristina was anxious for some action, and as soon as he jumped down from the flatbed she was ready to move.

"I'm going to jump one more rail and then lay under the last row of cars to see what's going on," she said and immediately stepped over the hitch next to her.

"Nooo...!" Ruben said. "There might be more men over there."

But it was too late. She was gone.

"Ooooh! What do we have here?" he heard one man say when he saw Cristina. "Hey, Jake, you want to share some of this lovely señorita with me?"

Cristina swung for his face, but he caught her wrist firmly with his large and strong hand.

"Mmm, a feisty one. I like that."

Ruben shook his head. He knew that if he fired his gun there would be 20 men shooting back at him before they could get out of there, and Cristina could get hurt. He went around the far end of the train car and slowly took a peek to see if he could make a plan.

"What kind of cowboy vest is that, ma'am?" He said zipping it down. "Now, that's what I call a fine set of titties."

"What you got there, Billy boy?" Jake said as he joined his friend. "Nice!" he said, stroking her breast, "Looks like there's enough here for both of us, partner."

Cristina could see that she was no match for two cowboy ranchers, so she decided to play along, hoping that her partner would come to her rescue soon.

"Mmmm…a couple of strong ones," Cristina said, stroking their cheeks. "I like that. And big hands too. I hope that means what I think it does. Why don't you boys drop these around your knees," she said stroking their crotches and then giving a tug on their belt buckles. "I haven't had my dinner yet." She undid Billy's buckle and he dropped his pants.

"Better yet," said Jake, pushing her to the ground, "why don't you take your pants off and get on your hands and knees. I'll take you from behind while you suck my partner's dick." He dropped his pants and began stroking his penis. "Do it!" he demanded as he tried to slap her face but missed.

"Hey, no need to get rough, Jake. She's just a girl, and she's going along with the program," Billy defended.

"Excuse me, Sir," Ruben said. He was about three feet behind the Jake, who turned around and almost tripped trying to step towards Ruben with his pants around his ankles.

As he tried to regain his balance, Ruben took one step forward and let go with a powerful uppercut to his adversary's jaw. Cristina watched in amazement as Jake's feet actually left the ground by more than a foot, and he fell to the ground, unconscious.

Billy bent over to pull up his trousers, and Cristina, still sitting on the ground, threw a handful of dirt and gravel in his face and punched him in the balls. As he stood erect and tried to wipe his face and get his bearings, Ruben took one more step forward and put the full force of his body behind his fist and into the man's midsection. Billy flew four feet into the side of the railcar, hitting his head on the protruding iron handle and falling to the ground.

Cristina looked at the two unconscious men and then at Ruben. "Not bad for…"

"For a short, fat Mexican?" Ruben taunted.

Cristina paused for a moment, and then nodded. "Ya. I think I will listen to you and stay close to you from now on," she said.

Ruben pointed to the boxcar next to them a slid the door open a couple of feet. "Get in," he said. "We will look out the other side to see what's happening and report back to Kelly and the others."

"Maybe we should tie them up first," she said, looking at the two men on the ground.

"Not necessary," said Ruben. "This one has a broken jaw, and the pain will keep him asleep for two to three hours. The other one has two or three broken ribs, the wind knocked out of him, and a concussion from hitting his head that will keep him down for over an hour."

"How do you know that?" she challenged him.

Ruben waggled his head. "After ten or twelve times you get to know. It's the same every time."

"Okay," she responded. "But can I cut their balls of first? Their pants are already down, and these dogs don't deserve balls."

"No! No ball cutting. You can't just go around cutting guys' balls off."

"Just the big mean one that tried to hit me, then."

"No."

"Well…how about just one ball…please?"

She tried to stomp her heel into Jake's crotch, but Ruben picked her up by the waist and sat her on the floor of the boxcar. "Get in," he said, and then he got in behind her. Ruben crawled past Cristina without making a sound and checked on both sides of a lone pallet on one end of the car loaded with sacks of grain. It was clear.

"Quiet now," he whispered almost inaudibly, and she nodded.

The pair moved across the car, and Ruben slid the door on the far side open very slightly and knelt down to observe the activity. He took his phone out to take pictures to send to Kelly and the other reinforcements. Escobar's chopper was almost right in front of the door. To the left were the hearse and Docksneider's BMW followed by a lineup of small trucks and the two semis. Cristina knelt down behind Ruben and pressed herself very close to get a good look.

"Ma'am…Cristina…would you mind not getting so close? It's kind of distracting me," Ruben said.

Cristina looked puzzled for a second before she understood the request.

"You mean to tell me there are 20 or 30 men out there who could blow your head off at any moment, and you're thinking about my tits?"

"Um, yes, I guess I am, ma'am. It's quite distracting."

Cristina shook her head and backed off. "Why are men such idiots? They're just tits."

Ruben took a deep breath and then slowly let it out. "You have no idea ma'am."

Chapter 32

Kelly was walking between the river and the trains as the pictures came in from Ruben. He had an AK47 with a 30-round clip that he had grabbed from the helicopter slung over his shoulder and a handgun on each hip with plenty of ammo. He stopped to look at the pictures and could see the small chopper on one end near vehicles. Escobar and Chavarria appeared to be stuffing garbage bags with money from the hearse, and the two semis were on the other end. Dozens of men were moving the contraband from the big rigs into smaller trucks that could use the freeways without any requirements to stop for weight checks or logs. He sent the photos along to his Apache pilot and texted Ruben.

Got the pics. Where are you? I'm by the tracks...can see your car up ahead.

Ruben got the message and called back.

"We're in a boxcar next to the action," Ruben whispered.

"We?" asked Kelly. "You better not mean that you have Cristina there with you, because I would have to kill you."

"It was a choice between her ripping my balls off or you killing me. I chose death."

"How could you take my girl into a battle zone, man?! I told you to drop her off with the boys."

"I tried, dude. You know how she is. Anyway, she's safe in here. There are lots of bad guys, but they're mostly manual labor workers and they don't seem to be armed."

"How can you be sure?"

"Well, we ran into a couple of them a while ago. No guns on them."

"Where are they now?"

"You know, um…taking a little nap."

Kelly shook his head. "Broken jaws or broken ribs?"

"One of each. Plus a concussion."

"So, how can I find you?"

"Just come straight across from my car to the last line of railroad cars and go to your left. We're in a red one right next to Escobar's little helicopter."

"Half of them are red, Ruben."

"Well, keep walking towards the northwest end until you trip over two guys with their pants around their ankles."

Kelly took a breath and waited a second to cool down. "I *am* going to kill you, you know."

"I know. Just give me a chance to call my dear, sweet Sylvia and my two boys first. Take care of my widow and fatherless children for me, partner. You're their godfather, you know…"

Kelly clicked the phone off and called the Apache pilot.

"Sergeant Pierce, where are you now?" Kelly asked.

"We got two Apaches on the big ball field, motors running, just behind the trees from the rail yard. The Blackhawks are still at least ten minutes out – could be half an hour. We have orders not to engage until they're here."

"Did the pictures help?"

"We don't see any sign of any mounted artillery that could take us out, but that doesn't mean they don't have any hand-held or shoulder mounted options. There are a lot of vehicles, but it doesn't really look like they were planning for any kind of aerial attack. The armed guards all seem to have handguns. I don't see any rifles. I'm confident we can take everything out with no problem, except that we can't have any casualties. Governor's orders."

"Okay. I'm heading toward the activity now. My partner is in the railcar right next to the little chopper, so do not destroy the chopper. I think we should scare all the people away with floodlights and flash bangs and maybe some machinegun fire. The hired help will scatter, and just the bad guys will remain. Then you can put a missile or two into each of the semi trailers and we'll have them surrounded."

"Great minds. Agent Bird and Martinez just mapped out the same strategy, but I'll be sure to tell them about your location and to avoid the small chopper. One Blackhawk is going to secure the truck and cargo in the river and rope off the warehouse and grab the computers. But when the other two come in, we'll put one on each side above the lines of railroad cars, and Martinez and I will have an Apache at either end. Law enforcement will soon be covering the entire perimeter. I'll strafe in from the Southeast along the access roadway without getting too close, lob in a few flash bangs, and all the helo units will shine their floodlights. Then Captain Boles will tell them to surrender peacefully."

"These are Colombian Army and cartel thugs. They don't know the meaning of 'peacefully' or 'surrender,' so don't expect a cakewalk. They will throw everything they have at you. And tell the cops outside of the tracks not to worry too much about the first rush of men. They're just cheap hired labor trying to make a living. We will have to go in and get the real criminals."

*   *   *   *

I'm underneath your boxcar. Lights and missiles coming in a while. They know your 20. Just sit it out.

Ruben read the text from Kelly.

"It's almost show time," Ruben told Cristina. "It's going to sound like a war out there pretty soon, so just stay low and get behind those sacks of feed over there."

Cristina nodded.

"Kelly's right below us. I'm going out to help him scope things out."

Cristina gave him a worried look.

"Don't worry. We'll let the helicopters and commandos do the heavy lifting, and we'll just help with the cleanup when it's over. They know where we are, so they'll keep the action away."

"Here," she said, taking off her vest. "Give this to Kelly."

Ruben put his hand on her shoulder with a nod and a smile and took the vest. "If it's me coming back in, I'll knock twice," he said. He took the gun out of her belt and handed it to her, then he went out the door to join his partner.

Seconds later came the sound of helicopters, soon followed by a line of bullets from the Apache's M134 Mini Gatling Gun, kicking up dust along the way. Flash bang grenades were lobbed in from all sides bringing flashes of daylight and a cloud of smoke. Then the floodlights from the Blackhawks lit the area like a ballpark at night, and the workers fled through the lines of train cars.

"Start the chopper!"

It was Escobar shouting from the hearse. The blades of the little chopper began to whir and turn.

"Fire One!" Boles commanded when the area around the semis was clear of men, and the Apache complied with a Stinger missile right into the payload.

"Fire Two!"

And the second truck was destroyed in a loud and fiery blaze.

Chavarria shouted to Escobar: "Sir, the cocaine! It is all

destroyed!"

"I don't give a fuck about those drugs. Just get the money into the bags!"

The chopper pilot was not anxious to go airborne with armed military helicopters all around him, so he crawled to the passenger's side and jumped to the ground beneath the turning blades. Ruben raised his pistol towards him just as the pilot turned to see the two men and froze in fear. Kelly zipped up his vest and pushed Ruben's pistol down. He waved the man on, signaling him to run. The pilot tipped his hat at Kelly and disappeared into the lines of railcars.

"The governor doesn't want anyone dead," said Kelly. "Besides, that was just a civilian Mexican pilot."

"Yeah, I wasn't going to shoot him," Ruben said, "or he'd already be dead."

Gun fire was sprayed at the helicopters as the smoke began to clear, and they could see Escobar and Chavarria by the hearse.

"Son of a bitch!" Escobar shouted. "Guillermo, you are going to have to fly the chopper."

"Yes, Sir," Chavarria responded.

"Put these two bags onboard, and let's go."

"But, Sir, it will be too heavy."

"We just have to go a few hundred meters to get across the river and out of sight," he said. "Hurry!"

"But the helicopters, Sir. They will shoot us down!"

Escobar laughed. "These American cowards are not going to shoot us. If they were going to kill us they would be shooting at us right now."

Kelly shook his head. "That son of a bitch is right. They'll just let him fly right out of here." He nodded his head toward the left. "Come on," he said, and Ruben followed him behind the wheels of the boxcar. Then they crouched and ran to the next boxcar, taking cover behind the wheels there.

"I'll go down one more, to the next car," said Ruben. "Then we'll have two angles on them, and we can keep the fire away from the other railcar."

Ruben crawled into the dark shadow behind the wheels of the next car and was startled by the voice of a young man.

"Good evening, Mr. Ruben. It's me, Carlos. You met me outside at the Roundup with Mr. Kelly," Carlos said as he moved a bit to allow some light to shine on his face.

Ruben's heart gradually retreated from his throat. "What the hell are you doing here?"

"Well, after I blew up the bridge and sunk the last truck, then Max scared away a car full of men that were going to kill you and Miss Cristina and everyone when you came out of the warehouse, and then we followed the little helicopter here, and the drug ring leader had a microphone on him, and the one in Mr. Kelly's pocket is also turned on too, so I knew where you all were and I left Max in the car over at the park and I came here to watch and see if I could help."

Ruben was dumbfounded and struggled to find words. "Just stay out of sight and don't get in my way. And...nice work."

Captain Boles was on the megaphone now. "The entire rail yard is surrounded by police officers and Border Patrol Agents, and our commandos in the helicopters have you outnumbered too. Throw down your weapons and come out to the open area in the center. Lie face down and spread eagle. We will give you two minutes to comply before we deploy our special ops forces. They can kill you or cuff you; it's your choice. Your time starts now."

A half dozen of Escobar's 18 men started walking toward the open space with their hands raised and throwing their weapons aside.

"Why, you cowardly traitors!" Escobar shouted, leveling his pistol and quickly shooting three of his men with perfect accuracy.

Kelly shot a few rounds into the hearse next to Escobar to stop his killing spree, and Ruben followed with several shots of his own. Escobar turned around in a blind rage, took cover on the other side of the vehicle, and started shooting.

"Load the chopper, Guillermo! It's time to go!"

Ruben bolted to one of the small trucks that had been waiting to be loaded, and Carlos was right behind him. All of the truck engines were running. He put it in reverse as Carlos jumped in the passenger's side and backed into the hearse, knocking Chavarria down with a jolt.

"Get up, you idiot! We have no time to waste!" said Escobar.

Kelly gave cover with a few shots as Ruben jumped out of the truck and ran to the front end of it, away from Escobar.

"Go back under the train car," he told Carlos.

"But…"

"Now!" Ruben demanded, and Carlos obeyed. Then he changed clips and fired towards Escobar, who was still stashing money into a black garbage bag.

Kelly made a dash around a couple of boxcars and headed for another one of the trucks. "Hey Lunchmeat, we're over here," he hollered.

Escobar fired a couple of shots toward his voice, but Kelly was already inside another one of the small trucks.

One of Escobar's loyalists had gotten up from his prone position and taken a truck from the second line and was heading for his boss. The Apache laid down a steady line of fire, giving him a perimeter he could not cross as a dozen troops rappelled from the Blackhawk on the far side. Escobar used the passenger's door for cover as he walked closer to Kelly's truck.

Kelly was about to step out of the truck as the Colonel aimed his gun directly at the Border Agent's head. A split second later, Escobar was hit in the side of the head with two golf ball-sized stones in quick succession, causing him to duck out of sight. Cristina looked to her left from the door of the boxcar, and Carlos looked to his right from in front of the next car. They gave each other a thumbs up and a smile. Cristina waved for him to get back under the train car and then quickly closed the door.

Kelly was running towards Ruben when he saw Carlos still standing in front of the boxcar. He ran towards him, grabbed him in a bear hug, and rolled back under the boxcar. He took off the his vest and handed it to Carlos.

"Put this on, and get back behind the wheels."

Cristina was concerned that Max might be with Carlos, so she opened the back side of the railcar slowly and carefully looked both ways for any stray men who might be relieving themselves. The coast was clear, so she jumped down to where the two unfortunate men that had a run-in with Ruben were still sleeping. The big one that tried to hit her was rolling his head from side to side and moaning.

"No – you can't wake up yet, pendejo."

She walked over and smashed her heel into his crotch. He let out a groan and then passed out completely again.

"Tiny little dick," she said and spit on him. She looked over at the tall skinny man's crotch and found his package to be much larger.

"Hmmm," she said, raising her eyebrows and nodding. Then she ran over to the next car and crawled underneath to find Carlos.

"Psssst...Carlos!"

"Don't worry, Miss Cristina. Max is still in the car at the park. He's listening to Mr. Kelly on the microphone in his pocket, so he knows it is still dangerous. I made him promise on your life that he will not come over here until it is over."

Kelly joined Ruben between the remaining small trucks and the line of boxcars. They could see Escobar standing by the open front passenger door of the vehicle now as the soldiers took cover behind the remains of the trucks on the other side. He had a perfect head shot lined up on Escobar and was trying very hard to obey the directive not to kill. The drug thug turned his head toward the Border Agent, and Kelly looked at him with one open eye, right down the barrel of his Glock. Escobar tilted his head slightly as a big toothy smile grew on his face. A familiar smile that Kelly remembered from three years earlier.

"We meet again, Mr. Smith," Escobar said. "It looks like, once again, you will not be killing me tonight. Or I would already be dead."

Kelly couldn't control his pent up anger and hatred any longer. He moved the gun slightly to his left and pulled the trigger, grazing the top of Escobar's right shoulder and zinging over the hood of Docksneider's BMW behind him. The kingpin did not flinch or avert his gaze as he rubbed the shoulder with his left hand.

"Very impressive, Mr. Smith. You ruined my suit without drawing any blood."

Suddenly Ruben butted his shoulder against his partner pushing him away, and a bullet immediately hit his shoulder. It was from one of Escobar's minions that he saw across the way aiming his sites on Kelly. Escobar immediately held his right palm up, signaling his men to stop. "You fools!" he shouted. "Do not give an entire army a reason to fire on us. Even these lily-livered Americans have their breaking point. Guillermo, grab these bags. We're leaving."

Ruben got down on one knee and held his shoulder.

"Ruben!" Kelly shouted.

"It's nothing, partner. Just a flesh wound."

"Yeah, I didn't think so. Right on the edge of the Kevlar, damn it. There's not a lot of blood, so it didn't hit an artery. Just lie down and stay low. We'll get help in a minute. What the hell did you do that for? That bullet was meant for me."

Ruben looked up at Kelly. "Better my shoulder than your heart, Kimosabe."

Carlos came out and started tending to the wound.

"I'll take care of him, Mr. Kelly. But you should not be out here without a vest," Carlos said.

Kelly watched as Chavarria stuffed a bag into the tiny helicopter and was running back for one more. Kelly's phone rang. It was Sergeant Pierce in the Apache.

"Can you guys make it back under the box car?" Kelly asked.

They nodded, and Ruben crawled off with some help from Carlos as Kelly answered his phone.

"Yeah."

"Get ready for a stinger, coming for the black money van...now."

Kelly saw it leave the Apache and he jumped under the boxcar as it whizzed towards its target. He heard the explosion and turned to see flames and millions of dollars in cash bursting into the air in the fiery plume. Another missile was launched, and it took out the entire line of small trucks across the way.

Chavarria was on the ground with his head covered, still several yards short of the doomed hearse.

"Let's go...now Guillermo!" Escobar called from the copter, and Chavarria made a dash inside and took the controls. Carlos, Ruben, and Cristina all joined Kelly near the railcar as the chopper lurched and chugged trying to get off the ground.

Kelly spoke into his phone. "Are you still there, Sergeant? You gotta shoot these guys in the little chopper down. These are the ring leaders, and Mexico is only a few yards away."

"I'm trying to get the go-ahead from the governor right now Kelly. I'm under orders, so all I can do is wait and see."

The little chopper finally seemed to get its bearings and started to rise very slowly above the rail yard.

"Until we meet again, Kelly Smith." Escobar got up and stood on the skid and waved to all of the helicopters around him as he continued to taunt Kelly.

"Sergeant! Now!"

Carlos reached into his pocket and pulled out the third grenade he took near the river, holding it out in his open palm. Kelly, Ruben, and Cristina all looked at each other. Cristina gave Kelly a "what are you waiting for?" look and then reached for the grenade. Kelly quickly grabbed her wrist.

"This is our only chance to have normal lives, Kelly! I swear I will never speak to you again if you don't let go!" Cristina said with a vengeful look on her face.

Kelly looked at her with a peaceful smile and steely eyes. "This is something I've got to do, baby."

Kelly took the grenade and looked at Escobar, still standing on the skid, as his chopper lurched slowly upward. He was puffing a freshly lit cigar and laughing as he flipped off Kelly and his companions.

"Now, Kelly!" Cristina urged. "Hit that fucker in the face!"

Kelly lasered in on Escobar and pulled the pin. "I've got a better idea," he said, and threw the grenade toward his target.

"It's a No-Go," said Pierce.

They all watched as the grenade hit Escobar square in the crotch and blew him and the chopper into a million flaming pieces. Burning hundred-dollar bills fluttered slowly to the ground across the entire area.

"How did you like that blow job, you son of a bitch!" Cristina shouted as she put her arms around Kelly's neck and gave him a kiss. "You died without a dick, you piece of shit!"

Chapter 33

Agent Bird ran over to Kelly as the commandos took the other men into custody. He looked at the flaming heap, half on top of the railroad cars and half on the ground.

"Hmmh," he said. "Catastrophic engine failure on takeoff." He gave Kelly a wink as two agents came out from behind the boxcar that Cristina had been in.

"Agent Bird, we've got two unconscious civilians down behind that car with their pants around their ankles. One has a broken jaw and one has broken ribs." All eyes went to Ruben, who was well-known for his bone-crushing punches.

Ruben looked at his shoulder and let out a moan. "Ooh, man! I could really use a doctor, guys. I took a bullet."

"Ruben, you know this could get you tossed out of the Patrol this time," Bird said, shaking his head.

Cristina turned to the side and ripped her blouse completely open, and then she turned to the agents. "I did it," she said. "They tried to rape me...I waited till they had their pants down so they couldn't chase me, and I kicked one of them in the face like this," she said with a powerful and impressive pirouette and swing of her leg, "and I smashed the other one in the chest with my head...do you want me to show you?"

Bird and the others waved her off, having seen the power she could wield. "No, no...that won't be necessary ma'am. The police might need to get a statement from you later. Pauley and Turk, you two escort Agent Garcia to one of the ambulances and get him taken care of right away. There should be a few around the perimeter. Then send some EMTs for the two men that assaulted the young lady here."

Max and Magda came walking out of the shadows. The boy ran to his mother, and they embraced tightly. Then Max looked over his mother's shoulder and pointed.

"Mama, that car is moving."

In the midst of all the flames and destruction there was one car right in the middle of it all that had remain untouched. It was a blue BMW, and it was rolling very slowly in reverse towards the exit. Bird nodded to two of his men who ran over to it and knocked on the driver's window. The car jolted to a stop, and the agent opened the door. Crouched out of sight was Jerrod Docksneider. They pulled him out, and he rose to his tall lanky stature.

"Bring me the keys," shouted Bird, "and give him to the military."

"Looks like you'll be needing a to find a new job, Mama," Cristina said to her mother.

"Uhh...I'll just take some time off, and you can work more nights at the club. You make more tips in an hour than I earn all week anyway."

"You are reporting all those tips to the IRS, aren't you Miss?" Bird said with a sly grin.

"Of course," she said sarcastically, then turned away and slapped her buttock. *"Pinche carbrón."*

"Kelly," Bird said, with a more serious tone. "The Intel detail comes with company car. It's looks like we'll be confiscating that one as part of a drug deal," he said tossing the keys to Kelly. "I'll have

Grace transfer it to the Border Patrol tomorrow. Since you came here in a helicopter, you'll need a way to get home tonight, so just go ahead and take it now."

"Oh, I can't really take that, Sir…"

"What?" Cristina screeched under her breath. "Yes you can," she told him through clenched teeth.

"Sir," said Kelly, "I really just took the Intel detail to help me with this takedown. I think I'll be going back to regular duty with my partner now, if you'll release me."

"I figured as much," said Bird. "I better have Grace just put it right into your name then."

"But, Sir…"

"But nothing," said Cristina clamping his lips shut with her fingers and pulling him towards the car. She opened the door and pushed Kelly into the driver's seat, then she ran around to the other side and got in.

Kelly turned the key and the space-age dashboard lit up.

"Oooh," she said looking at all the latest technological details in the luxury car. "What does this button do?" She pressed a button on the console and the windows all immediately went to a dark tint that gave them total privacy.

"You're in trouble now, Mr. Smith," she said as she began to crawl onto him like a panther.

Kelly reached for the side of his seat, and it began to recline. They were kissing passionately when the seat back came to a halt, hitting something in the back seat. Cristina reached over and knocked on the green bazooka case that was jutting through from the trunk.

"What's this?" she asked.

"Looks like a military case of some kind, probably for weapons," Kelly answered.

Cristina crawled into the back and Kelly reached over to try to open it. The latches were broken and he raised the lid a few inches until it hit the top of the trunk where it met the back seat. Cristina looked at Kelly, and he nodded, so she reached her hand inside. Her eyes became very wide, and she pulled out a ten-thousand-dollar bundle of hundred-dollar bills. Then she stuck her arm back in and felt around.

"Kelly this thing is almost full of these," she said excitedly shaking the bills in her hand.

Kelly took a few bills from her and stashed them in his pocket. "I'll have to show these to Agent Bird. This will have to be confiscated."

"But, Kellyyyyyyy...why? It will just sit on a dusty shelf in an evidence room until some bad cops steal it."

"It's drug money. People died because of this money."

"Yes...like my brother and my husband...and your wife. And confiscating it will not bring them back to life. My son deserves something since he has no father to provide a good life for him."

Kelly nodded his head and thought for a minute. "Just pull out ten bundles for Max's college education and put them under the seat. And...and ten for Carlos too."

Cristina nodded and counted out the bundles.

Just as she finished, there was a rap on the window, and they could hear Max frantically shouting for them.

"Mama...Mr. Kelly...Mama!" Max cried.

Kelly put his seat back up and opened the door.

"Mr. Kelly, they are going to take him away! Mama, tell them to stop!"

The two got out of the car and tried to get Max to settle down.

"Max, what's wrong? Who are you talking about?" Cristina asked, hugging her son.

"Carlos, Mama," Max said pointing over toward the boxcar.

"Come on," he said, pulling her by the hand.

She turned to Kelly and mouthed, "Lock the car," and went with her son. Kelly pressed the remote lock button and followed ten steps behind them.

Carlos was sitting on the step-up to the boxcar door crying, and there was an agent on each side of him, one with a clipboard and pen.

"Get away from him! This is my nephew. He lives with me," she said.

The agent didn't know if he should be amused or upset at the little Latina woman charging towards him.

"Maybe I should take a look at your papers," he said with a smirk.

Cristina took a step towards him with a clenched fist, but Kelly grabbed her from behind. She glared at the agent for a moment longer, then she shook herself free and crouched in front of Carlos.

"What's the problem guys?" Kelly asked.

"He smells like river water, and his socks are soaking wet, and his wet underwear is soaking through his pants," the agent responded. "Just doing our job."

"Well, I got this guys. He was in the river. He's the one who blew up the pontoon bridge and sunk one of their trucks. Then he tracked Escobar here. He's a hero."

Cristina was trying to comfort Carlos, who seemed inconsolable. She stroked his hair and kissed his forehead. "Don't worry, little man. We won't let them take you."

Carlos shook his head. That wasn't why he was crying. Then he handed her his phone with a text displayed from his girlfriend in Hipódromo.

It was in Spanish, and it read:

Carlos – I don't know how to tell you this. The men, they were here on our street. They burned many houses to the ground and they killed everyone. Your mama, your papa, your grandfather, and even your little brother Pepe. They are all dead. My family is gone too, but I was at the fiesta. I am so sorry. I love you. – your Estrella

A tear streamed down Cristina's cheek and she pulled Carlos up with her and gave him a strong embrace. Carlos wiped his tears with his sleeve and then took off his vest and handed it to Cristina.

"I think you need this more than I do, Miss Cristina."

She quickly put it on and zipped it to cover her torn blouse.

"So, what's the deal?" the agent with the clipboard asked Kelly. "She says he's her nephew living with her, and you say he's your nephew, and…"

"He lives with me," Kelly said.

"He lives with us," said Cristina, putting her arm around Kelly's waist and her other arm over Carlos' and Max's shoulders.

The agent tipped his hat, nodded, and walked off with his partner just as the bright lights and crescendoing sound of a large helicopter escorted by two smaller ones approached overhead. The large one landed, and a three-step stairway was deployed. A marine stepped out and stood at attention on the top step. Several camera crews from local stations were gathering as well. A moment later a tall, rugged-looking man with salt-and-pepper hair and a blue suit stepped out and descended with his entourage. It was Governor Franklin Basham.

"Find Agent Smith and bring him to me," he commanded.

"Governor!" shouted a young blonde woman with a Channel 9 microphone, determined and ignoring the trouble she was having with her high heels in the gravel. "Governor Basham…How did you learn about this drug operation, and how long have you been tracking them?"

"Governor," asked an older Mexican gentleman from Nuevo Laredo TV, "They say that you might have captured nearly a billion dollars worth of cocaine and heroine. Is that true? And who was running these drugs?"

The Governor just waved them off. "There will be a news

conference in the morning once we get all of the facts together. You'll get the full story then. Let me just say, Señor Espinoza, that this was not a Mexican operation. As you can imagine, truckloads of these kinds of drugs can only come from cartels in South America."

The Governor waved his hand amidst the uproar of reporters. "My press corps will take the rest of your questions," he said. A man and woman from his entourage faced the lights and cameras of the media clamoring for red meat. The National Guard unit already on the ground formed a line between the reporters and the Governor, and one member of his team led him over to Kelly Smith, who was still standing with Cristina and the two boys.

"Agent Smith, I presume?" said the Governor with his hand extended.

Kelly shook his hand. "Yes, Sir. It's a pleasure to meet you, and thanks for all your help and cooperation."

"Some pretty good work here, Agent. It was you in the news a couple of years ago with a big bust in Colombia, wasn't it?"

"Well, yes, Sir. This was the same Colombian Colonel running this deal. That's how I recognized him when I saw him in town and decided to follow up."

"It seems you had some pretty good eyes on the ground helping you out too."

Kelly looked at Carlos and Max. "Actually, Sir, these two boys were the ones who pointed me towards the pontoon bridge when I thought they would be coming across the North Bridge, and they tracked Escobar to the rail yard here too with a bug Cristina planted on him at the warehouse. Carlos here was the one who blew up the bridge before the final truck could get across."

The Governor raised one eyebrow at Kelly. "So this is the crack intelligence crew that got me to send the helo unit down I-35 and then over to here...?"

"Yes, Sir."

"Good work, men," he said as he shook both of their hands. "You too, ma'am."

"But it was my mother who originally planted the microphones at the warehouse that provided all the information that allowed Kelly to break this case. Mama!" Cristina shouted to Magda who joined the family circle.

Governor Basham shook his head and smiled. "It looks like a real homespun family operation here, son."

"It took a lot more than us to make this happen, Sir," Kelly said.

"Well, I'm going to need all of you to join me at the DoubleTree to help me get all the details straight. And, Kelly, I'd like you to join me at the news conference in the morning too. I'd like all the people to see what a real hero looks like."

"Well, Sir, there were a lot of heroes involved. And, if you don't mind, I'd just as soon let you and the Border Patrol and the National Guard be the heroes this time. I'm not much for cameras, and I don't really need the cartels to get me in their sites again. It didn't work out so well for me last time," he said, putting his arms around his new family, "and I'd kind of like to try to live a safe and normal life with the people I love."

The Governor nodded. "That's right. I remember hearing about your wife now. Really sorry for that. We'll keep your name out of it, son."

"Thank you, Sir. But we'll be happy to come over and tell you all about it tonight..."

Max tugged on Kelly's sleeve and rubbed his tummy with a pleading look in his eye.

"...as long as you'll have a couple of Mexican pizzas there for our young heroes, Governor."

The Governor chuckled and nodded. "And it looks like you could use a couple of cold Budweisers, and I'll have 'em send up a bottle of wine for the ladies."

"Beer for me," Magda interjected.

Cristina gave her a scowl as the men enjoyed a laugh. "Me too," Cristina conceded.

They said their farewells, and the Governor went off to talk with Boles and Bird and some others before he lifted off for the hotel.

"Now I will be fired from my job at the Roundup," Carlos said, starting to tear up again.

"Ha!" Cristina said, drying his eyes with her fingers and putting her arm around him as they all started to walk back towards the BMW. "Do you think your boss there wants me to leave and start working at the Chaparral Club a block away?"

"Of course not, Miss Cristina! All of his customers would follow you there."

"So, then you'll be working at the Roundup as long as you want. And, once he finds out what a hero you are, he will want to give you a big raise too."

Agent Bird left the Governor's circle and came over to talk to Kelly before he left. "Kelly, I won't be able to get you transferred out tomorrow, so I'm going to require you to take the rest of the week off, and you can go back to regular duty next Monday."

"Uh...thank you, Sir. And, I almost forgot," he said pulling a couple of hundred dollar bills from his front pocket. "There is a military case in the back of the BMW. It looks like it's for missiles or bazookas."

"If there are weapons in it, you can bring them to the Intel office tomorrow," Bird said.

"Well, no, Sir..." he said raising his hand with the money towards Bird.

Bird pushed his hand down. "Then just bring in the empty case next week."

"But, Sir, it's not empty. There's..."

Bird pushed his hand away again. "If there are no weapons, then

I don't need to know what's in it."

"But, Sir…"

"Agent," he said leaning down into Kelly's face, "if you tell me what's in it I will bust you down to desk duty until the day you retire. Do you hear me, Agent Smith?"

Kelly shrugged in frustration as Bird continued.

"All the money is accounted for," he said, extending his arm over all of the pieces of burnt cash lying all around on the ground. "And it all came from Colombian banks or cartel stockpiles, so there's no way of knowing how much there was all together. So it can't be money, which would just get stolen by dirty agents anyway."

Cristina pinched him in the side as if to say, "I told you so."

"It's a big case, Sir."

"I'll see you at the Governor's hotel room. Good work, Smith." He gave Kelly a pat on the shoulder, turned and left.

Cristina took Kelly's arm in both of her hands. "It's strange how you're even better looking now that you're rich," she said.

"Funny," Kelly said, "Now, how are we going to get all these cars home? And we need to stop at the hospital and see how Ruben's doing too."

"Well, we don't really need the old rust bucket any more. We can just leave it at the park."

Carlos' eyes grew wide. "Yes we do…I think we need it," he said.

"You're right. You and I will pick it up when we're done at the hotel."

"You mean, you really are going to bring me to your house? You weren't just saying that for those men?" Carlos said with wide eyes and a hopeful smile.

Max gave him a big hug. "You're my brother now, Carlos."

Carlos looked at Cristina. She raised her eyebrows and nodded, and Carlos began to tear up yet again.

A round shadow approached from one side. "What's up, guys?" It was Ruben.

"You're back? You took a bullet half an hour ago," Kelly said. "We were going to come and visit you on our way to the Governor's hotel room."

"Oh, well listen to Mr. Hoity-toity superhero, going to see the Governor."

"Hey, it's just a debriefing, so you'll have to come too."

"Ahhhh...I'm going to have to stop at the diner. Getting shot takes a lot out of a guy."

"There'll be pizza, Mr. Ruben," Max said.

Ruben brightened up. "Well, the Governor's never seen me eat pizza, but I think I can beat you guys out for the most pieces."

"So...the bullet...?" Kelly pressed.

"I guess the edge of the vest slowed it down enough so that it didn't go in too far. They just pulled it out, gave me a tetanus shot or something, and put about a gallon of very painful antiseptic in the wound. No stitches," he said, pulling back his shirtsleeve. "Just some superglue and a Band-Aid."

Ruben looked at Kelly and paused for a moment. "And, oh, by the way, your house burned down."

"What? But it's a crime scene. Escobar couldn't have gotten anyone in there to torch it."

"Uhhh...something about curtains and a rookie cop with a flare gun. The EMTs thought it was hilarious. Anyway, they got it in time, so just the porch and living room burned off. Your "panic room" and bedroom and kitchen should still be there."

"Swell," Kelly said. "Now I'm homeless."

Magda walked over to him and took his arm. "No you aren't, Kelly. You will stay with us. Cristina has a queen-sized bed. It will be no trouble."

"Mama!" Cristina whispered, nodding her head toward Max, but Magda just raised her eyebrows and shrugged.

"It's okay, Mr. Kelly," Max said. "You can stay with my mama. She's in love with you, and you're in love with her."

Kelly and Cristina were both speechless, and everyone seemed a little tense.

"But..." Max continued, looking Kelly right in the eyes, "...you will have to marry her before one year!"

The tension was immediately broken with resounding laughter from everyone in the group, and Magda walked over and smothered Max with a hug.

"Boys, you go with Abuelita or Mr. Ruben. There's no room in the backseat of the BMW. We'll meet you at the hotel."

"BMW?" Ruben asked Kelly.

Kelly pulled out the key remote. "Company car, compliments of Tom Bird and Jerrod Docksneider."

Kelly pushed a button which unlocked the car and turned the lights on.

"Nice," Ruben said.

Then he pushed another button, and the engine started to purr like a young kitten.

"Well, that's closer to a Batmobile than anything I'll ever have, so I guess you are the Caped Crusader from now on, partner. Just call me Robin. See you in a few." He headed out between the railcars with Magda and the boys.

Kelly and Cristina embraced as the crowd began to dwindle, the floodlights began to dim, and the Governor's helicopter left for the hotel.

"Soooo..." Kelly said, and kissed Cristina on the forehead, "...you love me, huh?"

"Mmmmaybe," she responded, squeezing him tightly. The she put her hands on his waist and pushed back a bit. "But I'm not sure I can stand living with you."

Kelly smiled. "Yeah…like you could stand living without me."

The couple turned, arm in arm, and walked slowly toward the BMW.

"What should we do tonight when we get home?" Cristina asked with a smirk.

"I don't know. How soundproof is your bedroom?"

"Not very. Mama and Max are sound sleepers, though. But I don't have any hero-sized condoms anyway."

"Well, we might just have to make a little cowboy, then."

"Or maybe a little Latina warrior princess."

"Or maybe one of each."

"I'm not sure you're man enough for that, Mr. Smith."

"That's okay. You're man enough for both of us."

Cristina laughed. They paused by the driver's door and kissed.

"Oooh, what's this, Mr. Smith?" she asked, rubbing her hand on his zipper.

"You're a naughty little girl, Ms. Chavez."

"You ain't seen nothin' yet, cowboy."

THE END

Epilogue

"It's good to see you up and around, Rick," Kelly said across the table as he tossed the napkin onto his plate after a huge dinner. "Any idea when you'll be getting back to work?"

It was the Sunday after the drug takedown, and Sylvia and Ruben had invited Kelly's new family over to get acquainted, as well as Rick and Sabrina. Chuy and Ruben Jr. were already becoming great friends with Max and Carlos, and Kelly had gone to Hipódromo to pick up Estrella for the weekend as well. There were eight of them at the main dining table, with the Garcia boys, Carlos, and Estrella on the end at a folding card table.

"Well, it's just my second day out of the hospital," Rick said, "so I'm still taped up pretty good, but they were able to save my spleen. As far as work…uh…"

He looked at Sabrina and she picked up the conversation. "The doctors say it'll be a few weeks. And then he's going to Austin to work on the Governor's security team. The security chief will be retiring in a year, so Hopefully Rick will be in line for that position."

"Wow, that's terrific, " said Ruben. Sounds like a pretty good gig. Congrats, man."

Rick looked a little sheepish and self-conscious about leaving the team in Laredo. "You know, I got a degree in Law Enforcement with a concentration in security, so…you know."

"Man – we're happy for you," Kelly said. "That's a great opportunity. A no-brainer. Good luck, and don't forget to say hi to us little people from time to time."

Sabrina smiled and gave him a kiss on the cheek, and Rick nodded.

"Thanks, guys," he said and kissed Sabrina on the lips.

Ruben smiled. "This is the first time I've seen you have eyes for only one woman, Romeo. I hope you're going with him, Sabrina."

She returned a tight smile with raised eyebrows and just a hint of a nod.

"Sabrina and Cristina, would you girls mind helping me clear the table?" Sylvia asked. "Everybody, just stay at the table. We have some warm blueberry pie and ice cream coming right up!"

"I picked the berries!" said Chuy.

"I'll get the dessert plates," offered Magda. The women all got up from the Garcia's dining room table, and Estrella went to help too.

"Don't forget the coffee," Ruben said as he leaned back in his chair with one arm behind his head and the other massaging his full belly.

In no time the table was cleared. The ladies had served dessert and were back in their seats.

"So, how do you like family life, Kelly?" Sylvia asked.

"Yeah, how do you like it, Kelly?" Cristina echoed.

Kelly almost choked on his first bite of pie. "Well, it's hard to beat the single life of frozen dinners, household chores, and being alone every night, but I'm adapting."

"Don't worry," said Magda. "Your honeymoon week is over, and you're no longer a guest. Your week to wash dishes starts tomorrow!"

"I guess I'll be buying a dishwasher on the way home," Kelly joked.

"Well, we'll miss having you right down the street so you can visit all the time."

"Don't worry. I'll still be working with this guy," he said, patting Ruben on the shoulder, "so I'll be around...and I'm sure these kids will be wanting to get together again too."

The boys all nodded their agreement, and Ruben dropped his shoulder and winced a bit from Kelly's pat.

"Sorry, partner. How's that shoulder doing?"

"Just a little tender, that's all. The hem of the vest slowed the bullet down pretty good."

"Yeah," said Chuy, "and the doctor told him he was lucky 'cause it got stuck in the fat."

"Go to your room," Ruben teased as his sons giggled.

"Boys," Sylvia scolded, "your father could have been killed."

That brought a somber mood to the table, so Kelly tried to lighten it up.

"So, I guess all of those midnight runs for donuts on the late shift have finally paid off."

With smiles returning to the table, Kelly changed the subject.

"I guess Docksneider ratted out the Deputy. He'll probably actually enjoy some of the 'perks' of being in prison. Maybe you should put in for that Deputy opening, Ruben."

"Not a chance," he responded with a forkful of pie in front of his face. "That's more of a job for Batman anyway."

Kelly and Cristina looked at each other and smiled.

"So," said Ruben, "That was quite something how, two days after the drug bust, an anonymous donor gave five million dollars and an entire city block right next to Dovalina Elementary to Sister Eddy's foundation to build an orphanage with 100 beds, a rec center for teenagers, and a playground for the community. That's right across the street from you guys, isn't it Kelly?"

"Ahm, yup."

"And then they gave each of my boys a hundred-thousand-dollar trust fund for college for my role in the war on drugs."

Kelly nodded. "Nice."

"It all came from some untraceable account in the Cayman Islands. Kind of strange how you and Cristina disappeared for a couple of days after the drug bust. Oh…and I saw Tom Bird the other day too. He had his mortgage paid off…anonymously. He told me to tell you, 'That must have been a really big case.' I wonder what that means."

Kelly looked at his pie and shrugged.

"Kind of funny that you didn't get anything, Kelly, I mean your house burning down and all, and you were the main man behind the drug bust. Is there anything you want to tell us?"

"Ahhh…nope."

"Ruben…" Sylvia whispered to her husband.

"Should we worry about you going to jail any time soon?"

"Daddy, Daddy!" Chuy cried excitedly, pointing towards the front window. "There's a big black car in front with a little white car behind it, and a man is coming to the door." Chuy ran to the door to meet the man.

"Run out the back, Kelly. I'll tell them I haven't seen you."

"Daddy, he wants you!"

Ruben went to the door with a curious look on his face.

"Ruben Garcia?" the man inquired.

"That's me."

"These are for you," he said, handing Ruben a set of car keys and a manila envelope with some documents.

Sylvia and Ruben Jr. joined Ruben and Chuy at the door as Kelly and Cristina smiled at each other.

"Enjoy your Crown Victoria, Sir, compliments of an anonymous donor. Have a nice day."

Ruben's eyes grew wide. He stared straight ahead at the black vehicle and swung the packet of papers into Sylvia's chest.

"A Crown Vic," he said, mesmerized as he headed outside and stood by the car. He pushed a button on the remote as his family gathered around him, and the roof started to rise and disappear into the back of the car. He pushed a button to unlock the car, and then he pushed the lock button.

"Push it again," Kelly said, joining the Garcias outside.

He pushed it again and the horn sang, "Bat-Maaan."

Ruben opened the door for his wife. "Get in. Kids, get in the back. We're going for a little ride around the block."

"Dad," Ruben Jr. said, "There's a box back here. Can I open it?"

"Go ahead," Ruben said. "What's in it?"

"It looks like some kind of black dress or something."

"Let's see," Ruben said pulling it out of the box. "That's my cape."

He tied it around his neck and drove off with the cape blowing behind him in the breeze. He greeted all of his neighbors with a honk of his bat-horn and a wave, and pulled back up in front of his house a few minutes later.

"Go in the house and finish your dessert, kids," Ruben said.

Kelly and Cristina were still outside, and Rick and Sabrina had joined them. Ruben turned to open the car door for his wife. Sylvia was holding the papers from the envelope in her hand and crying.

"What's wrong?" Ruben asked. "I know it's a nice car, but…"

"No," she said handing him a paper. "It's not just the title to the car. It's the deed to our house too…the mortgage was paid in full."

Ruben wiped a tear from his eye and struggled to keep his composure as he looked at Kelly.

Kelly put his arm around Cristina and Ruben put his arm around his wife.

"Here," Sylvia said to Rick. "There's an envelope in here for you too."

Rick opened it and found a check, then he embraced Sabrina tightly. "I'd swing you around if I could...but now you're coming with me for sure." He looked at Kelly. "Thanks."

"Dude, this is just too much. It's way too much..." Ruben said.

"No sweat, partner. It's just chump change." They all headed back toward the house.

"Like the man told you, Ruben...it was a really big case."

ABOUT THE AUTHOR

Jim Herrick is a retired 25-year veteran of the U.S. Border Patrol. He recently completed a tour in Afghanistan as a contractor for the Department of State/CBP as a mentor to Afghan Border and Customs Police advising on border security operations. He has a "Secret" security clearance and has been actively involved in a broad spectrum of border and security operations including anti-terrorism, tracking and surveillance, weapons and canine handling, and the investigation and apprehension of aliens and contraband that enter the U.S. illegally.

Jim's acquired knowledge and experience give him keen insights into the possible scenarios that can occur when you put powerful, callous, and violent drug cartels together with corrupt foreign military powers and governments, a permissive and ineffectual Mexican buffer, and a weak U.S. border. His creative imagination gives us an insider's peek into major events that are just waiting to happen, often based on real people and events that have "almost" happened.

Still active as a border and security consultant,
Jim now lives in New Mexico with his family.

Made in the USA
Charleston, SC
01 June 2015